8/10/12

Sherrie -

A Lover of hotCakes & Eggs

Enjoy

John

Batter Off Dead

Batter Off Dead

A Pennsylvania Dutch Mystery with Recipes

Tamar Myers

AN OBSIDIAN MYSTERY

OBSIDIAN
Published by New American Library, a division of
Penguin Group (USA) Inc., 375 Hudson Street,
New York, New York 10014, USA
Penguin Group (Canada), 90 Eglinton Avenue East, Suite 700, Toronto,
Ontario M4P 2Y3, Canada (a division of Pearson Penguin Canada Inc.)
Penguin Books Ltd., 80 Strand, London WC2R 0RL, England
Penguin Ireland, 25 St. Stephen's Green, Dublin 2,
Ireland (a division of Penguin Books Ltd.)
Penguin Group (Australia), 250 Camberwell Road, Camberwell, Victoria 3124,
Australia (a division of Pearson Australia Group Pty. Ltd.)
Penguin Books India Pvt. Ltd., 11 Community Centre, Panchsheel Park,
New Delhi – 110 017, India
Penguin Group (NZ), 67 Apollo Drive, Rosedale, North Shore 0632,
New Zealand (a division of Pearson New Zealand Ltd.)
Penguin Books (South Africa) (Pty.) Ltd., 24 Sturdee Avenue,
Rosebank, Johannesburg 2196, South Africa

Penguin Books Ltd., Registered Offices:
80 Strand, London WC2R 0RL, England

First published by Obsidian, an imprint of New American Library,
a division of Penguin Group (USA) Inc.

Copyright © Tamar Myers, 2009
All rights reserved

ISBN-13: 978-0-451-22592-4

Set in Palatino
Designed by Alissa Amell

Printed in the United States of America

For Liza Schwartz

Acknowledgments

The delicious recipes in this book are from *Pancakes A to Z* by Marie Simmons. She is the award-winning author of twenty cookbooks, most recently Sur La Table's *Things Cooks Love* (2008).

I am grateful to Jeff Freiert for suggesting the title for this book.

1

Minerva J. Jay was a glutton. There is no kinder way to describe a woman who wolfed down twenty-six pancakes at the Beechy Grove Mennonite Church Brotherhood all-you-can-eat fund-raising breakfast, and then complained when I cut her off after her seventeenth pork patty.

"Read the sign, Magdalena," she said. "I *can* still eat, and I will."

I favored Minerva with one of my infamous scowls. "The church needs a new roof much more than you need a larger dress."

"Was that a put-down?"

"Of course, dear, and one for which you really ought to be thanking me."

She dabbed at the corners of her mouth with an economy-pack napkin. "I beg your pardon?"

"Consider the obvious, Minerva. I'm eight and a half months pregnant, and I'm no spring chicken, which means my hormones are in all sorts of turmoil. Throw in the fact that this is a male child I'm carrying and that the father is a worldly physician of the Hebrew faith, whilst I am but a lowly Mennonite maid—well, no longer a maid, but not exactly a hoochie-mama, if you know what I mean."

"Does anybody? *Ever?*"

"Please, dear, my point is that I should be bouncing off the walls, becoming a total basket case. Instead, here I am, standing on sore feet that I can barely see due to my swollen ankles. Did I mention that my varicose veins are throbbing; that I'm as constipated as a mummy, thanks to my hemorrhoids, which make my bowel movements as excruciatingly painful as passing cacti; or that my bladder is squashed flatter than that last pancake you gulped down, resulting in my having to pee every ten minutes? Of course I didn't. And it would be entirely inappropriate for me to talk about my sleeping habits, but far be that from stopping me."

"Indeed."

"I mean, you try getting comfortable with a belly as big as mine. Oops."

"Was that another put-down?"

"Inadvertent, to be sure. But if you were to apologize for your rude behavior, after being politely rebuffed for consuming enough to feed a small third-world country or two buckeye matrons of the Presbyterian persuasion; *and* donate two hundred dollars; *plus* change places with me so that I might feed the male child within who is ruining what happens to be—and this I've only recently discovered—a remarkably comely temple for the Holy Spirit, I'll see to it that you get your eighteenth pork patty."

"Okay."

"*What?*"

"I'll take your place in the serving line, and I'll donate the money, but I'm *not* going to apologize."

"Fair enough."

"You can argue until the cows come home, Magdalena, but—"

"I agreed to your terms."

"So you did. Is this a trap?"

"Nope."

Minerva J. Jay was nobody's fool, least of all mine. "Tell me, if this fund-raiser is being put on by the Brotherhood, what are you doing helping out? Even when you weren't pregnant—despite being dressed in those horrible dowdy clothes of yours—there was no mistaking you for a man."

"Thanks—I think. Anyway, the Brotherhood, as you can see, has gotten rather small, thanks to Reverend Fiddlegarber, who stole half the congregation when he—uh—"

"Was kicked out for being a fraud? Face it, Magdalena, the man was evil."

"This just goes to show you that for a lot of people it's not the facts that matter, but the personality. At any rate, as senior deaconess of the congregation, I see it as my duty to step up to the plate whenever there's a need."

"How terribly holy of you, Magdalena."

"Hmm, do I detect a tinge of sarcasm? Well, never mind, dear. I choose to take the high road in order to expedite my breakfast. Just take this empty tray and hie thyself into the kitchen to fetch my hotcakes. And while you're there, scrounge around in the fridge, will you, and see if you can find some real butter. Nora Ediger tends to hide it behind the half-and-half at large functions, because she thinks the hoi polloi can't tell butter from margarine. But strictly speaking, seeing as how the butter was bought with church money, it belongs to all of us, and now that the crowd is waning, I'm thinking it's time to haul out the good stuff—don't you?"

"No."

"No?"

"For your information, missy, I like butter as well as you!"

"But it's full of trans fats."

"And the cheap margarine you serve isn't?"

"I'm sure it is, but you ate so *many* pancakes, Minerva, you couldn't possibly have savored each one. Be honest, now, doesn't it make sense to save what little real butter we have for those of us with more discriminating taste buds?"

"Is that yet another put-down?" With each word, her voice rose a billion decibels. "I'm telling you, Magdalena, it's busybodies like you who'll be the death of me!"

I gently rubbed the taut, stretched skin of the watermelon that hung suspended from my rib cage. "Please, dear, Little Jacob will hear you."

"Who cares? Do you honestly think he can understand?"

"I do, and yes."

"Don't be ridiculous. If babies understood language, they wouldn't babble nonsense for the first year and a half of their lives."

"I'm only trying to look out for your health, Minerva—since it's obvious that you don't." Uh-oh, I'd gone too far: with the exception of my husband, no adult likes to be babied.

"Hey, Little Jacob, can you hear me? Your mommy's trying to kill me with oleo. Kill me, kill me, *kill* me!" Minerva J. Jay cupped her pudgy hands to her mouth, the better to be heard as she bellowed, "Listen up, everyone: Magdalena's trying to kill me!"

"Stop it," I hissed. I undid my extra-large apron and threw it at her.

My name is Magdalena Portulaca Yoder and I am forty-eight years old. Normally my age would be none of your business, but since I am with child at this advanced age, and it is my first pregnancy, I may as well get every shred of sympathy I can garner. Also, and this is even less of your beeswax, this ever-expanding state of affairs was achieved entirely the old-fashioned way—no test tubes, no hormone shots, not even Viagra for my hubby.

Dr. Gabriel Rosen and I were experiencing a very troubled spot in our marriage when the improbable news of my conception was delivered by the impossibly beautiful Dr. Rashid. That was nearly eight months ago. The very troubled spot remains in our marriage, but fortunately she now lives across Hertzler Road and up a very long lane. I like to think that I've managed to sever at least one of the apron strings that tied her to my beloved husband, her son, but if that's so, then said strings have the ability to grow back—somewhat like lizard tails.

My people were originally Amish, and most of them arrived in this country in 1738 aboard the *Charming Nancy* (*The Descendants of Jacob Hochstetler* erroneously sets the date at 1736). From that time until now, my direct forebears filtered up (or down, depending on your point of view) through the ranks of leniency, so that by the time I came along, my family was no longer Amish, but Old Order Mennonite.

Since the 1830s we have lived in Hernia, Pennsylvania, which, by the way, is located *nowhere near Lancaster*. We are located in the south-central part of the state, just about a horseshoe toss north of wild and woolly Maryland. There are only four businesses in this town of less than 2,500 souls: Miller's Feed Store, the blacksmith shop (run by One-Eyed John), Sam Yoder's Corner Market (where the words *fresh produce* are an oxymoron), and last, but far from least, the PennDutch Inn.

The inn has been very successful, thanks to an early-on review from *Condor Nest Travel* magazine. Throw in a handful of murders, some torrid Hollywood romances, some embarrassing Washington disclosures, and a quick mention of a Japanese tourist who may have been stuck in the teensy-weensy elevator for some months after her last desperate cries were heard (it really was not my fault, and I do plan to get her out someday), and it couldn't help but be a moneymaker. In fact, so much moola did the PennDutch pull in, that she is now temporarily closed while I count it all and attend to the growing of my male child. In the meantime, the staff—Freni Hostetler—remains on duty to see that I, as well as my husband and our fourteen-year-old pseudo-stepdaughter, eat well.

"Magdalena!"

I started into reality. "Uh—what?"

Amygdaline Schrock is Hernia's second busiest body, after my best friend, Agnes Mishler. She had a firm grip on my dress sleeve, which meant I wasn't going to enjoy any pancakes until I heard her out.

"I thought you might be interested in knowing that a certain so-and-so is exchanging saliva with a certain who-does-she-think-she-is behind the church."

"Please, dear, I *do* plan to eat."

"Well, she's your friend; I just thought you'd want to know."

"Still— You don't mean Agnes, do you?"

"Well, I don't mean Santa Claus."

"But she's engaged to Harmon, and he lives in one of the square states and isn't due to visit for another three months, when he comes down for their wedding. Are you absolutely sure?"

"I saw it myself, Magdalena, and this wasn't any outsider named Harmon: this was our very own Kenneth Kuhnberger."

"Get out of town!"

"I beg your pardon?"

"That's just an expression my sister, Susannah, uses. It's not to be taken literally—although I do know of a real estate agent who lives in Sarasota. She specializes in selling homes down there to Mennonite retirees."

"And what makes you think I'm old enough to retire?"

"The fact that you used to babysit for me when I was a little girl, and you were already a senior in high school by then. On the other hand, it's possible that you were held back six or seven grades."

"Tell me, Magdalena, is it my name you don't like?"

Actually, Eh-*mig*-dah-lin is a nice strong name, reminiscent of my own. The fact that it refers to a cyanogenetic substance found in the seeds of apricots and bitter almonds only adds to its charm. What the woman doesn't seem to get is that she has the personality of a wolverine.

"No, *you* tell *me* something," I said. "Why do you think I would want to hear bad news about a dear friend?"

"Uh—so that you could do something about it?"

"Like what? I'm not her mother, for goodness' sake."

"Well"—she snorted—"you can't blame a gal for trying." With that, her talons released my sleeve and she stomped off to find another victim to demoralize.

"Save me a stack," I called pleasantly to my crew. "And I want six pieces of bacon—remember, I'm eating for two. I'll be right back."

And indeed I was, for the breakfast was being held in our fellowship hall, which is in the basement of the church, and it took me only two minutes to cut through the kitchen and up the back cement steps. As it was a cold and windy March day, no one in their right mind was up there kissing, and neither were Agnes and Kenneth Kuhnberger. But even though I'd been gone such a short time, a lot seemed to have happened during my absence.

None of the servers were at their stations. In fact, just about everybody in Hernia seemed to be crowded *behind* the serving tables—which, by the way, is an absolute no-no.

"What the ding, dang, dong is going on?" I hollered. "Sorry," I mumbled to the little one on board. "I'll try to clean up the language."

Amygdaline Schrock broke loose from the jumble of folks and took up her post at my elbow again. When she tried to grab my sleeve, I brushed her hand away in a firm but gentle manner.

"You got your wish, Magdalena: Minerva J. Jay is dead."

2

"*What?*"

"The second you left, she sank to the floor like an imploding building."

"Has anyone called 911?"

"Elmer Troyer did. He called both the dispatch center in Bedford, plus our very own chief of police."

I craned my neck for a better look but could see only a sea of backs. *Wide* backs.

"What makes you think she's dead? Does anyone here know CPR?"

"Karen Imhoff is a trauma nurse at Bedford County Memorial. She can't find a pulse."

"But I was gone only a minute," I wailed.

Amygdaline consulted an enormous watch that somehow managed to look both officious and cheap at the same time. "You were gone six minutes and nineteen seconds."

"I *was*? Oops, I forgot about detouring for a potty break on the way back, and wouldn't you know there was a line, and of course I just had to get behind Thelma Neubrander, who went on, and on, and on, and—"

"Just like you?"

I sighed. "If the shoe fits, but it better be a size eleven, and with my feet as swollen as they are—"

"Magdalena, quit stalling."

"I beg your pardon?"

"You're blathering like on a drunken writer, whereas the Magdalena I thought I knew would take charge."

"She would?"

"You bet your bottom dollar, and from what I understand, that's rather a huge fortune."

"Forsooth, although it still wouldn't be enough to win if the Donald played trump."

"I'm afraid you've lost me."

"Nothing; it was just some card-playing humor—which I don't do, mind you, except for rook and old maid, on account of real cards can lead to sin—"

"You're stalling again," she hissed. This time specks of her spittle peppered my face. They may have been minuscule, but I could feel them long after they'd landed.

Clearly, I had been goaded beyond human endurance. Perhaps, then, I can be forgiven for grabbing the lids of two empty metal serving trays and clanging them together like a pair of giant cymbals. *That* got everyone's attention, including the man-child's. The little fella kicked me so hard that I grunted in pain.

As a matter of fact, he kicked me twice. It was like he was using my abdominal wall as a place to push off from, so he could swim away to somewhere quiet and sane.

"Hey, take it easy," I whispered. "I would never kick you. And just in case you're looking for a way out, the portal's not due to open for another two weeks. So as they say in New Joisey, fuggedaboutit."

The murmuring of the crowd informed me that I was already losing their attention. I had to act fast.

"Stand back," I roared. "That means everybody except for Karen Imhoff and the victim—uh, I mean Minerva J. Jay."

My words were like a magic wand. Or perhaps it was the genuine faux-pewter trays; maybe they thought I'd box their ears with them. At any rate, the throng shrank back, forming a circle, into which yours truly stepped.

I knelt beside Karen, who was holding Minerva's head in her lap. "Is she really dead?" I whispered.

The throng leaned in, as if bowing their heads for prayer. "Let's just say that if I was at the hospital right now, I'd look for a doctor to call it."

"In that case, since everyone's already assumed a pious pose, let's really pray. Who'd like to go first?" My words had the same apparent effect on them as spraying Raid does on a pile of roaches; they fanned out in all directions, although to be perfectly honest, very few flipped on their backs and kicked their legs in the air.

I could hear Karen sigh loudly. It sounded like relief.

"What's that all about, dear?"

"I know this is going to sound awful, Miss Yoder, but I hate public, extemporaneous prayer: it's the stilted prayer language that really sets my teeth on edge."

"You mean like when folks use words like *thee* and *thine*?"

"Exactly. That's King James English, not biblical English. There was no such language as English when the Bible was first written. But you know, what really sets my teeth on edge is *just*."

"The word *just*? What's wrong with that?"

"For some reason it gets inserted into every unscripted prayer. Listen for it, Miss Yoder; you won't be able to miss it. Someone will get started praying, and the next thing you know, they'll say something like 'Lord, we *just* ask that you heal our sister Debra,' or 'Lord, we *just* ask that you give us the necessary wisdom to deal with this problem.' What does that mean? And if you ask them why they've inserted the word *just* into their prayers, they'll look at you like you're crazy. I guess they just don't hear *just* anymore."

"Well, I for one don't do it!"

"Ah, but you do: I've heard you. Virtually every born-again Christian does it."

"But not me," I wailed. "You're putting a word into my mouth that doesn't belong there."

"Excuse me, Miss Yoder, the crowd is edging closer again, so are we going to pray or not?"

With considerable effort, I managed to get to my feet. "I'm still looking for a volunteer to pray," I said. "And you can't use the word *just*. Anyone who does use it gets to make a one-hundred-dollar donation to the new roof fund. So think of it as a chance to give, folks."

The crowd murmured loudly as they scattered to the far corners of the fellowship hall—well, except for the blessed Karen Imhoff and the stubborn Amygdaline Schrock. At any rate, that left only the four of us, and since I was the wealthiest and, some say, the orneriest, I decided to give my own challenge a try. Alas, whether by intention or not, I failed miserably; all that matters is that the brotherhood had a thousand more clams in their coffers when I was through addressing the Almighty to mark the occasion of Minerva J. Jay's passing.

Hernia's only law enforcement officer arrived just seconds after my resounding *amen*, and I immediately filled him in. Police Chief Chris Ackerman is only in his midtwenties and so good-looking that women have been known to commit minor crimes just so they could have the pleasure of being thrown into his jail overnight. Jaywalking, loitering, even solicitation citations initially went through the roof. Gradually, however, as the people of Hernia learned that the Good Lord, in His wisdom, had chosen Chris to bat for the other team, this much-needed source of income dried up.

Once, believe it or not, in more prosperous times, we had a two-person police department, and on occasion even that was not enough. At first glance Hernia may not seem like a den of iniquity, but the Devil is just as hard at work here as he is anywhere else. Thank heaven, then, that murder follows me around like odor follows a troop of prepubescent boys, because over the years it has allowed me to become well steeped in the workings of the criminal mind. I say this without hubris. Indeed, I get very little credit—certainly no monetary reward—for solving the brutal deaths of others, and I am often subjected to great danger.

Why, then, one might legitimately ask, do I involve myself in such a dangerous pastime? Do I experience the same satisfaction one might feel if they've taken on the task of solving a particularly complicated puzzle? Absolutely not; the solutions to some murders are absurdly simple. Do I feel especially brave when I'm confronting a killer who has a gun digging into my well-formed ribs? Frankly, with my shapely knees knocking so hard, it's difficult to tell. Once I even soiled—uh, well, never you mind. But I will confess that another time I foiled a madman by jumping down into the pit of our six-seater outhouse.

"Miss Yoder!" Young Chris shook me with a good deal of force. "Miss Yoder, you're not going to faint again, are you?"

When you wake up and smell the coffee, you can only hope it's something better than what we serve at Beechy Grove Mennonite Church. "I'm as fine as frog hair, dear. I was lost in thought; it's still pretty much virgin territory."

"I was saying that we should go back to my office and talk."

"Talk? About what? I told you everything."

"Yes, but that was off the record, and in the presence of Miss Schrock."

"Why, I never!" Amygdaline was panting with rage. "Listen here, young man, I pay your salary, just as much as Magdalena does, so I have the same right to be privy to this conversation as does she."

"But you don't," I said.

"I beg your pardon?"

"Amygdarling, this is just a guesstimate, mind you, but I'm pretty sure that I pay at least ten times more in taxes than you do, which is neither here nor there, since I am Chief Ackerman's boss, as well as his sidekick, although at this stage of the game, I'm not the one doing most of the kicking."

"Chief! Did you hear what Magdalena called me?"

No doubt Chris's laugh was an attempt to smooth things over. "Amyg*darling*?"

"But I'm *not* her darling! The woman gives me the creeps. She's a self-admitted adulteress, you know."

"Inadvertent," I hissed.

"Hey, no fair; you can't hiss without an *S*."

"So?"

The chief of police grabbed my arm and steered me up the front steps, into the foyer, and then out to his cruiser. "Hernia is nothing like the quiet little Mennonite town I imagined it would be," he said, "and you are nothing like the typical Mennonite woman, are you?"

"Heaven help us if that were so, dear."

3

Hernia looks nothing like Lancaster, which lies at the other end of the state. The bucolic pastures of Lancaster are reminiscent of England, albeit one peopled with Amish folks, whereas our tiny plots are squeezed between mountain ridges and highways so twisted that the mere sight of them is enough to induce colic—without the *bu*. Or worse. Movie stars—mainly guests staying at the PennDutch Inn—who just can't seem to lose those extra ten pounds for that coveted role have their limo drivers race back and forth along Hertzler Road ad nauseam. In fact, this has happened so much lately that some local wag has dubbed that stretch *Hurl*zler Road—not that it's caught on.

At any rate, the town itself is almost equally divided between old historic homes and houses that are totally devoid of character. Fortunately, most of the latter are to be found clustered in one subdivision with the nonsensical name of Foxcroft. We have one main street, which is sensibly named just that, and the aforementioned four businesses. Our community gathering place is up on top of Stucky Ridge, where there is both a picnic grounds and a cemetery. Both places have lovely views.

I already have too many strikes against me to admit to being proud of Hernia, but I really can't imagine a finer place to raise a child. She—or he—can fish or swim in Miller's Pond in the summer; ice skate on it in the winter; attempt to dam up Slave Creek in the spring; go on hayrides and pick apples in the fall; and play in haylofts and count stars any time of the year. And if she is a very naughty child, which mine won't be, she can taunt the Amish as they drive by in their buggies, or fling "road apples" at the tourists and then run and hide. But she better run very fast, or else her mama will catch her, and then little Magdalena won't be able to sit down properly for a week.

Still, I couldn't be happier living where I am, which is more than most folks can say. I may have gurgled softly to myself with contentment.

Chris slammed on the brakes. "Are you all right?"

"Why the Sam Hill did you do that?"

"You let out this horrible groan, Miss Yoder; I thought maybe you'd gone into labor."

"Well, I might now, for Pete's sake!"

"No kidding?"

"Kidding."

"Whew. Don't string me on like that, Miss Yoder. When I was a kid I watched this movie—the one with Billy Crystal where he helps this calf be born. It was the scariest thing I ever saw. So, as much as I like you, I'm afraid I wouldn't be able to help if you went into labor and needed hands-on assistance."

"And that's a good thing, Chris, because if you ever did peek at what's hiding behind my sturdy Christian underwear, your next job will involve a tin cup—not that I'm advocating violence, mind you, but I'm sure you get my drift."

"I hear you, ma'am."

"Chris, have you ever seen a town as pretty as Hernia?"

"Yes, ma'am, plenty of them. In fact, most anyplace you look at back home in California is prettier than this."

Now, that got my goat. "Chris, after all this time you still refer to California as home. Is that because there are other *homo*sexuals there? No pun intended, dear."

Chris has a thick head of blond hair, a strong jawline, and teeth like Chiclets. He looks more like a movie star than most A-list actors do. When he threw back his head and laughed, I felt like I was watching a performance.

"Would it surprise you, Miss Yoder, to learn that I'm not the only queer in Hernia?"

"I beg your pardon?"

"You know, gay."

"Uh—well, there may be one or two in Bedford. But surely not in tiny little Hernia. And not any homegrown gays—except maybe for Willard."

"Miss Yoder, as we discussed when I was hired, it is not my job to expose who does what in this town behind closed doors, as long as they are consenting adults, and they are not doing bodily harm to each other."

"Ah, yes, the Sodom and Gomorrah clause. No offense, Chris, but it was the former chief, your mentor, who insisted on its inclusion."

"Nevertheless, Miss Yoder, you wouldn't want to know what *really* goes on."

"Yes, I would."

"Trust me, you wouldn't. Just last night I had to use bolt cutters and not for the usual reason either."

"So if was it wasn't to cut bolts—"

"I'll save you some time, Miss Yoder; it was for cutting handcuffs free from bedposts."

"What on *earth* would handcuffs be doing around bed-posts?"

"You see? You're not ready to know what goes on behind closed doors, not even in a conservative town like Hernia."

"But I am," I wailed. "I'm intensely curious—I am *ready*!"

By then we'd pulled next to the police station and it was time to resume acting like a grown-up, instead of the oversexed adolescent my raging hormones had turned me into.

"Last one inside is a rotten egg," I said.

Hernia City Jail was definitely not built for comfort. We've purposely kept our bunks hard and narrow, our mattresses lumpy, our pillows stained, all in hopes of discouraging recidivism. I know it's worked in my case: I was there only one night—in fact, just part of a night—before breaking out.

Unfortunately, not everyone is turned off by the grim accommodations. Some folks, like my sister, Susannah, have been in and out of Hernia's slammer so many times that they keep their own toothbrushes there. In my sister's case, even though she's cleaned up her act, her name has been carved into so many flat surfaces that she won't be forgotten until there has been a complete renovation, which is the second Tuesday after never.

It was during one of her many stints behind bars that Susannah fell in love with then chief of police Melvin Stoltzfus. For the record, I was always dead set against this match between my sister and the giant praying mantis, and I was horrified, but not shocked, when Melvin murdered my pastor, Reverend Shrock. It pains me to say that this horrible creature managed to break out of the state prison and is now on the loose. Rumors as to his whereabouts abound, the most consistent of which is that he is still in the Greater Hernia area.

Now, where was I? Oh yes, the Hernia jail. On the morning of Minerva J. Jay's untimely death, the rancid sludge in the coffeepot informed me that there had been no prisoners in residence for quite some time. This also meant that the Bloughs, the Amish couple who maintained the building, either were on vacation, or were experiencing some family tragedy. The sad fact that my gray matter continues to shrink at an alarming rate did not stop Chris from instantly reading my mind.

"They've gone to Sarasota—just like about half the retired Amish population around here. Is this something recent? I would have thought Florida vacations were too worldly for them."

"That's what the other half of our Amish think—and rather strongly so. It's a phenomenon that has divided Amish communities across America in recent decades. Those that do spend a portion of their golden years there are able to justify their actions with the fact that there is now already an Amish community in Sarasota to meet their spiritual and physical needs, so that they can still live apart. It was much more difficult for the pioneer retirees, so to speak."

In deference to my hemorrhoids (about which I've complained loudly in the past), Chris offered me his office chair. It boasts the only padded seat in the police station, so I wisely did not turn it down, as I've been known to do, just to prove my mettle.

"Sorry, I don't have any hot chocolate to offer you," he said, "but I have a huge assortment of flavored teas. They're all decaf, of course."

"Do you have Constant Comment?"

"You bet. I'll have to try that sometime; seems like everyone asks for it."

"You have any ladyfingers?"

"Only Archway lemon-filled rounds." Noting the look of disappointment on my face, he added, "Branch out a little, Miss Yoder. You might find that you really like them."

After we were settled in with our nosh (after all, I hadn't had a chance to eat any pancakes), Chief Ackerman didn't waste any time getting down to business. "Miss Yoder," he said, his voice assuming a supplicating tone, "I realize that you have certain— uh—limitations at the moment. But quite honestly, you are the best detective I have met."

I patted my bun, which is covered at all times by an organza prayer cap. It was a reflexive action; I really didn't mean to seem proud.

"Thank you very much, Chief, but as you well know, I am *not* a detective."

He shrugged his broad, well-muscled shoulders. "Labels. Who needs them anyway?"

"Well, they do make buying clothes a lot easier. But please, Chief, cut to the chase. Suppose my water should break right here. Would you know what to do?"

He turned a whiter shade of pale. "Miss Yoder, you know as well as I do that Miss Jay was the victim of homicide, and that the murderer belongs to your church."

I stared at him for who knows how long. No doubt my mouth was open and my shapely lips bedecked with garlands of drool. Finally it was he who took the initiative by waving a hand an inch or two in front of my face.

"Are you in there, Miss Yoder?" he asked, and not unkindly either.

Like an engine on a cold day, I sputtered to life. "I—uh—I'm in here, all right. I'm just wondering if my forehead is missing. How's my skull in general?"

His own forehead wrinkled, but he obligingly gave me the once-over. "You look just fine to me."

"That's what I hoped you would say, and I don't think that even *you* can read minds that well, Chief, without some assistance. But that's exactly what *I* believe: Minerva J. Jay was murdered."

4

"But that's silly!" We said it in unison. Then we both laughed inappropriately, and for an indecent period of time. When we stopped, it was only because the tea water was boiling.

"At least I have my hormones to blame it on," I said. "What's your excuse?"

"For the laughing, or my conclusion?"

"Both, and you may as well start at the beginning."

He selected the least-chipped mug, rinsed it with some of the boiling water, and then plopped the bag of Constant Comment in. "Don't spoil this with milk," he said. "Besides, I haven't got any." That said, he filled the mug dangerously close to the brim.

"I'm waiting, dear."

"Yes, I know, but I'm trying to soothe your savage breast first. You see, Miss Yoder, whether or not you personally had anything to do with Miss Jay's death is irrelevant to my way of thinking, but your presence at the breakfast was a sure sign of foul play."

I am *not* an umbrageous woman; nonetheless, I recoiled with indignation. Thank heavens I had yet to pick up the too-full mug, otherwise, Little Jacob might have learned that his mother had picked up some rather salty language from both his father and his auntie Susannah.

"What on earth do you mean by that?" I demanded. "And incidentally, I do not believe you intended to reference 'my bosoms,' as neither of my breasts has exhibited symptoms of savagery in the past several months."

He winced. "Miss Yoder, in the year or so that I've been here, several local people have died of natural causes, yet you weren't involved with any of them."

"I can't help it if all my friends are healthy," I wailed.

"No offense, Miss Yoder, but your wailing is very unbecoming. At any rate, the point I'm trying to make is that for some strange reason you seem to somehow, at some point, get tangled up with every murder case that comes down the pike."

"*That's* because you always call me when the going gets tough." I made a sincere effort to stand but succeeded only in bumping Little Jacob against the edge of Chief Ackerman's desk.

"Ouch," the chief said (Little Jacob couldn't quite talk yet).

It was really only a light tap, and the little feller was well protected by amniotic fluid, but it was just enough of a jolt to cause some of the tea to spill over the rim of the cup. Although I agreed with the young squirt from California that Constant Comment shouldn't be ruined by milk, I objected to his conclusion that I was the Grim Reaper, and most of all, I was extremely annoyed that he had the chutzpah to comment on my wailing.

"Chief, be a dear, will you, and run across the street to Yoder's Corner Market and get me some milk."

He looked alarmed. "For your *tea*?"

"It's the cravings, you know; they can't be helped. And while you're at it, see if Sam still has that jar of pickled artichoke hearts. I know it's been there for years, but—"

"That man is a thief. He rips off the Amish and the elderly, both segments of society who find it too difficult to get into bustling Bedford to shop for essentials. You can buy the same milk in the city for one-quarter as much, and I'll bet it will be fresher."

"Not if you keep flapping your gums, dear." I gave him a stern but motherly look. Alas, it didn't seem to have much effect on him. It was time to trot out the officious boss-woman glare. "A mayor with unfulfilled cravings cannot possibly concentrate long enough to sign her employee's checks, *capice?*"

He snapped to attention. "One percent or skim?"

"Whole milk, of course; Little Jacob is *not* on a diet."

"Yes, ma'am."

And away he went.

Call me a control freak, but after all, the boy was twenty-six, and I was forty-eight. In my day—never mind that; it was *still* my day, and would continue to be my day until Little Jacob arrived. Then it would be his day until he turned eighteen, or moved out of the house, whichever came first. Although from what I understood by listening to other mothers, being a parent is a lifelong commitment.

At any rate, it would have been a complete waste of time for me to twiddle my thumbs while Chief Chris Ackerman was chasing down milk and pickled artichokes. I am sure that there are those who don't agree, but if you ask me, the Good Lord wouldn't have given me a gene for snooping if He hadn't intended for me to use it. I do believe the Bible calls that sort of misuse a "buried talent." And furthermore, on my second try to extricate myself from my chair, I practically flew out of it, as if my posterior had sprouted wings—perhaps little bunting wings.

Therefore, it was with blessings from above that I glided over to the window and casually lowered the blinds. I wasn't interested in riffling through the stacks of papers on the chief's desk; it was the contents of his drawers that called to me.

The Hernia Police Department's single desk had been donated by the Commonwealth Map & Survey Company when it went out of business in the mid-1950s. The desk is made of solid wood, but painted battleship gray, and is large enough to spread a highway map on top and still have room left over. There is a shallow center drawer and two very deep drawers on either side. It was these deep drawers that held the most allure.

Depending on whether or not Sam had customers to wait on, or perhaps was in an exceptionally garrulous mood (Sam's six-hundred-and-eighty-four-pound wife, Dorothy, is the bane of his existence, and sometimes he feels the need to vent), the chief could be back in as little as two minutes, or as long as twenty. If I expected to find anything of note, I would have to get down on my knees and dig around in the bottom of each drawer—and then leave everything virtually intact.

"Hang on, Little Jacob," I said and, steadying myself with both hands gripping the lip of the desk, lowered myself into place.

The first drawer I perused contained nothing but old files. Since the majority of them mentioned me, they would have made good rainy-day reading, but I wisely skipped over them. The second drawer contained a variety of things: a pair of jumper cables; a box half full of Snickers bars; a grip builder; a black compact umbrella with a wayward spoke; and a large padded manila envelope, clasp side up. I pulled out the envelope and laid it on the desk, clasp side down. After that, I can't remember if I thanked the Lord first and gasped second, or the other way around.

In large, looping feminine script, written with black marker, were the following words: *To Chief Chris Ackerman, from Minerva J. Jay—Please Open In The Event Of My Death.* The fact that every word was capitalized could at least eliminate the possibility that Miss Jay had ever been a copy editor. The envelope, by the way, was sealed shut, as well as closed with the clasp.

I bolted to the window. The door to Sam Yoder's Corner Market was still closed, and there was no sign of Chris. What to do, what to do? Then I had a flash of inspiration, which, I'm sure you'll agree, could only have been heaven-sent. If steaming an envelope open worked for Agatha Christie's sleuths, why couldn't it work for me—a real-life woman of the cloak-and-shoot-dagger looks? With trembling fingers I turned the kettle back on high and, whilst my heart pounded at a dangerously high rate, held the envelope over the steam it soon generated.

Now, I don't know much about the dame herself, but it's my guess that most of her tea came to her by the way of servants, and that if she ever did really steam open envelopes, they weren't the sturdy manila kind. Nevertheless, after a good deal of puckering—both the envelope and my brow—I got the dang thing open. But wouldn't you know it, at the same instant I heard a sound that ranks up there with one of the ten most annoying sounds in the world, my wailing included.

"Fear not, Little Jacob," I said. "It's just your cousin Sam, laughing—although frankly, it sounds more like a donkey in heat braying for a mate."

My son's response was to wallop me in the ribs. No doubt he was punishing me for my crude reference to an ass desirous of sex; he was, after all, very much a minor and had every right to be upset. What a smart lad he was already turning out to be. Perhaps I should reconsider his name; Einstein Yoder-Rosen seemed a trifle pretentious, and I've never especially cared for Albert. But seeing as how he was the child of my dotage, and Sarah in the Bible had named the child of her old age Isaac, and Sir Isaac Newton was undoubtedly very bright . . .

Sam brayed again, sending Little Jacob into paroxysms of calisthenics. Finally the gravity of the situation permeated my thick skull; if I could hear Sam, then the door to Sam Yoder's Corner Market had to be open, which meant that at any minute the door to the police station would open, and the young, albeit handsome, whippersnapper from the Golden State would find me spying on him. I had to act fast.

The first thing I did was dump the contents of the padded envelope into my sensible, Mennonite-size purse (if I can't carry last Sunday's church bulletin in it without having to fold it, the bag is too small). All that fell out was a key. That's *it*—just a key. A house key at that.

Now, although it is neither here nor there, it is my assertion that every middle-class American is in possession of at least one key, the function of which escapes him or her. I had just such a key on my ring. It was supposed to be the key to the back door of my house, even though it didn't fit *any* of my doors.

Yet I was almost positive I was given this key by the builder himself, after the PennDutch was restored following the tornado that leveled it and left me lying facedown in a cow patty. But one thing I did know for sure: it had been manufactured by the same company that had produced the key in Minerva J. Jay's padded envelope, and a switch would surely go unnoticed for the meantime.

If only I could get the envelope resealed. The kettle method wasn't going to work; I knew from experience that once an envelope has been opened, it needs tape to be sealed. But maybe the chief had some glue— That's when I noticed a roll of stamps. Somehow, in the next minute and a half, I managed to detach the useless key and thrust it deep within the envelope, transfer some of the glue from the stamps to the envelope with my tongue, and then seal it. After that I returned said envelope to its proper place in the drawer. What I couldn't quite manage was settling my huge bulk back into the chief's chair before he stepped back in.

5

Banana Sour Cream Pancakes with Cinnamon Maple Syrup

Adapted from a recipe from Bette's Oceanview Diner in Berkeley, California, these are melt-in-your-mouth moist and tender. The Cinnamon Maple Syrup is easy to assemble while the pancakes are slowly cooking.

4 large eggs
2 cups sour cream
⅔ cup unbleached all-purpose flour
2 teaspoons baking powder
½ teaspoon ground cinnamon
¼ teaspoon salt
1–2 bananas, peeled and cut into thin slices

Cinnamon Maple Syrup (recipe follows)

1. In a large bowl, whisk the eggs until light and bubbly. Stir in the sour cream until blended. Sift the flour, baking pow-

der, cinnamon, and salt onto the liquid ingredients. Fold until blended.

2. Heat a large nonstick griddle or skillet over medium heat until hot enough to sizzle a drop of water. Brush with a thin film of vegetable oil, or spray with nonstick cooking spray. For each pancake, pour a scant ¼ cup batter onto griddle or into skillet. Immediately arrange 3 or 4 thin slices of banana on the surface of each pancake. Adjust the heat to medium-low. Cook the pancakes slowly until the tops are covered with small bubbles and the bottoms are lightly browned. Carefully turn and cook until lightly browned on the other side. Repeat with the remaining batter.

3. Serve immediately with Cinnamon Maple Syrup.

MAKES ABOUT TWELVE 4-INCH PANCAKES.

Cinnamon Maple Syrup: Combine 1 cup maple syrup, 1 tablespoon unsalted butter, and ½ teaspoon ground cinnamon in a small saucepan and cook, stirring to blend, until the mixture boils. Remove from heat and let stand until pancakes are ready to serve.

6

"Miss Yoder, you're up!"

"It's these ding-dang hemorrhoids—pardon my French, Little Jacob."

"You know, of course, that's insulting to the French people."

"Are *ding* and *dang* really swear words?" The first rule of good espionage is that *should* one get caught, one must rely on the D word: *deflect*.

"No," Chris said, "they aren't, but they *are* intended as replacements for swear words, so it is as if you said the real words."

I pretended to let that sink in. "I see your point," I said after an uncomfortable length of time had passed. "You know, Chief, it just occurred to me that you are no longer quite as sweet and respectful as you were when you first moved here from California."

His eyes widened in surprise. "I'm *not*?"

"To the contrary, dear, if you were a character in a book, you might even be labeled annoying. No doubt some impatient reader would toss the book across the room and promise never to buy another of that author's books ever again."

The drawer I'd ravaged was still slightly ajar, but young Chris absentmindedly closed it with his knee. "Wow! I didn't see that one coming."

"We never do, do we? Now, be a dear and hand me the goodies. You wouldn't happen to have an extra cup around here for the milk, would you? I'd drink from the carton, but I usually end up spilling on myself, and these maternity outfits are bling-blang expensive."

"You don't want it for your *tea*?"

"What? And ruin a perfectly good, albeit cold, cup of Constant Comment?"

In the end, until we received an autopsy report from Harrisburg, there was nothing young Chris and I could do but make a list of everyone who could have touched Minerva J. Jay's hotcakes that morning, and then jot down a few notes listing why he, or she, would have, or would *not* have, done the dastardly deed. There were "would haves" for every possible suspect, if only because Miss Jay was not a likable person.

This not to say, I must hasten to add, that disliking someone gives an individual license to murder—or Lord only knows, I'd be dead—but rather that everything else being equal, and one was bent on killing someone, then why *not* make it Minerva? I think I speak for everyone when I say that she was not going to be missed; even her pet cat, Mr. Patty-cakes Woo-woo, followed the paper boy home one day.

As for the "would not haves"—while young Chris was willing to cut a few of the older folks a break, I saw them all as having the *potential* to take a human life. I know, that sounds absolutely horrid of me, and perhaps it was the hormones speaking, but when you really think about it, you need to look no further than the Holy Bible (and the New King James Version at that), to see that this is true.

Folks in the Good Book were always smiting each other, and a lot of the smiters are supposed to be our heroes. Why, just look at King David. He sent poor Uriah into battle at the front of the line, just hoping he'd get killed, so he could do the palace hokey pokey with Bathsheba. Well, guess what? Uriah did get killed, which makes King David not only a murderer, but an adulterer, yet we recite his psalms frequently in church and at just about every funeral.

My point is that if the man who wrote "The Lord Is My Shepherd" was capable of such a dastardly deed, then the hunched-over little old woman with the unromantic name of Frankie Schwartzentruber can also be a dangerous killer. Of course, there was no way someone as inexperienced in life as Chief Ackerman could be expected to reach the same conclusion. So when I was quite through sharing my opinions, and pretending to listen to him (by which time I'd long finished the artichokes and the milk), I decided to hightail my fanny across the street and torture a man who'd made my life miserable as a child.

Sam Yoder and I are first cousins, except that we're not. That too is a long story, and not one to be covered here, except to say that I only recently found out that I was adopted—oh, not only that, but I'm also a full sibling to my nemesis, Melvin Stoltzfus, who happens to be an escaped murderer. Now, where was I?

"Magdalena, you look lost."

"Huh?" I was standing just inside the door to Sam's shop, and I must admit I seemed to have forgotten my agenda on account of something being not quite right.

"But as beautiful and radiant as ever. I swear, Magdalena, if there is anything sexier than a pregnant woman, it's you."

"For your information, Sam, I *am* a woman. However, in light of the fact that I need to pick your meager brain, I shall interpret what you said as a compliment."

Sam Yoder's Corner Market has just three aisles, and as the front door boasts a strap of sleigh bells, it is almost impossible for him not to keep track of his customers. His extra vigilance meant that either he had some particularly juicy (and perhaps helpful) gossip to share, or else he wished to pursue his sex comment further. Just for the record, Sam is an *ex*-Mennonite, having left the fold in order to marry a Methodist.

"Trust me, Magdalena, I have never doubted your womanliness—not since you blossomed in the fifth grade like an Israeli desert. And of course my brain is yours for the picking, although I prefer to think of it as intellectual foreplay." He winked lasciviously.

"Shame on you, Sam; you're a married man."

"Yes, but unhappily so. The last time Dorothy and I consummated our marriage—"

I clapped my hands over my ears, but not so tight I couldn't hear the rest of his statement. "Even so, I am a happily married woman."

"Yeah, finally. But how long will that last? You and Gabe don't have a trouble-free marriage."

"Who does?" If I said it breezily, perhaps it was due to the hole between my ears. I made this shocking discovery only recently, when I suddenly realized how little I knew—about anything. Rest assured, however, I was not about to reveal my embarrassing condition to anybody, least of all Sam Yoder.

"You're a stubborn woman, Magdalena. The more you stand your ground, the more irresistible you become. Right now you're hotter than Angelina Jolie."

"You're a wicked man, Sam. May I assume that the chief told you all about Minerva's untimely demise?"

My former kinsman snorted. "You call that untimely? I'd have run her over with my delivery truck years ago if I'd thought I could get away with it."

I couldn't help gasping. Even for a Methodist that was going a bit far.

"And you call yourself a Christian!"

"Just hold your horses, Magdalena, until you hear what I have to say. But in the meantime, knowing you as I do, would you care to have a snack? I'm working on a couple of boxes of stale cookies and a gallon of slightly off orange juice; can't afford to throw away inventory just because of due dates. Speaking of which, you look pretty close. Would you like to sit down? I can pull my chair around from behind the counter."

It saddens me to say that the offer he'd just made was by far his most generous ever. But alas, this sort of miserly behavior is quite in keeping with Sam's character. When asked for food to contribute to family gatherings, he donates day-old bread and cold-cut packages that have been pried open by cautious customers. However, one must remember not to pile the coals of scorn too high on my pseudo-cousin's head. I mean, surely a good deal of the blame must lie with his maternal ancestress: persnickety Priscilla Peabody of Parsippany, whose parsimony was legendary. It was said she could squeeze blood from a persimmon, but I again digress.

"I hate alliteration," Sam said.

"What?"

"I said, 'You don't look so hot.' Don't get me wrong, you still look hotter than Angelina, but you look kind of sick."

"Uh-huh. I think I need to use the bathroom."

He pointed to the rear of the store. "Well, you know where it is. Just don't blame me if you see anything lying around—you know, like magazines and such—because it's my *private* bathroom. I don't normally let customers use it."

"Don't worry." I hadn't taken more than three steps when I felt my thighs become drenched with warm liquid.

"Magdalena! You could have at least held it in a few seconds longer!"

Believe me, I was mortified. Then terrified. It wasn't time yet, not for *that* to happen. It was still two weeks too early. Besides, there was no way I was going to even *begin* the process of welcoming Little Jacob into the world in Sam Yoder's miserable excuse for a grocery store.

"I didn't! I mean, it's nothing; just a little too much coffee this morning, that's all."

Sam may have been a slimy, slithering sleazebag, to put it kindly, but he wasn't a brainless slug. When it sank into his elliptical bald head that my water had broken, he lunged for his desk phone.

"I'm calling 911," he said. "Then I'm calling Gabe. Anyone else?"

"Oprah? Sam, it isn't what you think. It's just an embarrassing little episode of—holy Toledo!" I all but dropped to my knees as Little Jacob, no doubt inspired by Sam's lunge, dove for the nearest exit. Honestly, it was an abdominal pain the likes and intensity of which I'd never before experienced.

Sam's dialing hand froze while a smirk spread across his smarmy face. "Why, Magdalena, I do believe you swore."

"I did not! But since you're going to call, call *now*."

"All right, all right." He leaned on his checkout counter while he talked, and he talked far too long. My Amish cook, Freni, could have baked yeast rolls from scratch while he alternately nodded and mumbled.

"Well?" I demanded, quite reasonably after two real minutes (as measured by the clock above the counter) had passed. "What's taking so long?"

"Shh! I can't hear what she's saying if you insist on prattling in my ear."

I wasn't anywhere near his ear, a fact for which Sam should thank his lucky stars. "Jumping junipers and a pear tree," I screeched as a second pain shot like a lightning bolt down my abdomen to my nether regions.

Instead of getting off the phone, Sam stared at his watch while talking louder. "Yes, that was her. Look, you've got to send someone out; I can't do this alone."

The hairs on the nape of my neck stood up as I, true to form, assumed the worst. "Do *what*?"

"But I've never birthed a baby before," he all but shouted into the phone.

"And you won't now! Give me that dang thing!" Normally, given his strength, playing keep-away with Sam would be a losing proposition for me. But by leading with my belly (sorry, Little Jacob) I was able to unnerve him to the point where I could have grabbed a million dollars in cash from his register. Wresting the phone from him was child's play.

Nonetheless, Sam had to catch his breath. "You don't want to know, Magdalena."

"Yes, I do," I hollered into the receiver. "What *is* going on?"

The person on the other end of the line swore at me for shouting but caught herself after the third invective. "Why, Magdalena Yoder, is that *you*?"

"*Thelma Liddleputt?*"

"Indeed it is. I don't believe we've spoken since the tenth grade."

"And there's no time to speak now, dear, unless it has to do with the situation at hand. Where is the ambulance, and what is all this about Sam birthing my baby?"

"Uh—I take it he didn't tell you?"

"No, we've been too busy having tea and crumpets. Of course he didn't tell me—he just got off the phone!"

"Magdalena, sarcasm does not become you; it never did. Remember that time in biology class when we were lab partners and we had to dissect a—"

"Tell me where the ambulance is, Thelma, or I'll crawl through this phone line, belly and all, and do to you what we did to that frog—oops! I'm sorry, Thelma, I really am. The Devil made me say that."

There followed an unforgivably long pause. "I'll forgive you, Magdalena, but only because you're in the final stages of labor, and due to the mass poisonings at your church, there isn't an ambulance available in the tri-county area."

7

"This is no time for games, Thelma. Minerva J. Jay was the only victim of our pancake breakfast, as you well know."

"You wish. After you left, twenty-three people came down with food-poisoning symptoms and we had to call in the rescue squads from Somerset and Blair counties to transport the victims to Bedford County Memorial Hospital."

"That's just not possible."

"I don't lie—like *some* people I know, Magdalena. Remember the time in English class when Mrs. Seibert asked you if you'd finished your term paper, and you said that you had, but you hadn't even begun?"

"We're all works in progress, dear. Even you. Anyway, I'm not in the final stages of labor, because I've only just begun. I'll just have Chief Ackerman drive me into town."

"I'm afraid that won't be possible either. Your chief of police was pressed into service transporting the victims, but now he's stuck on this side of the bridge."

"Bridge? What bridge?"

"The one that spans Slave Creek. Isn't that the only way in and out of Hernia, except for that painfully circu—uh—circu—no, it's not circumference, uh—"

I may have lied to Mrs. Seibert, but at least I passed her course. "You mean circuitous," I may have snapped. "What about it?"

"Goodness me, Magdalena, there's no need to get snippy, just because you're about to have a baby with no one but that creepy Sam Yoder to assist you."

"I'm not about to—holy guacamole and a bowl full of chips," I roared. The third contraction was more like a wave of contractions, each one stronger than the last, and if my language strayed from snack items, it really was not my fault so much as it was Eve's. It was she, after all, who first bit into the forbidden fruit and then offered it to Adam. As part of Eve's punishment, the Good Lord cursed her with the pain of childbirth.

Until now I'd never really given that particular part of the creation story a whole lot of thought, but suddenly it had relevance, and, if I might be so bold, it seemed perhaps more than a wee bit unfair. I mean, far be it from me to tell God how to structure his punishment scale, but shouldn't Adam—and I mean this in the generic sense—also have to share in the pain of childbirth? Little Jacob got into my womb with some outside help, and if getting out of it was going to hurt so ding-dang much, then by rights my husband, Gabriel, ought to be made to share in the pain (Lord, that is only a suggestion, mind You).

"Magdalena, are you there?"

"No," I panted, "I'm off gathering mushrooms in the steppes of Mongolia."

"Is that sarcasm again?"

"You think? Finish telling me about the bridge, Thelma, or you don't get invited to this baby's dedication." As a Mennonite, I belong to a denomination that not only eschews, but practically abhors infant baptism. My ancestors faced death at the hands of the established church in Switzerland during the late 1500s, rather than submit to what they viewed as a senseless practice. The dedication of an infant to the Lord, however, has a sound biblical basis. Of course, Thelma needed no invitation if she merely wanted to attend the church service, but she knew that I was referring to the reception that would later be held at my house.

Thelma sighed. "Oh, all right, but you're so bossy. Always have been. Anyway, one of the ambulances was crossing the bridge when this big truck carrying farm machinery comes barreling down the hill from the other direction. The ambulance driver—that was Rory from up in Altoona—just managed to squeeze by, but the truck jackknifed and slammed sideways into the rails. Magdalena, there's no way you're getting across Slave Creek unless someone carries you across in a stretcher. Even then, how will you get there?"

"Sam," I bellowed, "get your truck!"

"I can't," he whined. "I tried to take my Dorothy into town last week and two tires blew. I haven't had time to fix them." Alas, he was probably telling the truth; the last time Dorothy had been weighed at Miller's Feed Store, she'd tipped the grain scale at six hundred and eighty-four pounds.

"Magdalena," Thelma snarled, "did you just shout in my ear?"

"You would too if a watermelon was pressing down on your pelvis."

"Aha, just as I thought. You're a very lucky woman, Magdalena Yoder; this is one of those what I call 'zip-zap' deliveries. Only one in a thousand women gets to be this lucky."

"Aaaaaaaaaaaaaaaaaaaaaaaagh!"

"Which is not to say that it isn't without some discomfort.

But like you said, you're about to give birth to a watermelon. You can't expect to get off scot-free."

"Errrrrrrrrrrrrrrrrrrrrrrrrrrrrrgh!"

"Do you feel like you need to push?"

How in the Sam Hill could I answer that question when I was panting as hard as if I'd just run the Pittsburgh marathon?

"Magdalena, did you take birthing classes? You know, like Lamaze?"

Oh, that I had! Mine has been a somewhat rocky marriage, and there have been a lot of things I've been intending to do but that I have put off until "things get better." Of course, they never quite have.

"I'll take that as a no," Thelma said after my telling pause. "So, here's what you'll do—"

"Unnnnnnnnnnnnnnnnnnnnnnnnh!"

I gasped for air like a stranded carp. I had no doubt that this last contraction had done more than position Little Jacob for a "zip-zap" exit. The bugger was already on his way.

"But—I—want an—ep—i—dural!"

"It's too late, Magdalena, even if there was a doctor standing right there. By the way, are you wearing panty hose?"

"*What?*"

"Oh, that's right, I remember now; you wear sturdy Christian underwear and thick woolen stockings when the weather's cold. Well, the good news is that the stockings can stay—"

I dropped the phone and instinctively lowered myself to a squatting position; Little Jacob had let it be known he was tired of our conversation.

"So that is how this little fella came to be born in Sam's tawdry market, and me without a single drop of painkiller in my system," I explained to the cluster of loved ones gathered around my bed in Bedford County Memorial Hospital. It was eight hours after the fact, and this was my bazillionth retelling of the story, but the first time that the entire bunch could assemble at the same time. The bridge had just been cleared.

If I must say so myself, Sam had done a remarkably good job of the delivery. He'd cut Little Jacob's cord with a sterilized box cutter, cleared the little fellow's air passages, bathed him, and swaddled him in an old apron that had been washed so many times, it was as soft as a pima cotton jersey.

My pseudo-cousin had even rustled up a semiclean set of sweat duds for me. It was the first time I'd ever worn pants. I might have been bothered even more by this very clear violation of Scripture had it not been for the fact that I had nothing on underneath them. Well, what's done is done, right? Since then I'd been bathed by a coterie of nurses (I donated their lounge, after all) and dressed in a sex-appropriate gown—that is to say, one of my very own new flannel nighties that the Babester had brought from home.

"*Nu*," my mother-in-law demanded, "you call dat a story? Mitt dis von I vas in labor for five days, not five minutes."

"Actually, it was closer to twenty-five minutes from start to finish. Once he poked his head out and looked around, Little Jacob seemed to have second thoughts."

"Yeah," Sam said, "and that's when I had to—"

"But all's well that ends well, right, Little Jacob?"

As if on cue, my seven-pound, two-ounce bundle of joy simultaneously mewled and yawned. Of course this indescribably cute response elicited oohs and aahs from everyone in the room, but as well it should. I'm not prejudiced, mind you—a fairer woman was never born—but Little Jacob was the single most perfect and harmoniously formed newborn I had ever seen.

"Mags," my sister, Susannah, said, "are you going to breast-feed?" The poor dear not only has a deficit of bosom, but she is able to, and does, carry a pitiful pooch named Shnookums around in her bra.

"Oh, gross," my pseudo-stepdaughter, Alison, chimed in. "Mom, ya don't mean ya really are going to feed him with your— I mean, that's disgusting!"

"*Going* to? I've already nursed him three times; your little brother is a bottomless pit."

"Ya mean *that* too?"

"You better believe it. If Lake Erie was breast milk, he could drain it dry."

"That's my boy," the Babester said proudly.

"No, Mom," Alison said, and there was an unusual sense of urgency in her voice. "I mean, like, is he really my little brother?"

"Listen, dear," I said, "you're my foster daughter now, right?"

"Right."

"But more than that, you're the daughter of my heart. So, therefore, Little Jacob is your brother. Case closed."

Alison beamed. "Mom, you're the best!"

Freni Hostetler, who is both my Amish cook and a mother figure, nodded vigorously. Due to the fact that she lacks a neck, her stout body rocked back and forth like a spinning top about to topple over.

"Yah, Magdalena, I am very proud of you. And to think that you had this baby with only Sam Yoder as a midwife! Ach, it was a miracle."

"Amen," Freni's husband, Mose, intoned.

"But tell me, Magdalena," Freni continued, "how soon will you have the brisket?"

"I guess that all depends on when you smuggle it in. And the sooner the better, I say. I'm famished."

"Hon," the Babester said, "I think she means 'bris.' "

"What's that? A little brisket?"

"Ach," said Mose, stroking his beard, "I think maybe some-one should tell her."

"Tell me *what*?"

"Hon," Gabe said, but his eyes were not on mine, "a bris is a ritual circumcision. We talked about that, remember?"

Dare I admit that I had? But the conversation had occurred ages ago, and it had been theoretical, when Little Jacob was still just a little heartbeat who might never develop a whatchamacal-lit. Besides, I'd given birth to a human being just eight hours ago. How could I be expected to remember *anything* at the moment?

"Maybe vaguely," I said. "But since we have thirteen years to go before that's an issue, I don't think we need to talk about this further now. We don't want to give our little precious nightmares, do we?"

"*Oy gevalt*," my mother-in-law, Ida, said. "Now she's *shikkur*."

"Ma," Gabe said with surprising sharpness, "Magdalena is *not* drunk; she's just confused." The Babester then turned to me tenderly, this time making eye contact. "Hon, thirteen is when you get bar mitzvahed. You get circumcised when you're eight days old."

"*What?*"

"What's circumcision?" Alison said.

"Snip, snip," Susannah said crudely.

"Ach," Freni gasped.

"Snip, snip *where*?" Alison demanded.

"Down below," I said meaningfully. It was the only term my adoptive parents had ever used for genitalia, male or female, *and*, I'm ashamed to say, Alison knew exactly what I meant.

It was her turn to gasp. "All of it?"

As long as gasping seemed to be the thing to do, Ida wouldn't be left out. "Such an imagination dis child has. Tell her, Gabeleh."

I gasped. *"Now?* In mixed company?"

"It's in the Bible," my sweetie said. "Starting with Abraham—although he was circumcised when he was an old man. But Jesus had his bris when he was just eight days old."

"Oh, all right," I said, "you may as well explain. You're a doctor, after all." The truth is that every time Gabe, who is *not* a Christian, brings up Jesus to score a point, he wins a point.

My husband, the doctor, wasted no time. "It's called a foreskin. Think of it as a hood of skin that extends over the end of the penis. During a bris—which is a ritual circumcision—the skin is surgically removed."

Much to my amazement, Alison appeared neither shocked nor titillated by the information. "Doesn't it hurt?"

"Put it this way," Gabe said. "For a year after my bris, I couldn't talk *or* walk."

Freni's hands flew to her cheeks. *"Ach, du leiber!"*

"It's a joke, dear," I said. "Most babies don't talk or walk—at least well—until they're a year old."

Ida beamed. "My son the comedian. Und to tink dat Shoshanna Rubeninger let dis von go."

Susannah stamped a long, narrow foot. "Well, I think that circumcision is a barbaric and outdated custom."

"Actually," Gabe said, sounding not in the least bit perturbed by the outburst, "there is evidence now that suggests that circumcised men are not only less likely to get cancer of the penis, but also less likely to contract AIDS."

Alison turned to me. "So, Mom, whatcha ya think? Maybe it's a good thing."

"But he's so tiny," I wailed, perhaps not altogether unlike a baby myself.

The Babester leaned over and silenced my anguished cry with a kiss. "If we do it now, hon, he won't remember a thing. Honest."

"Bullhockey," Susannah said and stamped her slender foot harder.

That's when the Babester started humming "If I Were a Rich Man" from the musical *Fiddler on the Roof*. As I don't go to movies, I hadn't seen that version, but we had driven into Pittsburgh and watched it performed onstage. I must admit that I'd been a reluctant participant in this worldly pursuit. But as soon as the character Tevye started to sing about tradition, I was hooked. Tradition is, after all, what we Mennonites and Amish excel at, and I mean that in the humblest of ways.

"If you can find a mohel who will perform a bris on a baby whose mother has every intention of raising him as a Christian," I said, "then have at it."

Ida clapped her hands to her face in sheer amazement. "She said mohel, Gabeleh! Since vhen does dis von learn to speak Jewish?"

My husband kept right on singing and snapping his fingers, even as tears of joy began to course down both cheeks.

8

The bris of Yaakov Mordechai (Jacob Mordecai) ben (son of) Gabriel Rueven (Rueben) v'Magdalena Portulaca (and Magdalena Portulaca) was the single best-attended event in all of Hernia's history. I'd issued a general invitation to the townsfolk, expecting maybe a few of the more curious souls, certainly not everyone and their cousins in surrounding counties. In fact, we had to change the venue four times, finally settling on the Augsburgers' barn, which is by far the largest in this area.

Although the mohel wore thick glasses, he was steady of hand, and I am pleased that Little Jacob did not suffer any additional loss. Of course I fainted during the actual cutting part, but I'm told that such a strong reaction is not too unusual, especially for one who was not raised in the tradition. And, of course, Little Jacob did feel pain and screamed his head off, but after fifteen minutes he cried himself out and fell asleep.

Just as I was beginning to relax a bit, and actually think about getting a bite to eat—something I hadn't done since the day before—young Chris Ackerman pulled me aside.

"How are you doing, Miss Yoder?"

"Fine. Now, I ask you, Chris, doesn't he look like he belongs on a jar of Gerber's baby food? I mean, a more perfect baby you've never seen, right? And I'm not just saying that because I'm his mother."

"I must admit that he's very cute, Miss Yoder—even though I don't do babies."

I recoiled in shock. "You don't like babies?"

"No offense, Miss Yoder, but they're kind of icky."

"*Icky?* Pus is icky, Chris, and so are boiled turnips, and half-naked parboiled people at the beach, but not babies."

"Are you saying they're all cute?"

"Indeed I am!"

"Even that Schultzendorfer kid who looks exactly like a possum?"

"Okay, so maybe the Good Lord made one exception."

"Aha! So you see it too—the marsupial thing he has going on?"

"I'm not blind, Chris."

He shrugged, happy to be validated. "Who knows, maybe the kid will grow out of it."

"Or not. Melvin Stoltzfus was born looking like a praying mantis and he never grew out of—oh, my Land O' Goshen! I'd completely forgotten; Melvin is Little Jacob's uncle." I threw myself into young Chief Ackerman's strong, but entirely safe, arms and began to sob.

"There, there," he said as he patted my back. "From what I've heard about the man, I don't think he'd hurt the boy—not unless he felt threatened by him directly. I mean, isn't Melvin's strong suit murdering adults?"

"It's not that, you idiot—oops, did I say that? If so, a thousand pardons. My point is that an innocent little boy may have the genetic predisposition to grow up looking like an insect with eyes that swivel independently of each other."

"Is that all you're concerned about? Then fear not, oh inbred one. You obviously inherited the good-looking genes in your family, and as for your husband—woof; you can't get any handsomer than that."

I pulled free from my shameless embrace. "Uh, down, boy; the Babester is already spoken for."

"Yeah, I know. Sorry."

"Look, dear, did you drag me away from my dear Little Jacob, not to mention the food, just to talk about babies?"

"No, ma'am."

Suddenly the straw that littered the barn floor became intensely interesting. "Miss Yoder, you know those twenty-six people who got food poisoning the day Minerva J. Jay died?"

"I am *not* responsible, Chris. Just because I am the most senior deaconess, *and* in charge of a new search committee for a new pastor, does not make me culpable for what happens at the Brotherhood breakfast. I was helping out only because they needed an extra pair of hands; I most certainly did not have an ax to grind."

That pipsqueak from California had the audacity to laugh. "Miss Yoder, you're a hoot when you get all wound up. Anybody ever tell you that?"

"Who are you kidding?" I said, and wagged my finger in his face, presidential style. "I'm a hoot *and* a holler, but I'll have you know that my sex life is none of your business."

Poor Chris didn't know what else to do but laugh. Fortunately it is something he does very well.

"No, no, Miss Yoder. What I mean is that—well, never mind that just now. What I brought you in here to tell you is that nobody got sick that day except for the deceased."

I sighed impatiently. "Of course they did. That's why the ambulances were all tied up and I had to wait so long to get to the hospital. Why am I telling *you* this? You were there, for crying out loud!"

"Yes, but, Miss Yoder, I got their lab reports today along with Miss Jay's autopsy. The reports show that none of those twenty-six people had food poisoning."

"Why, that's impossible! They all had to have their stomachs pumped, and some of them were in the hospital for days afterward. Irene Sprunger is still in the hospital, too weak to make it to the toilet on her own."

"Miss Yoder, it was mass hysteria. There was nothing wrong with any of them that could be attributed to your pancake breakfast."

"*What?* Are you sure?"

"As sure as I am that Little Jacob is one cute baby boy. Apparently this kind of thing is not all that uncommon. As for Miss Sprunger, as long as she sincerely believes she was poisoned, there is a good chance that her body will continue to respond that way."

"And Minerva J. Jay?"

"There were enough drugs in her bloodstream to kill an elephant."

"Oh, really?" Shame, shame, shame on me for feeling even a second's worth of schadenfreude, although, in my defense, it was only because hearing this news vindicated my intense dislike of the abrasive and gluttonous Minerva. (Even more shame, I think, should go to the Germans, who felt enough schadenfreude to have deemed it necessary to invent such a word.)

"Yes, but the strange part is that they were a weird cocktail of drugs, not something you'd normally find in the system of someone who was trying to get, or maintain, a buzz."

"A buzz?"

"I forgot. You're not a drinker and you've probably never even taken—"

"I *get* it," I said. The sad truth is that I'd been buzzed by an entire hive of bees on three separate occasions, but all of them inadvertent, to be sure. How was I to know what a mimosa was? Or a hot toddy? Not to mention hard cider. In my opinion, if the Good Lord intends for us to stay away from alcohol, He shouldn't allow it to be served under such beguiling names. Then again, mine has always been the minority opinion.

"Yes, well, the drugs included prescription sleeping pills, tranquilizers, and antidepressants. Given that Miss Jay was herself on antidepressants and tranquilizers, the addition of this combination proved to be lethal. Despite her size, she didn't stand a chance."

"Are you officially declaring this a murder case?"

"Yes, I am."

"I see." I began counting silently, knowing that I wouldn't get past four—oops, I only made it to three.

"I need your help, Miss Yoder."

"With what?"

"Don't play coy, please. This woman's killer has had eight days to get a head start and cover his tracks."

"What makes you think it's a man?"

Then young Chris did the nearly unforgivable; he grabbed my biceps and squeezed it tightly. The message he sent was loud and clear: he was the boss, and all I had to do was to listen to him. Needless to say, I yanked my arm away to let him know that no one was the boss of me. Especially not a man half my age.

"Miss Yoder, the lab tests show that the drugs had been cooked into the pancakes, thereby altering their chemical states somewhat. Weren't all the cooks that morning men?"

I took a tissue out of the pocket of my blue broadcloth dress and pretended to blow my nose. I honked as loud as a Canada goose and moved that wad of paper hither, thither, and yon, just so young Chris wouldn't see the smirk that was impossible for me to corral and squash into submission.

"Actually, dear," I mumbled, "Frankie Schwartzentruber is a woman."

"*Who?*"

"Frankie only comes up to my chest on account of she's all hunched over. She has her hair pulled back tightly in a bun, and she wears a lot of beige and brown, so she's easy to miss."

"Oh, you mean that elderly Asian woman who belongs to your church? I didn't see her on pancake day."

"She's not Asian, dear. Frankie's had five plastic surgeries more than Joan Rivers ever dreamed of. Her last facelift was performed in Bangkok by a surgeon who has self-esteem issues and uses her own face as a template. But the procedures are very inexpensive, I hear."

Young Chris grinned. "I'll keep that in mind. Anyway, Miss Yoder, as usual, because these are your people and you know their ways, I'd like to count on your help."

I cocked an ear to the other side of the cavernous barn. To the best of my knowledge, my little precious was not even mewling. Then again, he might have been bawling his head off and I wouldn't have heard him, thanks to the masticating jaws of hundreds of apparently starving people chowing down on the traditional Jewish delicacies provided by Shmoe's Deli out of Pittsburgh. (You would have thought we'd invited locusts, not people, to the bris.)

"Look," I said, "in the past I've been more than happy to use my not inconsiderable brainpower—and I say that with all humility—as well as my above-average people skills—ditto on the humble thing—to solve most, if not all, of Hernia's baffling crimes. But, as my sister is wont to say, that was then, and this is now. Then I had just myself to consider—well, and sometimes a hunky man—but now I have a *little* man to consider, one that is totally dependent on me. Forgive me, therefore, if I don't feel like putting my life in jeopardy once again."

"Harrumph."

"You can't say that, dear. Nobody says *harrumph* in real life, and most especially not a man your age."

"What am I supposed to do, then? Swear?"

"You've got a point, but I'm still not going to do it."

Defeated, he hung his handsome blond head. "Well, I guess this means I'm going to have to go with Plan B."

"I guess it does—wait one Mennonite minute. What is Plan B?"

"Sheriff Hughes said that since we're understaffed so bad, and he's actually got a surplus of rookies this year, I could have one of them. On loan, you know. Just for this case. The kid grew up in Hernia and knows everyone in town, and we wouldn't have to pay him on account of—"

I couldn't believe my ears, which, by the way, were flapping like those of an elephant about to charge. "Do you perchance mean Percival Prendergast the Third?"

"Yeah, that's him."

"Nix on the knave," I cried. "The boy is a charlatan! He wasn't raised in Hernia; he only spent his last two years of high school here because the coach was tired of having a losing football team. Yes, he may have been a football star, but he roomed and boarded with a family of transplants who moved here from Chicago. He's as much of a Hernian as Oprah Winfrey—who, by the way, *would* have made an excellent vice president."

"Harrumph again. Let's face it, Miss Yoder, when it comes to local knowledge, you have no equal."

I hung my head as the rules of modesty dictated, mock or otherwise. "Well, I wouldn't say that exactly—"

"But more important, when it comes to sleuthing, it's like you're a natural-born prodigy or something."

"Chris, dear, I didn't fall off the turnip truck."

"Huh?"

"What I mean is that flattery won't get you anywhere. I've made up my mind, and the answer is no."

"Yeah, I got that. But I'm just saying that not one of those detectives on TV could compete with you. If you were, like, in my Methods of Detecting class back in California, you would have wiped the floor with the rest of the cadets. The instructor too."

"*Really?*"

"Like the time you solved that livestock-mutilation case and proved to Silas Marner that it wasn't aliens killing his sheep—that was brilliant. Even the sheriff said so."

"He did, didn't he?"

"The sheriff really respects you, Magdalena. And that's the thing: the entire community of Hernia respects you."

"They *do*?"

"You ought to hear what they say behind your back. 'There goes the smartest and best-informed woman in town.' Why do you think you got elected mayor?"

"Because I'm rich and pay a lot of the town's bills."

"Yeah, but is Donald Trump mayor of New York City?"

Do you see what flattery can do? To my knowledge, the Donald has never run for public office, and Mayor Bloomberg, who *is* the mayor, is super-rich, but young Chris had managed to pull the wool over my eyes like a backward burnoose.

"Hernians elected me because they respect me?" I asked.

Chief Ackerman's beautifully coiffed blond hair fell into his eyes as he nodded vigorously. "Uniquely qualified: that's you. Nobody else could possibly interview the seven people who volunteered in the kitchen that day and get the same excellent results. But"—he shrugged as he forced back what might well have been a bogus tear—"since you're not going to do it, I guess that's just not going to happen the way it should."

It must have been the Devil standing next to me that caused what happened next. My mouth opened of its own volition and the words just poured out like water from a suddenly unplugged gutter.

"Hold your horses, young man! Don't you *dare* tell me what I'm *not* going to do, because I *am* going to investigate this case, and that's that. Case settled." I slapped my hands against each other to drive the point home. "*However*, this investigation is going to have to wait a couple of weeks until I can at least walk like a normal human being, and sit down without the aid of a doughnut ring. Is that clear?"

"Yes, ma'am, but—"

"There's no need to worry your pretty head, Chris; the killer isn't going anywhere. His—or her—objective was to get rid of Minerva, and now, as our erstwhile president infamously said, 'mission accomplished.'"

"Oh, Miss Yoder, I can't thank you enough. Like I said—"

"No offense, dear, but put a zip on the lips."

Do you see what the Devil made me say? And that was mild compared to what was to come.

9

Shame on me. I put on my gumshoes that very afternoon. I'd just fed the little one, and even though I was still so sore I had to sit on a foam doughnut, and had all the energy of a teenager come six o'clock Monday morning, mentally I was itching to get back in the game.

My reentry strategy was simple. Minerva lives—well, she *lived*—in a remodeled farmhouse about eight miles south of Hernia on Thousand Caves Road. She bought the house in the late 1980s, and I remember the event well, because she made a big flap about it. She was pursuing a life as a real estate agent at the time and was promoting the Thousand Caves area as the new retirement utopia for the fresh-air crowd. There were woods to roam, streams in which to trout fish, a lake with paddleboats, and, of course, spelunking in the myriad caves and sinkholes that gave the region its name. Lots could be had in one- to three-acre sizes and for a fraction of what one would pay anywhere else.

What Minerva didn't tell the retirees is that the 183 acres that comprised Thousand Caves Retirement Village had been purchased from a struggling Amish farmer, who couldn't make a go of it because that particular patch of Pennsylvania was so riddled with caves and sinkholes that the surface of cleared land resembled Swiss cheese. Even if he could manage to get his horse and plow to safely turn over a field, come a heavy rain, half the crop would disappear underground.

Then there too was the matter of her sales brochure. The photos were taken somewhere in the Pacific Northwest and depicted towering Douglas firs, and a sparkling lake with water so blue that one couldn't help but think of Aaron Miller's eyes (the man whom I *believed* I was married to, and who is the scum beneath the slime beneath the sludge beneath the ooze beneath the mud at the bottom of the pond, and I am *not* bitter, thank you very much). In reality, it was a pockmarked landscape studded with miniature trees, and the so-called lake was a man-made brown puddle that kept disappearing into an underlying cavern.

And although the farmhouse that Minerva bought had been built on a solid chunk of land, the same could not be said for the other potential lots. Of the dozen lots sold, only two were viable as home sites. Minerva had advertised that county utilities were available, but she didn't say when, and didn't say where. When the two brave couples who had bought into Minerva's grand scheme learned that she had her own generator and pumped her water from an underground stream, they sued and won the right to back out of their contracts.

Today Thousand Caves Retirement Village consists of the loneliest house on planet Earth. If I had an imagination—which, sadly, I don't, or a sense of irony—I could probably envision a murder mystery being set in this strange landscape of seemingly bottomless pits and elfin tress. One could, theoretically of course, toss a body into one of these black gaping holes and it would never be found, because even a thousand and one detectives from

Dalmatia, each with their own Dalmatian, would not be enough to scour each and every man-size opening in the porous limestone that underlies the thin layer of topsoil.

I'd been to Minerva's house only once before, and that was many years prior, when she, uncharacteristically, hosted the Mennonite Ladies Sewing Circle. Perhaps I just spoke too harshly, but I also remember that everyone was surprised when Minerva volunteered to do so, and that virtually everyone in the group attended because we were all curious to see what living out there was like. But I, for one, was so "freaked-out"—as Susannah would say—by what I saw that when I got home that night I fell on my knees and thanked the Good Lord that I lived in a bustling community like Hernia.

After all, not a day goes by that I don't hear the clip-clop of a horse pulling an Amish buggy—sometimes even twice or more a day—out on Hertzler Road, and once a family of Parisian tourists rapped on the kitchen door and demanded that I tell them how to get to Rio de Janeiro. (I told them that the most direct way was to continue on down Route 96 to Cumberland, Maryland, then head east until they caught I-95, which they should follow all the way to Miami. After that they should swim like mad until they got to the coast of Brazil, from whence they could get further directions.)

Now, where was I? Oh yes. I hadn't been out to Thousand Caves Road for many years, but nothing seemed to have changed—at least not for the better. There was no sign of the two homes that had been started, and Minerva's solitary house looked just as lonely and out of place as a petunia in an onion patch. Still, it was a very nice house, so Minerva's finances must have been halfway decent.

The house was set close to the road, because there wouldn't have been much point to a lawn in this earth-eating landscape.

Even from a hundred yards away I could see the brightly colored bands of crime scene tape that crisscrossed the front door, forbidding entry to the curious—of which we have plenty hereabouts, I assure you. Anticipating that very thing, I'd brought along a pair of scissors and a roll of duct tape (I fear that one day this marvelous invention may be our only means of repairing the fractured world we live in). Before getting out of the car I checked to make sure that my cell phone was charged; it was. Then I hoofed it to the porch and snipped away.

The key I'd purloined from the chief's desk drawer fit the front door perfectly. I'd been almost positive that it would. What I found odd was that it had now been eight days since Minerva's death, and the chief had yet to mention anything about the envelope being tampered with, or that Miss Jay had left him with yet another puzzle to solve. Perhaps he really didn't care if he solved it, and that was why he'd been so eager to fob it off on me, the untrained amateur. Curious, isn't it, that *fob* should mean two very different things. Land O' Goshen, there I go again, interrupting the narrative flow, which is something a real novelist would never do; thank heavens that I am merely an innkeeper with a phenomenal memory. (This is a fact, so it is by no means meant to be braggadocio.)

Even a house that has been shut up for only eight days takes on a musty odor, but Minerva's house was as fresh as one might expect a house out in the wilds of weirdom to smell. I concluded, therefore, that someone, probably Chris, had been there recently, also looking for clues. And since jumping to conclusions is what I do best, I outdid myself that afternoon and got in a great deal of exercise.

Could it be, I reasoned, that the chief had been shown the key before it was sealed in the envelope, and that he'd agreed to fetch me the milk on the day of Minerva's death because he *knew* I'd snoop around? Perhaps he still hadn't mentioned it because his search of her house had revealed nothing that shed light on her case, and he was actually hoping that I would break and enter. Well, if the latter was true, I didn't know of what use my piddly detecting abilities were going to be, because once I noticed that the house didn't smell particularly bad, the second thing I noticed was that it was in total disarray.

Now, I'm not referring to your typical teenager it's-*my*-room-why-can't-I-keep-it-the-way-I-want? kind of disorder, or the slovenliness that I normally associate with my sister. I'm talking about the everything-dumped-out-on-tabletops-desks-or-floors kind of thoroughness that I've observed before, but only after the police have gotten through searching a place. Where was I to even begin looking? Perhaps I'd be just as well off checking to see if Minerva kept any unopened bottles of water or juice in her refrigerator, and then after gingerly lowering my still sore nether regions to the couch, flipping through the stack of photo albums on her coffee table. After all, they say that the camera doesn't lie—it's Photoshopping that fibs up a storm—and from my personal experience family albums can be a treasure trove of information: most of it embarrassing, of course.

I'll spare you the descriptions of the ad nauseam snaps of the chubby baby Minerva, or the pudgy preadolescent, or the plump early adolescent, or the quite frankly fat high school student, or the alarmingly obese college woman, just as I'll spare you descriptions of her parents, whom I remembered as not being very nice. And, most probably, no one really cares to know about the disturbingly large number of dogs Minerva owned during her middle school years alone, or that one of them was named "Minerva's Revenge." Ditto, I'm sure, regarding the fifty-seven photos—I counted them—that depicted Mimerva in her senior prom dress, although there was not one picture of a boy in that album.

Suffice it to say, there was a photo album dedicated to just about every topic one could imagine, and each was neatly labeled on the outside—all except for one. This last album was tucked into the middle of one of three stacks, but was in every other way unremarkable. As I began to flip through it I noticed that the photos displayed inside were also unlabeled, and that George Hooley's hangdog face was one of the likenesses included.

"Chef Boyardee!" I exclaimed, invoking the name of my favorite childhood supper; Mama was not much of a cook.

I looked at the photo just before George's. Lo and behold, there were Frankie Schwartzentruber and James Neufenbakker standing next to each other, and they had their arms wrapped around each other's waists. What was that, an April Fool's joke? Whatever it was, it had been taken at least ten years earlier, which explained why I'd glossed over it so easily: James still had some hair and Frankie's eyes had yet to be yanked up to forty-five-degree angles.

The very next photo was of the perpetually smirking Merle Waggler, and it was almost exactly four years old. I could date that photo because it had been taken for inclusion in the church directory. Norma Rae Fields had been in charge of selecting the backdrop that year, and her choice had been a boil pink and earwax orange chenille bedspread with half the nubs missing. Since our policy has always been that "she who does the work calls the shots," the rest of us had naught but to grin and bear it (although some wag went so far as to whisper privately that she was half tempted to actually *bare* it, in order to distract from the hideous bedcover).

But the aforementioned three were not the only members of the Beechy Grove Mennonite Church Brotherhood I spotted in that unlabeled book. Separated by many other faces, several of whom I recognized, and some whom I didn't, I happened upon an excellent photograph of the handsome Elias Whitmore, and immediately below this, a thumbnail-size likeness of the Zug twins. The former had also been taken with Norma Rae's chenille monstrosity as a backdrop, but the snapshot of the twins was no doubt the product of some sort of camera gimmick and, given that they were both looking away, possibly even taken without their knowledge.

The remainder of the album was a total waste of my time, given that my comely visage was nowhere to be found. I say that with Christian charity and a generous dollop of humility, so you know that my heart is in the right place. But let's just be fair for a moment; I *am* the mayor of this thankless little burg, as well as its primary benefactor. I am also its perennial whipping girl. And, as previously noted, I am *not* unattractive. Therefore, why would one *not* want a photograph of me to dress up the otherwise ho-hum pages of her collection of local mug shots?

"Then, phooey on you too," I said, and slammed the book shut.

The sound of the album cover closing with such force took me somewhat by surprise, and I leaped to my feet. Whilst, like the Shulamite, I may have thighs as beautiful as jewels, a navel as round as a goblet which lacks no blended beverage, and breasts like the twin fawns of a gazelle, unlike the Shulamite, I have two very large feet—both of them left. In my attempt to stand on them, one of my clodhoppers struck a leg of the coffee table, and the resulting jolt was responsible for the toppling of a fancy-schmancy vase. When that shattered, so did my last nerve, and I was out of there like kids from a one-room schoolhouse on a Friday afternoon.

After all, there were no clues to be gleaned from Minerva's erstwhile residence that the chief himself hadn't already uncovered. If and when he chose to divulge the information, then I would bother to add it to my mental data bank. Until then, I'd be better off following the more direct approach.

&

All of the Suspicious Seven had been in attendance at my son's bris—except for George Hooley. A banker, George lives and works in Bedford, the nearest real town. However, the man was born and raised in Hernia and has been a lifelong member of Beechy Grove Mennonite Church. George is a contemporary of mine, and many are the times we had to share double desks in elementary school. In both my adoptive and birth lineages, the man is also a cousin of some sort, but to what degree I am uncertain, and have never been motivated enough to sort out.

A generous biographer would say that George Hooley is tall and gaunt with sunken cheeks; his eyelids hang slack, and his lips are gray and shriveled, yet he manages to project an air of someone—or something—well preserved. He is not unlike a sachet that has been closed in an airtight drawer for a very long time. In fact, George Hooley even smells of lavender and other floral scents. On the plus side, he is a dapper dresser, never to be seen without a suit, tie, and pocket handkerchief. Some of the less charitable folks in our community refer to the man as Fastidious George—of course, not to his face. If you ask me, that's a lot better than some of the nicknames the Amish use to distinguish the members of their large broods, and quite openly at that. Of course, that's just my humble opinion.

George Hooley has repeatedly described himself as "a confirmed bachelor." Perhaps there really is such a thing—and indeed, George Clooney comes to mind—but in a community as tightly knit as ours, we are well aware that certain of the "confirmed bachelors" and "maiden ladies" in our midst are quite content with their status, and do not really wish to be paired up with anyone of the opposite sex. Nonetheless, George Hooley goes to great pains to enact a role that has fooled no one since he was in the third grade and made the serious mistake of volunteering to play the part of Little Bo Peep in a school skit. Rather than ham it up, as the other boys might have, George made such a good shepherdess that most of the parents watching the performance were unaware that Bo Peep was really a boy Peep.

At any rate, not quite three weeks after the bris, while Little Jacob and his papa were sleeping (neither of them had slept much during the night), I called on George at the bank. Perhaps I should say that I attempted to call on him.

"Who did you say you were again? And what is it you want?" After fielding my request to see him, Miss Assistant Manager cum Miss Screener of Scum had disappeared into the office quite clearly marked George Hooley, whereupon I'd heard two voices: one hers, one his. Had she been in there so long that she'd forgotten everything I'd said?

"Look, dear, tell him I'm the wealthiest woman in Hernia—perhaps in all of Bedford County—and that my investments with this bank total well over two million. Of course, if he's too busy to see me . . ." I waggled my eyebrows and nodded toward the door, through which could be seen the bank across the street.

"Is that a threat, Miss Yoder?"

"Oh, so you do remember my name. Well, keep reminding yourself what it is, so that when I buy this bank I won't have to waste so much time training the staff. That is, if I decide to keep any of you on board."

"But, Miss Yoder, I—we—haven't done anything wrong."

"In the meantime, him tell that my accountant will be in touch—"

Miss Assistant Manager popped back into the office, and then almost immediately out again, this time with George Hooley hot on her tail. Behind him wafted the scent of bath salts and the odor of dry-cleaning fluids.

"Magdalena! How nice it is to see you." We Mennonites are not into the "kissing cousin" thing, but George acknowledged our kinship by grabbing my hands and holding them in his for all of one second, and almost two-thirds of the next.

I flashed Miss Assistant Manager a so-there look. Admittedly that is not the Christian way to act, but we are all works in progress, are we not?

"*Cousin* George," I said, "I need to speak to you privately."

"Certainly. Magdalena, if this is about why I didn't attend the bliss of your baby, I can explain."

"I think he means *bris*," Miss Assistant Manager said. She hadn't budged an inch.

"No, he didn't," I said. "And it really was bliss. Just ask my husband—or his mother. Now if you'll *excuse* us."

"Well," she said, "I'm not going anywhere. It's my job to sit out here and screen—I mean assist—customers."

"George," I snapped, "your office now!"

Perhaps George's reaction to my tone harkened back to forty years ago when I had to periodically get tough with him in order to stop him from organizing my side of our shared desk. Whatever the reason, it was as if he'd been released from an evil spell and was momentarily free to do my bidding. So, while Miss Assistant Manager glared at us, I marched him back into his inner sanctum. It was he, however, who locked the door behind us.

"Have a seat, Magdalena." He gestured to a pair of black leather armchairs that faced the largest desk I had ever seen.

Although I took him up on his offer and slipped into the closest chair, my intention was to sit ramrod straight and immediately launch into my investigation. However, the leather was exceptionally soft and smooth.

"This is really nice," I said.

"Lean back and put your feet up," George said. "Then you can enjoy the massage features. There are four zones, and right now it's set on all of them, but you can pick and choose. The control is right there beside your purse."

I did as bid, but not before tucking my skirt securely under my calves. George might not be batting for my team, so to speak, but that was no reason to give him a peek at home base. That said, I picked up the device, which was the size of a potato, and pushed the ON button.

There are few words in my vocabulary to describe the sensation that George's leather chair ignited in my exhausted, post-delivery body. I honestly thought I would never be privileged to experience such pure physical enjoyment of this earthly shell ever again. It started as a tingle that began to build gradually, and then grew stronger and stronger, ever rapidly, like a river in flood stage, a thousand streams emptying into an accelerating current, heading toward a dam that would surely burst—I leaped to my feet.

"Get behind me, Satan!"

George blinked. "I beg your pardon?"

"That chair is of the Devil. How *could* you, George?"

"Uh—"

"On the other hand, what's done is done, right? If the sin's already been committed, so to speak—*not* that one actually occurred, mind you—but *if* it's been, then what would be the harm in lingering longer in the gentle embrace of such a manly chair, yet one whose manhood does not interfere with the guilty pleasure of one's sweet surrender?"

"That's because it's a chair, Magdalena, not a man."

"Indeed." I sniffed. "But admittedly not just any chair. By the way, how much did it cost?"

"Thirty-five hundred dollars."

I calculated the amount it cost to keep the Babester (an aspiring mystery novelist) and his mother fed and clothed in the style to which they'd been accustomed in New York. That came pretty ding-dong close to $3,500 a month—every month—whereas the chair was a onetime purchase.

"Does it come in other colors?"

"Besides black, there's dark brown, golden brown, reddish brown, deep tan, pale tan, and pink."

"Hmm."

"But you didn't come here to furniture shop, Magdalena. My guess is that you're here to grill me like a weenie. Isn't that the quaint expression you're so fond of using?"

"Sarcasm does not become you, George. And why on earth would you think that?"

He locked his well-manicured fingers together and twiddled his thumbs as he mocked me further. "Let's see . . . could it possibly be because you're playing detective again, and because I was one of those serving John Q. Public at Minerva J. Jay's untimely, but most probably deserved, demise?"

"Why, George Hooley, what kind of mouth is that for a good Mennonite boy to possess? 'Deserved demise' indeed!" I glowered at him only briefly, so as not to encourage permanent lines on my forehead. "Such a cold-blooded comment is not befitting someone of your professional ranking, not to mention that you are on the fast track to become a deacon in our church."

"I *am*? Since when?"

"Since—well, you do know that the Lord works in mysterious ways, don't you, George?"

He sighed and leaned back in his own comfortable chair. "And none quite as mysterious as you. Am I right? Although frankly, Magdalena, you're as transparent as a CT scan."

"Vous êtes très drôle," I said, exhausting my high school French. "But I'll overlook your insults if you'll elaborate on why it is that you believe our poor Minerva got what was coming to her."

When fastidious little bankers snort, it's not unlike kittens sneezing. "Our *poor* Minerva? Name one person in the entire county who was sad to hear that she died."

"Uh—Wanda Hemphopple, out at the Sausage Barn. I wouldn't be surprised if on slow days, Minerva accounted for almost half of her business."

"That was a business relationship. Name someone else."

"So what if I can't? It doesn't matter; God loves us all. He even notices when a sparrow falls."

"The sparrow probably caught Minerva looking at it."

"George!" I said sharply, surprising even myself. "What did Minerva ever do to you that you should hate her so much?"

He stared at his desk miserably, then at each of his walls in turn, while I waited patiently. Finally he could stand it no longer.

"Can you keep a secret, Magdalena?"

"Of course, dear." I pretended to lock my lips and throw away the key. It was a gesture I'd learned from Alison.

"You need to swear to it."

"Don't be silly; we're both Mennonites. Just like the Bible says, our *yeas* should be *yeas*, and our *nays* should be *nays*. But speaking of neighs, what did one horse say to the other when—"

"Magdalena! This is no time for riddles. I need you to give me your word as a woman of the cloth that you will not breathe a word of this to anyone."

A woman of the cloth? The poor man's gears must have broken a sprocket or two. It was my sister, Susannah, who swaddled herself in fifteen feet of filmy fuchsia fabric, and for whom a trip to Material Girl in Bedford was more of an inducement to good behavior than the promise of eternity spent in Heaven would ever be. I know we're not supposed to judge, but if it weren't for the fact that we Christians are justified by faith, and not deeds, my only sibling would be on the fast track to you-know-where in a very large handbasket lined with an entire bolt of brightly colored polyester.

"You're thinking of Susannah," I said slowly, whilst moving my lips in an exaggerated fashion, to make sure he got the message.

"No, I'm not. Your sister's a divorced strumpet and a lapsed Presbyterian to boot. I'm referring to you. In the absence of a regular minister, you are our de facto leader. That, Magdalena Portulaca Yoder Rosen, or however you choose to style your name, makes you a woman of the cloth in my book, just as surely as if you were an Episcopal priest, or a Reform or Conservative Jewish rabbi."

It is said that the high tide floats all boats—well, let me tell you that flattery does the same thing. I don't think there is a person alive whose ego can't be inflated at least a little by the right words, delivered by the right sycophant, at the right time. Yes, on an intellectual level I knew that I could not be compared to a rabbi or a priest, seeing as how I lacked (at least) another six years of education, but to have a respected banker compare me to them got my dinghy to bobbing like a fishing cork on Miller's Pond come spring.

I patted my bun to make sure the bit of cloth we refer to as a prayer cap was still in place. "Do you really think so?" I asked. "I mean, I've studied very little theology. What's the use in raising questions, I always say, if one isn't prepared to accept the answers—not that I couldn't come up with a good answer if I really tried. Besides, one can always trot out the tried but true 'When we get to Heaven someday the Good Lord will explain everything.' "

George nodded solemnly. "Yes. And my first question will be: why did You create someone as frustrating as Magdalena?"

I was stunned. *"Moi?"*

"Admit it, Magdalena; you'd rather do anything than get down to brass tacks."

"Brass tacks hurt."

"Enough of this nonsense. Do you, or do you not, agree to keep the following information absolutely confidential on the grounds that you are, in effect, my clergy substitute?"

Clergy substitute was almost as good as priest or rabbi, perhaps even better: I would have a title, but none of the responsibilities. In the world of religious nomenclature, I might even be described as a sugar-free lay minister.

"I agree," I said, perhaps with a wee bit too much enthusiasm.

George left his desk and came around to stand over me. I suppose that his intent was to express his earnestness, but his expression simultaneously brought to mind President Richard Nixon and Ichabod Crane.

"She was blackmailing me," he whispered.

"Over what?"

He leaned so close, I could smell a MenthoLyptus lozenge on his breath. "It's a good thing you're sitting down, Magdalena," he whispered, "because you're not going to believe what I'm about to tell you."

10

Dutch Baby with Cardamom Honey Apples

Sometimes called a popover pancake, this audacious-looking flapjack is made in a large skillet. It puffs up, rising dramatically as it bakes in the oven. It is topped with sautéed apple slices laced with ground cardamom and sweetened with honey. Golden Delicious apples are best for this recipe because they keep their shape when cooked. The pancake takes 18 minutes to bake—just enough time to put together the apple topping.

3 large eggs
¾ cup milk
¾ cup unbleached all-purpose flour
1 tablespoon sugar
2 tablespoons unsalted butter

Cardamom Honey Apples (recipe follows)

1. Preheat the oven to 400° F. Place an 8-by-10-inch cast-iron skillet or other heavy skillet with a heatproof handle in the oven.

2. Combine the eggs, milk, flour, and sugar in a medium bowl and whisk until smooth. Using a pot holder, remove the skillet from the oven and add the butter; tilt the pan to melt the butter and coat the skillet. Add the batter all at once and immediately return the skillet to the oven.

3. Bake until the pancake puffs up around the edges, 18 to 20 minutes.

4. To serve the pancake, slide it from the skillet onto a large platter. Pour the Cardamom Honey Apples into the center. Cut into wedges and serve, distributing the topping evenly.

Cardamom Honey Apples: Peel, quarter, and core 2 large Golden Delicious apples. Cut into thin wedges. Heat 1 tablespoon unsalted butter in a medium skillet until sizzling. Add the apple wedges and cook, stirring gently, until lightly browned on both sides. Sprinkle with ½ teaspoon ground cardamom and stir to coat. Add ½ cup honey and heat to boiling. Remove from heat; stir in 1 tablespoon fresh lemon juice.

11

"I'm all ears, George."

He reached out and patted my arm. "I hope you're not offended, Magdalena, but I don't find you attractive."

"Ditto, dear."

"No, really. I'm told that you have all the attributes one would normally desire in a member of the opposite sex, but they do nothing to excite me."

"And no offense to you, George, but your parts don't light a fire in my loins either."

He seemed a bit taken aback by me giving him tit for tat. "I don't think you understand. It's not just you I'm not attracted to; it's all of the fairer sex."

"In other words, you're gay."

"Oh, how I hate that word!"

"I'm sorry, George. Do you prefer *homosexual*?" We were still whispering, by the way, albeit a bit loudly.

George reared like a horse that had spotted a snake lying across the trail. "*What?* No! No labels, please. Call me a confirmed bachelor, if you must—or a gentleman's gentleman. Really, Magdalena, you don't seem a bit surprised by my revelation."

"Hmm."

"She could have ruined my career, you know. Who would want to trust their money to a bank managed by a—a—known—well, you know."

"George, these days what one does in the privacy of one's own bedroom—and I'm not saying that it's right or wrong—is of little interest to the public."

"Maybe in cities like Pittsburgh or Philadelphia, but here in Bedford, it most certainly does matter. This is still a Christian town, Magdalena, and here folks vote by what their Bibles say. You, better than most, should know that."

"Yes, but trust me, George, the good folks of Bedford really don't care about your personal life all that much."

"You're being cavalier," he shouted. "I'm trusting you with the biggest secret of my life, and you won't even take it seriously."

I bit my tongue whilst I prayed for guidance. Although my prayers for patience usually go unanswered, sometimes, if I am able to quiet my inner dialogue, I feel that I am able to discern that "still small voice" that the prophet Elijah mentioned in the Book of Kings. To explain to George that virtually everyone in Hernia and Bedford had already guessed that he was gay would undoubtedly hurt his feelings, as well as acutely embarrass him. On the other hand, the knowledge that his personal life was not germane to his career as a banker could lift a huge burden from his shoulders and allow him to live life more abundantly.

"I do take you seriously," I finally said. "As it so happens, I have a friend who is a banker in a town just this size, and that friend is also gay, but it doesn't appear to have hurt his career at all."

"Yeah, but I bet that town isn't in Pennsylvania."

"Oh, but it is."

"Which town? Where?"

"I'm not at liberty to say—not until my friend comes out of the closet."

"Aha, so nobody knows that your friend is gay!"

"Actually, I'm pretty sure that everyone does."

"*How* do they know?" he demanded.

"I'm not really sure; it's no one thing in particular. Maybe because he never married and doesn't date. But it doesn't matter. The point is that they know, and that they haven't boycotted his bank on account of it. Also—and I hope I'm corrected if I'm wrong—the folks at church have always treated him warmly as well."

"Yes, they have—I mean, *they* know as well?"

"Perhaps not everyone at his church; I don't think it was ever the subject of discussion. But still, I'm sure that there have been some folks who just sort of picked up on it."

"Picked up on *what*? I act just like the other men—darn, Magdalena, you were really talking about me, weren't you?"

In a move quite uncharacteristic of myself, I grabbed his hands, which were as light and cold as yesterday's biscuits. I couldn't, however, look him in the eyes, which were as dark and moist as the raisins in hot-cross buns.

"Forsooth."

"That's a *yes*?"

"Undeniably so."

He made no move to pull his hands from mine while he pondered his new reality. In the meantime, I felt as if I'd taken a child to the edge of a precipice and forced him to look down, just so he could experience the view.

"Magdalena, are you saying what I *think* you're saying?"

"There's no telling, dear, because I'm not psychic, and even if I was, I certainly wouldn't admit it, given that the Bible comes down rather harshly on that subject and I personally prefer a life of hypocrisy to one of open sin, having already spent too much time in the latter's trenches, but were I to speculate on your current state of mind, I'd guess that you are feeling curiously relieved, although understandably concerned about your bank's future, not to mention run-on sentences. Rest assured, however, that naught shall differ between yesterday's deposits and today's, unless, of course, you consumed an inordinate amount of bran for supper."

"No offense, Magdalena, but has anyone ever told you that you're nuts?"

"All the time."

"It doesn't bother you?"

"Au contraire. If the shoe fits, I always say, then make sure you buy a pair. By the way, I must say that the ones you're sporting are very spiffy. I've been admiring them and would like to get some for Gabe. I hope you don't mind me asking, but were they expensive?"

"Over three, can you believe that? My dear sainted mother would have a stroke if she were alive to hear that. Of course they *are* Ferragamo."

"Just three bucks for a snazzy pair like that? What they say about bankers must be true, George; you are a parsimonious lot."

"That was three hundred, Magdalena—not three dollars."

"Oops." Of course I was feeling foolish, which gave me the perfect amount of adrenaline to tackle yet another thorny issue. "Tell me, George, why is your assistant such a ferocious watchdog, and why do the two of you give the impression that there is something a trifle indecorous occurring twixt the two of you?"

He beamed. "That's what you thought?"

"Ah, so she's your beard."

"My *what*?"

"Your decoy."

"Magdalena, that's positively indecent of you!" He licked his thin, pale lips. "Besides, how would you know about such things?"

"Because the PennDutch Inn has catered to the rich and famous almost since it opened. You wouldn't believe how many actors—and actresses—involve themselves in relationships that are merely for show. Why, there's this one top-earning actor who—oops, I better stop now. This guy would sue me if I as much as whispered his name, even though everybody knows who he is."

George's eyes were as big and round as lemon tarts. "Would I know his name?"

I stood. "Look, dear, I really must be going. But you should know first that even though I wish you all the best, I can't take you off my list."

"*What* list?"

"Of suspects, of course."

Forget about lemon tarts, moist raisins, and light biscuits. George's face took on the cold, hard look of the fourteen-year-old fruitcake that Emma Kranebull gave Mama for Christmas one year. My parents used it for a doorstop until Papa stepped too close and broke his littlest piggy and two metatarsals. I was given the honor of disposing of the offending object, whereupon I threw it into Miller's Pond. Of course it immediately sank. Crazy Felix Neubrander went scuba diving in the same pond seven years later and brought up what he thought was a gold brick . . .

"Magdalena!"

"Yes?"

"I said, 'Get out of my office.' "

"Certainly. But you could have asked me nicely."

"I did—several times, in fact."

"My, aren't we snippy!"

"Good day, Magdalena." He actually pushed me over the threshold. "And as long you've got your list of suspects out, may I suggest that you put the Zug twins on top?" Although worded as a question, it was most definitely an order.

There was only one person in the entire world capable of ordering me around. At that moment he was a very short—just twenty inches—bald guy who pooped in his pants willy-nilly and burped with panache. Before I put the screws to anyone else, this little man was getting his midmorning feeding, and I was getting a load taken off my chest. I mean that literally.

Although my beautiful, semiauthentic, nineteenth-century Pennsylvania farmhouse sports a front porch replete with rocking chairs and a proper front door, I almost always enter through the kitchen in the rear. The kitchen is where one is sure to encounter my cook, and kinswoman, Freni Hostetler, and because of the warmth and pleasant atmosphere, this is where I've set up Little Jacob's day bassinet.

However, I was to discover that upon this occasion the big love of my life was cradling the tiny love of my life tenderly in his arms. There is nothing sexier, in my opinion, than the sight of a man caring for an infant. I might have initiated the begetting process all over again, had I not still had a somewhat sore nether region from the act of spitting out a complete human a month earlier. Instead I extended warm greetings to everyone in the room, which also included Alison.

Upon hearing my voice Little Jacob let out a wail that could be heard as far as the Maryland state line. I must confess that my heart swelled with sinful pride at this confirmation that my son had inherited at least one of my traits, albeit perhaps not the most attractive. His cry was, of course, hunger motivated, so I flung my pocketbook on a corner stool and rushed over to perform the most motherly of deeds.

"Well," the Babester grumbled, as his offspring latched on to me as tight as a leach, "I guess now I'm superfluous."

"Nonsense, dear. As soon as he's done he'll fill his diaper. From what I've observed, changing nappies is something you do very well."

"Gross," Alison said. "Everything about this kid is gross: the way you feed him, the way he poops. This family ain't nothing like it used to be, ya know? It's Little Jacob this, Little Jacob that—it's all about the stupid kid. If ya ask me—which nobody does anymore—I say send that brat back where he came from."

"Alison!" the Babester said sharply.

"Alison!" I said in horror. The thought of Little Jacob returning the way he arrived was too awful to contemplate—especially now that he'd grown a bit.

Freni adores Alison and thinks of her as a granddaughter, but her Swiss-German genetics make it all but impossible for her to express physical affection. Instead of hugging the girl—and I'm sure Alison wouldn't have enjoyed that either—Freni flapped her stout arms, which made her look like a black-and-white turkey trying in vain to achieve liftoff.

"Yah," she said, "this family is very much changed. But now you have a baby brother."

"So? What good is that? He can't talk, and he don't even listen when I talk to him. How am I s'posed to boss him around?"

"Yah, maybe now he is not so much fun. But someday he will be a very good friend to you. You must trust me, Alison; a brother—or a sister—is the best friend to have."

"Yeah? Do you have brothers and sisters, Freni?"

"I had nine brothers and five sisters," she said, her plump round face lit by the memories of bygone years.

"What d'ya mean ya *had* 'em? Ya saying that ya ain't got 'em no more?"

"Freni's seventy-five," I explained gently. "She's also the youngest child in her family."

"Oh, I get it; all the rest of them are dead."

"Ach, not all!" Freni turned her attention to a pot of stew that was simmering on my institutional-size stove. "I still have one brother and two sisters. Each is a blessing. You will see."

"Ha! I don't even think so," Alison said before stomping from the room in a prerequisite teenage snit.

"I don't understand," I said. "She seemed so excited at first. You would have thought *she* was the mother when we first brought Little Jacob home."

My handsome husband, who'd relinquished his chair for me, stooped to plant a kiss on my forehead. "It's a normal reaction, hon. First she had you all to herself, and then she had to share you with me, and now there's him. How can she compete with a helpless baby?"

"But she doesn't need to compete!"

"Yes, but she doesn't know that—not on an emotional level. Listen, I've had some cross-training in basic psychology. Why don't I talk to her and see if I can't get her to understand that she's still every bit as much a part of this family as she was before?"

"Would you?" My heart swelled with love.

"Of course."

"A good man," Freni muttered. "Never mind what they say."

"*What?*"

"Ach!"

It was too late. With Little Jacob as firmly attached as a nit, there was nothing to stop me from leaping to my feet and cornering her over the stew pot.

"What did you mean by that?"

My stout little cook didn't even have the nerve to turn and face me. "What is this *that* of which you speak?"

"Freni," I said sternly, "dissembling is lying just as much as telling an out-and-out falsehood."

"Hon," Gabe said, his tone pleading, "leave her alone. She can't help what anyone else says."

"Yah," Freni said, sneaking a peek at me through the corner of her right eye, "this is very true, because I do not even know this Mr. Dis Embling."

I sighed. No matter how long he lived in our community, my Sweet Baboo would always be an outsider. Hernians were graded like diamonds; not by clarity and color, but by the year in which their ancestors first set foot on our sacred soil. Not to brag, but my ancestor Jacob Hochstetler (indeed, I share him with most Amish and many Mennonites in Hernia) passed through the area in 1750 as a captive of a Delaware Indian raiding party. That unfortunate fact makes me a triple-A, gem-quality Hernian of impeccable credentials. It wasn't until 1820 that the village was founded, but again my ancestors were represented.

The third-tier cutoff date is usually given as 1860, the fourth is 1900, and the last, which barely counts for anything, is 1946. After World War II the book on new arrivals was closed; marriage to a triple-A gem did nothing to change an immigrant's status. As one local wag described it, "Putting a cubic zirconia and a diamond in the same ring doesn't make the CZ a diamond." To be sure, though, the gentlefolk of Hernia will never mention this distinction to your face, for with the exception of the occasional cold-blooded killer, they shy away from confrontation.

"Okay," I finally said, "subject dropped. But I need to have a serious discussion with the both of you."

"Ach!" Somehow Freni managed to squeeze out from between me and the stove. It must have been instinct that propelled her to Gabe's side. He might not be blood, but he was the only other possible ally in the room.

My dearly beloved was on his feet, a look of genuine concern written all over his classically handsome features. "What is it, hon?"

"Sit back down, dear, because you're not going to like what I'm about to say."

12

But there would be no sitting for the man who had cared enough about me to finally sever his mother's apron strings, and a full month before our son was born too. Although it had been a grizzly operation, the only victim appeared to be Ida. She now lived alone in what was formerly Gabe's house, across from us on Hertzler Road. In the intervening weeks my husband seemed to have transferred most, if not all, of his concern onto me. Yes, it did get a little wearing to have him follow me around like a puppy all day, but a good Magdalena would just shut her mouth and count her blessings. At least I didn't have to assume all of Ida's former duties, such as cut his meat for him at dinner—well, not unless it was exceptionally tough.

"How did his checkup go?" he demanded. "Tell me everything the doctor said; don't leave anything out. I knew I should have driven you. It's only been a month; it's far too early for you to be driving yourself. I don't even know how you even could be sitting now."

"Month, shmonth," I said. "In Africa the women give birth in the fields, and then go right back to work."

Freni shook her head. "That is too soon. We Amish women wait at least one day before we help the men to bale the hay."

"You're kidding," Gabe said. "*Aren't* you?"

"She *is* kidding," I said. "Plus she composed a rhyming couplet. The next thing we'll hear from her is the pitter-patter of iambic pentameter."

"Ach," Freni squawked. "How you talk! I am too old for such a thing to happen."

Gabe smiled. "As for the African women thing, that sounds more like missionary lore than fact. But back to you, Magdalena; what did the doctor say? How did Little Jacob's one-month checkup go? How are you doing?"

"Uh—you see, that's why you should be sitting down, dear. I didn't *exactly* go to the doctor, except for maybe sort of."

Gabe stared. "What does *didn't exactly* mean, exactly?"

"She did not go at all," Freni said, crossing her stubby arms in front of her ample bosom, "because the appointment is in two days."

"Magdalena, is that true?"

"But I was very close to the doctor's office," I said. "I went to the bank."

"Bank? What for?"

"To put the screws to George Hooley; he's a member of my church."

"I repeat my question: *What for?*"

"To investigate the privates," Freni said, in the ultimate act of betrayal.

"I am not a private investigator, merely an undeputized postpartum woman in charge of a postmortem event."

"*Mag-da-leen-a!*" When Gabe does his ventriloquist bit, spitting my name out without moving his lips, it's time to get to the point.

"Remember Minerva J. Jay, the woman who died while eating pancakes at my church?"

Gabe cocked his head. To tell the truth, he looked maddeningly handsome.

"Hmm," he said. "Wasn't that the day my wife gave birth on the floor of Sam Yoder's Filthy Corner Market?"

"If you don't mind my saying so, dear, sarcasm really *does* become you. But yes, that was the day, and even though the paper said that Miss Jay died of undisclosed circumstances, they were disclosed to me, and—"

"You're working on another murder case?"

"But the suspects are all Mennonites, so they can't be so bad."

"*Huafa mischt,*" Freni muttered.

"What?" Frankly, I couldn't believe my ears.

"You heard her," Gabe roared. "Horse manure! They may all be Mennonites, but one of them is a killer. Am I right?"

"Agreed. But the weapon of choice was pharmaceuticals. Just as long as I don't ingest anything during my investigation, I shall be as fine as frogs' hair." By the way, I owe that colorful description to my southern friend Abigail Timberlake.

"This one is meshugah," Freni said in a louder voice. *Meshugah* means *crazy* in Yiddish, not Amish. Unfortunately my kinswoman learned this word from my mother-in-law, who usually applies it to me.

"Et tu Brute," I said, deeply hurt.

"Ach, such a terrible thing you say!" She blinked behind her grease-and-flour-covered spectacles. "What *did* you say?"

"That you're a traitor, Freni. I thought you were my friend."

"Yah, but this I do for your good."

"And you, Gabriel Jerome Rosen," I said through clenched teeth, "are being totally unfair to me. All I am doing is helping out a young man who is totally overwhelmed and, frankly, unprepared to be the sole police officer in this community."

"But you're the mayor; you hired him. Don't get me wrong, Mags, I think he's a nice young man, but every time you help him you're putting your life on the line. And now you have more than just yourself and me to think of; you've got our little man here. Do you honestly want our son to grow up without a mother?"

There are times when arguing with the Babester is like trying to stop global warming by scattering a tray of ice cubes on the lawn. "I'm already committed to this case," I said. "But just as soon as I've—we've—arrested a suspect, I'm turning in my nonexistent badge and hanging up my metaphorical spurs."

"What does this mean?" Freni demanded.

"It means she's feeling guilty," the Babester said. "This is her last case."

Freni nodded, an action that caused her entire body to shake. "Yah, we shall see."

"So what will you do about the baby?" Gabe said. "Express your milk?"

I'd heard somewhere that breast pumps were not entirely comfortable, that they were not unlike the electric milk pumps Mose uses on my two dairy cows, Matilda Two and Prairie Queen. Perhaps they didn't hurt at all. I didn't care, because I wasn't about to find out. The times I'd spent with Little Jacob at my breast had been the most fulfilling hours of my life, bar none.

"I'm taking him with me," I said.

"The Hades you are," Gabe said. Of course he didn't use the Greek word.

"I know that you're his father and that you're concerned," I said, "but I'm the one who carried him for almost nine months inside me and then had to expel him through my pelvic region without an epidural. For now, my vote trumps yours."

"Yah," Freni said, and nodded even more vigorously than before.

Yes, it was unfair of me to play the birth card—on second thought, no, it wasn't. Like I'd said, I wasn't taking him to a play date with Eliot Ness; I was merely going to question upstanding members of my church. Believe me, I would never, ever intentionally use my son for nefarious purposes, but as long as he was along for the ride, would it be so bad if the oochy-goochy-goo factor kept the pharmaceutical killer a little off guard? I think not. (Please bear in mind that I'm the head deaconess in my church; ergo, my opinions should count for something.)

My first victim was James Neufenbakker. I've known Jimmy since I was a mere lass in pigtails and flour-sack dresses, except that back then he was known to me as *Mr.* Neufenbakker, the little kids' Sunday school teacher. During the week Jimmy worked as a coal miner, a grueling job that he held for forty years, but somehow he still managed to outlive two wives. Jimmy has been retired for the past ten years or so, and although he no longer teaches Sunday school, he's very active in the brotherhood. Oh, and for what it's worth, I currently teach the adult Sunday school class that Jimmy attends.

One can be kind to a fault when describing someone, *or* one can choose to be honest. That said, to put it kindly, Jimmy Neufenbakker looked very much like the male sea lion I once saw at the Pittsburgh Zoo. His small bald head featured watery brown eyes, and his upper lip sprouted bristles that were too sparse to be called a mustache. He appeared to lack shoulders (although he did have functioning arms), and his body expanded exponentially to an enormous rear end—even by Mennonite standards. Alas, I cannot claim that he had flippers instead of legs, but he did walk with a shuffle, and his feet were exceptionally wide.

Because of the mass he had to move, and his peculiar gait, it took Jimmy a good two minutes to answer his doorbell. Meanwhile, I waited patiently, tapping my foot whilst singing children's hymns to keep Little Jacob quiet in his car seat.

"Oh, it's you," he said, suddenly opening the door. "I thought it was that pair of feral cats that's been hanging out under my front porch lately. They screech and holler just like that before they get down to mating, and then they start right back up again. I've tried everything in the book to get rid of them: hosing them down, borrowing a neighbor's dog overnight—I even bought a bottle of wolf urine off the Internet. Seeing as how you know just about everything—or think you do—what would you suggest?"

"But I don't know everything: there are two mountain dialects of Laotian that I'm struggling with, and the concept of string theory is still a little frayed in my thinking."

"Humph. But you're still a smarty-pants, Magdalena." He slipped a pair of spectacles out of the breast pocket of a dingy white shirt and perched them on an almost nonexistent nose. "What's that you've got balanced on your hip? A basket of some kind?"

"It's a car seat, and inside is the cutest baby ever born in Hernia."

"Ha! That's a mighty provocative statement. I was born in Hernia, you know."

"I know, Jimmy, and I was thinking about that on my drive over here. You see, it's a scientific fact that babies have been getting progressively cuter over the years—some sort of biological necessity predicated on the Cold War and then it's subsidence—but of course in nature there are always exceptions. So I got to thinking about you, and how handsome you are. That's how I came to the conclusion that you must have been an exceptionally cute baby—no, undoubtedly the cutest of your generation, that so-called, misnamed, Greatest Generation. If only Tom Brokaw had been ten years younger, he might have seen that it was the leading edge of the baby boomers who marched for civil rights and fought to end racism and sexism in the workplace—but I digress. My point is that you have been officially dubbed by *moi*, mayor of Greater Hernia, as our second cutest baby."

"Magdalena, you're full of baloney, just like you've always been. But as long as you're going to flap your gums, you may as well come on in. No use exposing that baby to the elements and who knows what all those wild cats carry."

At the second mention of uninoculated cats, I couldn't get Little Jacob indoors fast enough. Unfortunately, I had no choice but to shuffle in behind him. Once inside, I remembered with a sinking heart something I'd heard another brotherhood member say: "I'd rather hold our meetings out at the dump than in Jimmy Neufenbakker's house."

There are folks whose houses are merely messy, and folks with relatively neat houses where dust bunnies multiply at the same rate as their mammalian namesakes. Then, of course, some houses combine both forms of slovenliness, whilst others add food and grime to the mix. Poor Jimmy's house, bless his heart, had both the smell and look of an exploded garbage truck—not that I've had a whole lot of experience with those, mind you.

"Have a seat," he said as he gestured to a caved-in easy chair.

The crater was almost filled with a mix of pulverized crumbs and lint, so, theoretically at least, one could almost sit on it. The only other option was a sagging sofa, but it was piled high with dirty clothes, empty milk containers, and newspapers, all topped by a three-foot-long stuffed toy lion with one eye missing. There was certainly no place I would be willing to set the car seat down, not even at gun point.

"Silly me," I said, my desperation mounting by the second, "I forgot to lock my car."

"It would be silly if you did; no one locks their car in Hernia."

"Yes, but times are changing. I mean, if we can have murders in Hernia, can car theft be far behind?"

"So that's why you're here! I should have surmised as much. You have me pegged as a suspect in the Minerva J. Jay murder. Well, let me tell you something, girlie. I don't much care for one of my former students—and may I add, a very hardheaded, obstreperous student—accusing me of breaking one of the most important of the big ten. So take that little runt of yours and get out of my house. I don't have to answer even one of your questions, seeing as how you're not even a real policewoman, but a busybody. That's what you are: a busybody."

I was too shocked to say anything for a good minute and a half, much less move one of my comely, but admittedly oversize feet. Little Jacob was certainly not a runt! Virtually everyone who saw him—murder suspects excluded—invariably commented on what a healthy-looking baby he was. As the shock wore off, I had the almost overpowering urge to respond to that verbal attack on my progeny, yet at the same time the rational side of me began to mobilize with what might be a more useful rejoinder.

"How very interesting," I said as I edged backward toward the door, "but I never said that Minerva was murdered."

Jimmy shuffled toward me at the same rate. "Oh, come on. You wouldn't be here otherwise. Yes, at first I thought you might have come to see how I was getting along. As you well know, I do a lot for the church, Magdalena, and a logical person might think that in turn the church would care about me. Someone might even ask if I need a ride into Pittsburgh to see my cardiologist, now that turnpike driving is getting to be somewhat scary for me."

"I'm sorry, I didn't—"

"Remember that I had a quadruple bypass in 'ninety-four? That I have a pacemaker? That I suffer from emphysema? But that I still volunteer at things like the pancake breakfast, standing on my feet for hours, just to raise a little money for new hymnals?"

My heart went out to him, of course, but that didn't mean I found him any less threatening. I fumbled for the doorknob, which was both clammy and greasy. Once I turned it, I pushed the door open with my posterior cheeks.

"Jimmy, I honestly didn't come here to accuse you of anything. I merely wanted to ask you if you thought Minerva might have enemies. You see—and you must keep this confidential—if indeed Minerva was murdered, her killer could have been anyone who was there that morning; not just the kitchen crew."

Shame, shame, triple shame on me for thinking that Jimmy sounded like a barking sea lion when he laughed. Where was my compassion? Surely a man with that many ailments deserved a huge dose of human kindness, and here all I could think of was how much he resembled a marine mammal.

"Magdalena, you haven't changed a bit since the third grade, have you? Where is the information in what you just said? What am I supposed to keep confidential? That a *possible* murder could have been committed by *anyone*?"

My left foot found the porch floor and was quickly followed by my right. "There you go; you just answered your own questions. And really, dear, there's no need to see me out. I can do a follow-up on Minerva over the phone."

Jimmy's watery brown eyes seemed to crystallize into obsidian. His normally pallid complexion turned blotchy in front of my eyes, and he began to quiver with rage. His sudden mood swing put me right back in the third grade when he was *Mr.* Neufenbakker and had the right to smack me with a ruler if I so much as squirmed during my Bible lesson.

Perhaps it was his declining health, or perhaps it was the way he'd always been, but Jimmy Neufenbakker was as emotionally stable as a two-legged giraffe on roller skates. I needed to get out of there before he lost his balance completely, and took Little Jacob and me with him. Alas, I was too late.

13

"Stop!" he roared.

What is it about the adult-child relationship that never quite changes? Or could it be that because Jimmy had been physically abusive to me, that he once had the power to order me around, I felt that I still needed to obey him? Whatever the reason, I stopped and did my own quivering—not from rage, but from fear.

"Minerva!" he roared again. "So you really want to know what I thought of her, do you? Then I'll tell you: that woman was a *t-r-o-l-l*—" He checked himself abruptly as he inclined his small bald head toward the infant seat I cradled. "No, I probably shouldn't even spell that in front of him."

"Who? The little runt? Trust me, he can take it."

The red blotches shriveled before my eyes. "Yes, but it isn't a Christian thing to say. And it was wrong enough of me to call you a smarty-pants."

"Pants, shmants. I've already forgotten about that. Now, were you saying that Minerva was a troll, like the kind that lived under the bridge when Billy Goat Gruff came trotting along? Because honestly, dear—"

"No, you idiot, that's only a children's story! Now look what you made me say."

I took five steps backward and felt for the first step that led down to the walk. "Ah, she was a trolley off her tracks! Well, personally I couldn't agree more. But in what way did she strike you as being—well, nertz to Mertz?"

"Magdalena, you're certifiable, you know that?"

"Yes, but a padded cell with documentation is better than one without, *n'est-ce pas*?"

"She was a trollop, you numbskull!"

"*Oy vey*. Little Jacob, cover your ears." Of course the fruit of my womb was unable to do anything more than gurgle a response to my directive, so I took the time out of my escape to tuck his blanket up around his ears. "Please, Jimmy," I begged, "no more of that vulgar language."

"I'm sorry," he said at once, "but you really do have a thick skull."

"Not the N word; the T word."

"Oh, come off it, Magdalena. That little fella was not the product of a virgin birth, and just saying the T word in front of him is not going to turn him into some sort of deviant."

"Well, I never! Okay, so perhaps I did, but it's none of your business. Besides, now who's not answering questions?"

Jimmy Neufenbakker snorted. "If a simple answer is what you want, then I suggest you ask the Zug twins."

With that he shuffled backward until he could slam the door. Not a second latter a feral cat yowled from beneath the porch. Almost immediately its loud, mournful cry of distress was drowned out by Little Jacob exercising his lungs. Clearly it was time to make a hasty exit, even if I had to leave my dignity behind.

Little Jacob, we soon learned, found riding in automobiles to be very soothing. Sometimes it was the only way we could get him to fall asleep. Thus it was that after leaving the somewhat temperamental Jimmy Neufenbakker, I took the tyke on a rather extensive tour of historic Hernia.

Although many tourists are initially drawn to our town by its predominantly Mennonite and Amish culture, a goodly number now come just to gaze at our plethora of Victorian-era homes. To be absolutely honest about it, the most spectacular of these houses were built by our nonpacifist brethren: the Baptists, Methodists, and Presbyterians. At any rate, for me it is always a pleasure to drive, or even walk, through this neighborhood, and Little Jacob immediately proved that he was a chip off the old block.

I had just turned down Crabapple Street when I noticed Frankie Schwartzentruber out in her yard. She appeared to be bending over to examine something in her flower bed, but since the dear old lady suffers from such severe osteoporosis, it is difficult to tell when in fact she is standing erect. Frankie has been a de facto member of the Beechy Grove Mennonite Church Brotherhood ever since her husband, Simon Schwartzentruber, was killed during a brotherhood game of horseshoes thirty-five years ago.

Of course it was a freak accident; Simon wasn't even in the game, but a bystander, watching from the other end of the pit. The game might have proceeded without a hitch, had not Magnus Amstutz, a veritable giant of a man, but a novice player, thrown a pitch so hard that it sailed a good six yards past the stake and slipped around Simon's long, slim neck instead. Simon was pronounced dead at the scene. As for poor Magnus, he was so traumatized by the event that he quit Beechy Grove Mennonite

Church and moved to Washington, D.C., to become a lobbyist for one of the tobacco companies. "If I'm going to kill people," he is quoted as saying, "I may as well make money from it."

Now, where was I? Oh yes, I was about to put the screws to Frankie Schwartzentruber. The woman may be an elderly widow, and as short as a third grader, but may I remind you that it is said that the Devil can take many forms. Since her back was to the street, and she didn't appear to have heard either my car engine, or the doors slamming, or the clack of my heels on the pavement, I cleared my throat loudly.

"Expel sputum on this sidewalk, Magdalena, and you'll get down on your hands and knees to clean it up."

I recoiled in surprise. "Frankie, who knew that *you* knew the S word?"

"You're not the only college-educated woman in this town, Magdalena." She turned slowly. "I know I'm being generous about your two years at the junior college, but hey—noblesse oblige, right?"

"How very kind of you, dear."

"Magdalena, why are you here?" Her eyes, which were slightly crossed (no doubt due to how tight her face had been pulled), focused on my bundle of joy for the first time. "Well, why didn't you say that you had the little one with you? Come inside before he catches his—well, before he catches cold."

I must confess that I hadn't been inside the Schwartzentruber house since the day after Simon's funeral, when I came to pick up my empty casserole dish. Simon carved cuckoo clocks for a living. He sold the clocks through a small catalog, and by word of mouth out of his house. I'd heard that he was one of the best cuckoo-clock-makers in the country and that his prices reflected this. Having never been in the market for a timepiece from which sprang a wooden bird with the sole purpose of insulting me, I'd never bothered to ask just how much one had to pay for a genuine Schwartzentruber. Whatever the price, Simon must have done pretty well for himself, because his widow had never appeared to be in need, and the house was still ticking away like a hundred time bombs.

"Rather gives you the creeps, doesn't it?" Frankie said.

"What?"

"So it's true, then, that you're hard of hearing? And all along I thought you were obtuse."

"But I'm neither! Hardheaded maybe, but I mean that literally. My birth mother practically overdosed on milk and calcium supplements, and of course I was raised on a dairy farm. Why, you could drop me headfirst from a silo and the worst that could happen is that I'd bite my tongue. But in answer to your first question, yes, it is creepy in here—no offense, of course—and if those birds all start in at the same time, I might just jump out of my brogans."

Frankie's pale, thin lips formed a split-second bow. "Don't worry: I disconnected all the birds the day I buried Simon. I never could stand them."

"But all these clocks—you have to wind them—why do you still run them?"

"I can't stand the silence either, but the ticking I can take." She hobbled around to peer into the carrier slung over my arm. "Just like I thought; this little fellow seems to like it as well."

Indeed, the new numero uno man in my life was fast asleep, and either was having pleasant clock-induced dreams or was passing a smidgen of gas. "Hmm," I said, "I don't suppose you'd sell me a couple."

"Oh no, I couldn't possibly do that! These are my retirement, you know."

"But you're already retired—aren't you?"

"Well, I don't work at a job outside my home, if that's what you mean, but I edit the monthly newsletter for the CCCCP, and that takes a lot of work."

"It also sounds vaguely obscene. What does it mean?"

"Cuckoo Clock Collectors of Central Pennsylvania. But you know, Magdalena, you're right. I've been hanging on to this collection and living off Social Security, and to what purpose? I think we should spend it now, while there's still time."

"Absolutely! What will we spend it on?"

"Don't be silly, girl, that was the *royal we.* But speaking of which, I've always wanted to go to Egypt and see the pyramids. My papa was a builder—okay, so he only paved parking lots, but construction is in my blood. Do you think it's too late for me to travel that far?"

"Well—"

"And then maybe a trip to Israel. It gets such bad press, you know, partly because it lets foreign reporters file negative stories about it while on Israeli soil. Can you imagine Saudi Arabia doing the same thing?"

"Why, no—"

"Magdalena, for such a verbose person, you suddenly seem to have clammed up."

"I haven't clammed," I claimed calmly. "I am just being careful lest I employ alliteration, which, as you know, is the bane of effete snobs across the educated spectrum—not that I consider you to be one. A snob, I mean."

"Hmm, I shall choose to take that as a compliment. Now, let's cut to the chase: *why* are you here? You never did answer that question."

"Forsooth, I say, speaking, of course, as one who can handle the truth. How about you? Do you prefer the unvarnished truth, or should I lacquer it up like a Stradivarius violin?"

"I'm eighty-two years old, Magdalena. It's beginning to look as if I might die of old age before you get down to brass tacks."

"What an odd expression," I said before attempting a reassuring smile. "I'm sure you have plenty of time left. Who knows, maybe even a few years. As to why I'm here, no doubt you've already guessed that it has something to do with Minerva J. Jay's untimely demise."

Frankie's eyes uncrossed for a split second, and then arranged themselves into diagonal slits. "So that's it," she hissed. "I'm on your short list of suspects."

"At least you hiss with an *S*, dear. Don't you just hate it when folks don't?"

"You're strange," she said, still hissing. "No doubt it's that Stoltzfus blood you got from your birth father. Look what it did to your brother."

"That murdering maniacal mantis is not my brother—ding, dang, dong! *Now* look what you made me do. And in front of my sweet, innocent son."

"Magdalena, if you weren't such a brilliant woman and a boon to the area economy, I'd personally lead a drive to have you committed."

"Which I am, dear. A more committed wife, mother, and erstwhile amateur sleuth has probably never before crossed your threshold. So tell me, did you like the deceased?"

"Is that a trick question?"

"Should it be?"

"Sit!" she barked. "And put that baby contraption on the floor. It's got to be ding-dong heavy—to borrow your pseudoswear words."

"You forgot the *dang*; that makes all the difference."

"Just shut up, Magdalena, and listen—I mean that with Christian love, by the way. Isn't that what you always say?"

I set the carrier next to an overstuffed armchair that looked to be clean, and plopped my patooty on it. "What's good for one goose is not necessarily good for another."

"As I said: shut up. Now, what was I about to say? Oh yes, while Simon was alive, Minerva was the bane of my existence. She was a shameless flirt, you know, and of course my Simon was a physical specimen par excellence. Wouldn't you agree?"

I'd known Simon my entire life and could never remember a time when he was not a scrawny, pigeon-chested little man with a neck like a swan that was topped by a bobbling head. There is a breed of duck called the Indian Runner that comes close to fitting this description, but I've never been sexually attracted to it—well, at least not on an ongoing basis.

"Your Simon was definitely something else," I said.

She nodded with surprising vigor, her white prayer cap bobbing back and forth with dizzying speed. "So you see the problem, then. She even sent him love notes on scented paper, the kind you have to buy in Bedford at the stationery store."

"What did they say?" There were moments when I adored my avocation, and this was one of them.

"What do you *think* they said? They were love notes, for pity's sake. Honestly, Magdalena, if I were a judgmental woman, like some I know, I might be tempted to think you were a little slow on the uptake."

"Do you still have them? And if so, may I read one?"

"Certainly not! What are you, a voyeur?"

I sprang to my size elevens. "I take umbrage at that remark! My interest was purely task related, speculating as I did that said documents might contain some clues as to who might want Minerva dead." I spread my fingers to dramatize what I hoped was a tone of resignation. "But—if you refuse to cooperate, I will be forced to conclude one of two things: a. the letters do not exist, or b. they exist but contain something that might indict you."

Although it took her considerably more effort, and she probably wears a size four, Frankie Schwartzentruber had also found her feet. "If I was going to kill Minerva, I would have done it long ago, when my dear Simon was alive. Of what use it would it be to me now?"

"Revenge?"

"*Revenge?* Why, I'm a Mennonite, for chocolate cookie's sake! The R word is barely in my lexicon."

I picked up the car carrier and edged toward the door. "That may be, dear, but you seem to be exhibiting a great deal of agitation at the moment."

"Which means what? Magdalena, you have the ability to get under my skin like a saline drip. Now, before I truly regret my actions, get out of my house."

"Gladly. But first let me say, that saline drip comparison was brilliant. Was that a simile or a metaphor? I can never remember which is which."

"Out, out, out!"

If you ask me, it was pretty poor of a card-carrying, bonnet-wearing Mennonite to slam the door behind me.

There are those who say that I'm a slow learner, but I refuse to listen to them. I must continually shrug off negative comments and forge ahead like Lewis and Clarke. But as to whether or not the aforementioned explorers had any naysayers, I cannot say, and I have no Sacagawea to guide me, so perhaps it was a poor analogy.

But at any rate, unlike Sacagawea, I had the opportunity to leave my darling little papoose for the duration of my quest, and that's exactly what I did. From Frankie's house I drove straight back to the inn and, after tanking up both the rascal and myself on yet another round of nutrients, set out for one final turning of the screws that day.

In retrospect, it was a move best left for the morrow.

14

Elias Whitmore. Now there's a Mennonite who is hands down more sexy than an Indian Runner duck. Then again, Elias is only half Mennonite; his father was a Methodist udder-balm salesman who charmed young Rachel Beiler off her feet—literally. Rachel was only sixteen, and Johnny Whitmore a decade older, but rather than press statutory rape charges, the girl's parents unfortunately saw a golden opportunity. The couple was wed in West Virginia, and honeymooned in South Carolina, both states, where, I am told, just about anything goes, as long as one can come up with three Scripture verses to defend it—oops, perhaps I'm being unkind. For that I repent.

At any rate, financially speaking, the Beilers made a good call, and thus Beiler's Udder Massage, or BUM, as it's called in the trade, was born. But poor Rachel was never even given the benefit of counseling, and less than a month after giving birth to her son, she hanged herself in her parents' barn. To be fair, the girl's parents claim she was always unstable, and I didn't know her well enough to hazard a guess one way or the other. I mean, who is to say what's normal?

What's important to know at this juncture is that Johnny Whitmore drank himself to an early death, and the Beilers were killed in an automobile accident a year ago Thanksgiving weekend, when they were broadsided by another vehicle. The couple in the other car was distracted by an argument they were having over who used the last teeth-whitening strip. In the twinkling of an eye, the handsome young grandson of self-made multimillionaires went from working in a car wash to running his own company.

Although strictly speaking Elias Whitmore is probably wealthier than I am, since his is not a self-made fortune, I do not count him as Hernia's richest citizen. Besides, when it comes to philanthropic donations, BUM lives down to its name. True, Elias does donate one morning a year to whipping up batter and flipping hotcakes, but as head deaconess I happen to know how much Mr. Whitmore drops in the offering plate every Sunday, and it could be a *lot* more.

I like to think of Buffalo Mountain, which I can see from my front verandah, as the Beverly Hills of Hernia. Although really just a long wooded ridge, Buffalo Mountain does offer some splendid views of our countryside and therefore is real estate appropriately priced out of range of our average citizenry (which, sadly, is not saying much). Those folks who have been able to take advantage of these lots positioned closer to Heaven have been, for the most part, successful artsy types, and owners of small businesses in Bedford and surrounding communities. Then there is Elias Whitmore.

Zigler Bend Road, which winds its way to the top of Buffalo Mountain, is as crooked as a serpent's tongue, and thus the delight of teenage boys for miles around. To reach the summit alive is akin to climbing Everest, but I made it in one piece just as the sun was setting over Miller's Pond and my homestead to the west. After enjoying the view for a long minute, I made a sharp left and continued north along the ridge until I got to Stopper's Gap Road. Since the latter isn't so much a road as it is a pair of axle-breaking ruts, I parked the car in a clearing that already contained at least two dozen other cars. From there I hoofed it the rest of the way up.

To say that Elias lives in a log cabin would be a fact, but it's also an understatement along the lines of: the Taj Mahal is an attractive tomb. Tree Tops, as Elias calls his wooden palace, is three stories high and contains just over five thousand square feet of heated space. One might jump to the conclusion that this quiet young Mennonite man, this member of my church, might find such a large house lonely, and one might be right, were it not for the fact that Tree Tops was the site of one continuous party.

Okay, so maybe I've exaggerated; maybe the parties end at ten every night, and the partygoers are all Scrabble-playing Christians who listen only to inspirational music, and Elias acts more like a chaperone than a playboy host. Nonetheless, the Devil himself has to be lurking in the shadows outside that oversize pile of sticks, just waiting for a chance to snatch some poor teen's soul out of the loving hands of the Good Lord. Elias claims that he started having these parties when he discovered our young folk necking in the woods along Stopper's Gap Road. But if you ask me, the problem has only gotten worse since the parties began, as word of "something happening on top of Buffalo Mountain" has spread far and wide.

Even now, from a hundred yards away, I could hear the thumping rhythm and shrieking vocals of something called Christian rock. Freni, who is denominationally challenged, calls this an oxymormonism. Jesus didn't have an electric guitar, she says. Neither did the disciples jump around to the beat of Jewish hymns. Of course I can agree with her line of reasoning only so far; any further and I'd have to become Amish, which would mean giving up my car and Big Bertha, my whirlpool bathtub with seventy-odd delightfully pulsating jets.

At any rate, the oversize log cabin lacks a doorbell. Instead, there is a life-size brass woodpecker attached to the door, which one is supposed to rap against a brass plate. It is actually a clever idea—assuming anyone inside can hear over the din.

Eventually I gave up on the brass woodpecker and used my knuckles, which, by the way, are the envy of real woodpeckers. That did the trick. The so-called music stopped immediately, and a few seconds later the door was opened by a wide-eyed waif in a black sweatshirt that featured Jesus Himself bedecked in a crown of thorns. The rest of the waif's outfit consisted of ragged blue jeans and the hideously ugly footwear Alison refers to as muck-my-lucks.

"Who is it?" I heard Elias call from somewhere within the bowels of his wooden house.

"I think it's your grandma," the child said.

"I don't have a grandmother," Elias said, sounding slightly closer. "Tell whoever it is that I'll be there in a minute."

"He'll be here in a minute," the waif said, her gaze never leaving my face.

"In the meantime, dear," I said, "I think I'll step in. You don't want me freezing my *tuchas* off, do you?" Thanks to my Jewish husband and his mother, I had a small Yiddish vocabulary that allowed me to add a little spice to my daily discourse without making me feel like I needed to wash my mouth out with soap.

The urchin was quick, however. "Are you a neighbor? Because these windows are double sealed, ya know? Besides which, Elias says he can hear yinz guys classical crap all the time."

"*Yinz?* Me thinks thou must have originated in Pittsburgh."

"Huh? What about Pittsburgh? Yinz didn't say anything bad about it, did ya? Because that's where I'm from."

"What's not to like about Pittsburgh? It's got Mystery Lovers Bookstore in Oakmont, and some very fine restaurants. Say, isn't yinz supposed to be second person plural? Like y'all?"

"Huh?"

"Not to mention the fact that you said *yinz* and *ya* in the same sentence. At the very least, one should show consistency."

"Oh, I get it; you're that crazy aunt of his."

"Hardly."

"Well, yinz is too old to be a friend."

"Call me Methuselah with a handbag."

"You're really weird, ya know? And I bet yinz weren't even invited, were ya?"

"Case in point, and the answer is no, but I—"

"Then yinz can't come in. Elias is very strict about not allowing outsiders into these parties. Unless you're on the list, ya can't come in. Not without prior screening."

"Outsiders? Screening?"

"You know, like unbelievers. Ya wouldn't believe how many times they've tried to sneak in and sabotage things."

"I'm neither an outsider nor an unbeliever," I said and gently pushed the elfin creature aside as I scurried into the light and warmth of the double-sealed cabin.

"Intruder!" the spunky sprite bellowed in a voice that was practically demonic in its magnitude and depth. The throng of once singing (and I call it that with Christian charity) young folks pressed around me, their eyes as wide as the waif's. Perhaps they sought to overpower me with the sheer force of their amazement.

"Peace be with you," I wailed. Wailing, I've learned, is not only annoying, but deeply unsettling. Nobody really wants to get too close to an adult wailer, for fear of being whaled.

The crowd stepped back, but I learned that it was not on my

account when the very handsome Elias Whitmore strode in, still buckling his pants. "Hey," he said with a sheepish grin. "It's only you."

I held out both hands and pretended to study them. "Are yinz sure? The left side of this person looks a little unfamiliar."

He laughed. "Hey, everybody, this is Miss—uh—Mrs.— Yoder—whatever. She's the head deaconess at my church. She's cool, so you can get back to whatever you were doing."

Any behavior strong enough to kill a cat was not going to be that easy to override in a room full of teenagers and young adults. No matter where we went for a moment of privacy, at least three people followed. Finally Elias had had enough.

"Let's go up to the crow's nest," he said. "Half of it's enclosed, so it won't be too cold or windy."

As I followed him from the room, the vigilant waif grabbed my sleeve. "You don't look like no deaconess to me," she hissed without a single sibilant S. "On account of that, I'm keeping an eye on yinz."

"Right, or left, eye?"

"You're like really, *really* crazy, ya know that?"

Elias Whitmore virtually pulled me away before I had chance to respond.

There were no lights in the crow's nest. This was intentional on Elias's part, so that one could not, by merely flipping on a switch, spoil the view. And surely the view from Elias's crow's nest was unparalleled in its magnificence anywhere east of the Mississippi.

Not only could I see my farm, but I could see the lights of Bedford, which lay twelve miles to the north. The bright glow on the northeastern horizon had to be Pittsburgh, which is a full hour away by a lead-footed driver like me, and to the south a much dimmer glow suggested Cumberland, Maryland (one is wise to take along provisions when visiting that state).

I gasped in awe. "Wow!"

"Wow is a palindrome, you know."

"A man, a plan, a canal, Panama," I said without missing a beat, although my ticker was beating a good deal faster than it had been at the start of the evening. Elias was turning out to be quite the wonder boy: handsome, charismatic, and now, apparently, intelligent as well.

"Miss Yoder, you really are smart," he said, which was a smart move in itself.

"To be honest, credit for that palindrome should go to Leigh Mercer, who published it in *Notes and Queries* all the way back in 1948. But we didn't come up here to discuss this fabulous view, or the beauty of the English language, did we?"

"You tell me; this was your idea."

"Touché—whilst a French word, is quite useful nonetheless. At any rate, I want you to know how much Beechy Grove Mennonite Church appreciates your involvement, which really is remarkable considering your—uh—youth. Your mother must have been a great inspiration to you."

If a handsome young man snorts in the dark, one might ask, is it still a derisive, disgusting noise? The answer would be an unequivocal yes!

"I hate it when people suggest that my involvement in church has to be some kind of legacy from my mother. Why can't it be because I love the Lord and feel that Beechy Grove is the best place for me to serve Him, as well as grow spiritually?"

"But we don't even have a pastor at the moment!"

"Yes, but there are others from whom I can learn."

"Such as?"

"You definitely are a good organizer, Miss Yoder."

Sometimes one must lunge to catch the bullet before one can bite it. "And?"

"And what?"

"You know, the spiritual growth stuff."

"Yeah, about that—well, you're a pretty good example of what not to do. That should count for something."

"Why, I never!"

"Sorry. I was just being honest; isn't that what good Christians are supposed to be?"

Ha! We'd see about that.

"How did you feel about Minerva J. Jay?" I asked, like a bolt from the blue.

Not only did he have the temerity to laugh, but what came out sounded natural and easy. "Finally, you get to the point of your visit. So, I gather I'm one of your suspects."

"Perhaps I'm not at liberty to say."

"I'd understand perfectly if that was the case. However, if perchance I am *not* on your list of suspects, then I insist that you add me to it at once."

"*What?*"

"Well, you'd be stupid not to. Everyone knows that Minerva was poisoned that morning, so whoever the culprit was, he or she had to be someone with access to the kitchen. Including you, that makes eight."

"Including *me*?"

"Yes, why not you?"

"But I'm a Menno—"

"As are we all, Miss Yoder. Certainly you've demanded an independent investigator."

"Mr. Whitmore," I said, adopting my Sunday-school-teacher voice, "please remember that I am the one who is supposed to be asking questions." I tried to give him a slightly stern yet benevolent glare—even if it was wasted in the dark. "You said that 'everyone knows that Minerva was poisoned.' How do they know that—assuming that she was indeed poisoned, of course?"

He cleared his throat, which signaled to me that he was buying time. "Well—uh—it's obvious. She ate our pancakes; she died. It doesn't take a rocket scientist to figure that one out."

"Why always a *rocket* scientist? How are they any smarter than the human genome folks? Besides, it seems like nobody cares about the space program anymore, which is a crying shame, if you ask me, but also a great relief. Can you imagine how fast we'd have to scramble if we did discover life on other planets, like, say, Mars? How will we know if those beings have souls? And if they do, will they too need to be saved from their sins? And what if missionaries who aren't quite as Christian as the rest of us get there first—like, say, the Catholics? Or some other religions altogether, like the Mormons or Scientologists?"

"You really *are* crazy," he said uncharitably.

But there was a method to my madness, and it was the art of keeping people off their toes—or their game, as the young people call it today. Just when he thought I'd become totally harmless, I pounced.

"Why did you hate Minerva so much?"

Even in the dark I could see Elias go through a complete transformation. His muscular physique seemed to swell like a puffer fish, his short blond hair bristled, and when he spoke, his voice shook with rage.

"You really want to know, do you? Then I'll tell you!"

15

Heavenly Cloud Cakes

Sour cream, eggs, and flour make pancakes as light as air—so light that at Bette's Diner in Berkeley, California, these ethereal offerings are called Cloud Cakes. Serve with warm Berry Sauce or Raspberry Maple Syrup.

3 large eggs
2 cups sour cream
⅔ cup unbleached all-purpose flour
3 teaspoons baking powder
¼ teaspoon salt

Berry Sauce or Raspberry Maple Syrup (recipes follow)

1. In a large bowl, beat the eggs until they are thick and light in color. Gradually stir in the sour cream until blended. Sift the flour, baking powder, and salt together in a separate bowl. Gradually stir the dry ingredients into the egg mixture.

2. Heat a large nonstick griddle or skillet over medium heat until hot enough to sizzle a drop of water. Brush with a thin film of

vegetable oil, or spray with nonstick cooking spray. For each pancake, pour a scant ¼ cup batter onto the griddle or into the skillet.
Adjust the heat to medium-low. Cook until the tops are covered
with small bubbles and the bottoms are lightly browned. Carefully turn and cook until the other side is golden brown. Repeat
with the remaining batter.

3. Serve with Berry Sauce or Raspberry Maple Syrup.

MAKES ABOUT EIGHTEEN 3- TO 4-INCH PANCAKES.

Berry Sauce: Combine ¼ cup water and 1 tablespoon cornstarch
in a small saucepan and stir until the cornstarch is dissolved.
Add one 10-ounce box thawed frozen strawberries or raspberries
in sweetened syrup. Heat, stirring, until the mixture boils and
thickens. Remove from the heat and stir in 2 tablespoons orange
liqueur, if desired.

Raspberry Maple Syrup: Combine 1 cup maple syrup and ½ cup
unsweetened frozen (or fresh) raspberries in a small saucepan.
Heat until the mixture begins to boil. Cool slightly. Press through
a sieve to puree the berries into the syrup. Serve warm.

16

"Because she killed my dad!" Elias's voice thundered through the treetops.

"I beg your pardon?"

"Miss Yoder, do you have a hearing problem?"

I jiggled pinkies in both ears to make sure they were clear of wax. "No. But this is the first time I've heard about this."

"That *woman*—Miss Jay—was a slut, pardon my crude use of language, Miss Yoder. Anyway, she and my father were having an affair while my father was drinking himself into an early grave. All the while she was trying to get him to marry her so that she could get her hands on his share of BUM. Of course it didn't work. He used her, just as she was using him, and he died of cirrhosis of the liver without ever intending to pop the question. How did she contribute to his death, you might ask?"

"Indeed I might."

"You see, he tried to go on the wagon a number of times. However, the scheming Miss Jay did everything she could to derail him—if I might mix a metaphor."

"Why not? Everyone else does."

"He'd check himself into a rehab facility, but then halfway through his treatment she'd come up with some horrific-sounding emergency that would compel him to quit, so he'd have to start all over again. On one occasion she had a message smuggled in that said she'd been diagnosed with stage-four lymphoma and had less than a month to live. Could they please spend that month together in Acapulco, because she wanted to die on a tropical beach? Being the romantic drunk that he was, he bought it."

"That's awful! But surely—"

"Surely *what*? Surely my father should bear some responsibility for not being able to withstand the wiles of Minerva J. Jay?"

"Men are not helpless creatures, dear; if they are, then they have no business running the government."

"No disrespect intended, Miss Yoder, but women should not be involved in positions that give them power over men. If you doubt me, then look up what the apostle Paul has to say on the subject."

"What about Deborah the judge? That was like being president back then."

"Whatever you say, Miss Yoder. Are we through here?"

"Almost, but first let me say that I choose to interpret your sarcastic rejoinder as complete acquiescence. That said, how did you deliver the poison to her pancakes and no one else's?"

That shocked him into a moment of silence. "I could ask you the same thing, you know," he said at last.

"Yes, but I'm the interrogator. Now, please answer."

"It *wasn't* me. But I can answer that for you; the pills were dropped into a single bowl of batter, and then Miss Jay with her enormous appetite ate that entire batch."

"Hmm. I suppose that would work—if the killer knew the cakes were headed out to a specific customer. But we were working at breakneck speed. We were all taking turns, dashing about madly, filling in as needed. What you're suggesting would have taken some planning."

"*You* were dashing about at breakneck speed, Miss Yoder, because that's your modus operandi."

"It's genetic; I can't help it! It's a disease."

"Nevertheless, any one of the rest of us, by keeping a calmer head, could have planned an entire griddle full of cakes for that glutton. It was a given that she would show. Oh, and by the way, before you point out that I have one of the calmest heads—which I do—I must likewise point out that your maniacal behavior would also make a perfect cover for that insidious crime."

"How dare—"

"Good night, Miss Yoder. Please watch your step going down the spiral staircase. And peace be with you."

🍮

"He's awesome," Alison said.

It was less than an hour later, and we were sitting around the kitchen table enjoying a hearty supper of beef cabbage soup and corn bread. Little Jacob, of course, was growing fat on his own special diet. Freni had been driven home by her husband, Mose, via horse and buggy, so my dearly beloved was the only other adult there.

"He's a murder suspect," I said.

"And no, you can't date him," Gabriel said.

Alison slammed her spoon down on the table, sending specks of broth out into the universe. "Aw, man, you guys are like the meanest parents there are."

Oh, what music to my ears. That my pseudo-stepdaughter should refer to my husband and me as her parents, even in a fit of anger, meant that she had truly come to accept us as such. Biologically she was the fruit of my quasi–first husband's loins. Aaron, you see, was the cause of my inadvertent bigamy because he was legally married to, but separated from, a strumpet up in Minnesota, one to whom he is still hitched. They, however, neither wanted to raise Alison, nor cared enough about the child to turn custody of her over to me. Thank heaven all that would change in just eight weeks when the court could declare Alison officially abandoned and our petition to adopt her would be finalized.

I flashed our future full-daughter a placating smile. "When you turn eighteen, you may date anyone you wish. Although I must warn you that in the meantime you should work really hard on developing a taste for Christian rock music. He plays it for a couple of hours every night for the benefit of his groupies."

"Yuck. I don't like religious music—no offense, Mom. And whatcha mean by *groupies*?"

Gabe winked at me. "She means the girls that hang around him, right, hon?"

"Yes, but I'm not making this up. Alison, dear, before you came to live with me—with us—I had big-name stars stay here at the inn, and none of them had quite this guy's charisma."

"Oh, man," Alison said as she lurched for her spoon, "this reeks big-time. How come you had big stars stay here before I come along, and since then only piddly people like what's her name?"

"Babs is not piddly!"

Gabe sighed. "I'll say. You don't have to be a person who loves people to go nuts over her singing. Even Ma loves her, and she's critical of everyone."

As if on cue, the swinging door from the dining room flew open. "Did I hear my name taken in wain?"

I couldn't help but groan. Ida Rosen used to be the mother-in-law from Hades, but ever since she found out that her shikse daughter-in-law (that would be me) could produce an heir, she has been the mother-in-law from the suburb next to Hades.

"Ma," Gabe hastened to explain, "I was just saying how much you love Barbra."

"Yah, a good Jewish girl, that one." She pulled a chair out opposite Alison and, unbidden, hiked her rather hefty heinie up to the seat. The chair groaned as well.

"Do you want some beef cabbage soup, Grandma Ida?" Alison knows there is no love lost between the two of us, but she adores us both.

"From a can?"

"Absolutely not," I declared indignantly. "Freni made this from scratch."

"Den mebbe a litle."

"Ma," Gabe said quietly, "your accent's getting stronger again."

Ida pretended not to hear. "*Nu*, Magdalena, I vas reading dis article in *Hadassah* magazine und I tink about you."

"Really?" I was mildly curious; still, I wanted to slap my lips for betraying me.

"Yah. It said dat your Jesus vas a Jew."

I waited patiently for something enlightening to follow.

"Did you know dat?" she said, a bit piqued when no response from me was forthcoming.

"Why, yes I did."

"So, He vas a convert. Den it is not such a bad ting for you to convert, no?"

"No! I mean, He wasn't a convert; He was born Jewish."

"Even better! But imagine such a ting! All the goyim say dat He vas a Christian, und now you, who are an expert in such tings, say He vasn't."

"Of course Jesus was a Christian," Alison said. "Every dummy knows that—oops, sorry, Grandma Ida."

"No, Alison," I said softly, "to be a Christian means that you are a *follower* of Christ. Jesus was not a follower of Himself."

Meanwhile Ida was shaking her head. "Vas His mama a Jew?"

"Yes," I said. "Born that way as well."

"Den dis I don't understand; vhy do so many Christians hate de Jews vhen der own Jesus und His mother vere Jewish?"

Gabe and I made eye contact but said nothing. Surely Ida knew the answer to that question. She was a survivor of Nazi Germany, for crying out loud. She'd been exposed to anti-Semitism all her life. If she'd been called a Christ killer once, she'd been called it a thousand times.

"Yeah, why?" Alison demanded.

"Because," I said at last, "they blame the Jews for killing Jesus."

"But I thought it was the Romans," Alison said.

"Yes, directly—but it was *all* of us who put Him up there on the cross; it was the sins of the world that He volunteered to die for."

"Really?"

"Really."

"*Oy veys meer.*"

When Alison descends deep into thought, her brows literally meet. "What I don't get is that these people, the ones who blame the Jews for Jesus' death, how come they ain't thanking the Jews instead? I mean, if Jesus died an old man, He wouldn't o' taken away nobody's sin, and they wouldn't have crosses and such for the front of their churches. They'd have to hang up canes or wheelchairs instead."

As sacrilegious as that was, I couldn't help but smile. The girl had a point; one could hardly subscribe to a faith that relied on a sacrifice, and then not have a sacrificial victim. I was about to add an enlightening theological comment of my own when I saw Ida giving Alison what looked like a thumbs-up.

"What was that about?" I demanded.

"It weren't nothing," Alison said.

"You mean it wasn't nothing, dear," I said.

"Yeah, that's exactly what I meant," Alison said.

"Yah, das vhat she meant," Ida said without missing a beat.

I looked from Alison to Ida and back again. Something was going on between the two of them.

"Out with it!" I roared. Beneath the blanket Little Jacob stopped nursing, but only for a second. With his strong nerves and insatiable appetite, my bundle of joy was indeed a chip off my old bun.

It was Ida, bless her grandmotherly heart, who went first. "This one," she said without a trace of an accent, "is not having such a good time at school."

I turned to Alison with alarm. "You're not failing algebra again, are you, dear? Because we can get you a tutor."

"Mom, it ain't that."

"Oh, sweetheart," Gabe said, "is that Lipinski girl picking on you again because you're uh—well, you know."

"Ya mean because I'm a carpenter's dream?"

Ida found her accent again. "Vhat does dat mean?"

"It means that I'm flat chested, Grandma Ida."

"*Nu?* Better dat you should have too litle den too much. Even vhen I go shluffie on my back, dey—"

"TMI!" Gabe cried. "Too much information!"

"Anyvey, her chests, dey are not de problem. De problem is dat some of de children are anti-semantic."

I started. "*What?* They're opposed to the use of connotative meanings?"

"Oy," Ida groaned, "dis von is meshugah for sure."

"They call me Jew girl!" Alison blurted.

I was momentarily stunned. Alison was no more a "Jew girl" than I was a "Jew woman." And what was wrong with being either?

"Is that an insult?" I asked.

"The proper term is Jewish," Gabe said quietly.

"But she isn't." I turned to Alison. "Who calls you that?"

"Walter Gawronski even calls me a stinking Jew girl. He says that I have Jew cooties."

"Did you tell him you were a Mennonite?" The Gawronskis were newcomers to town, having immigrated here from southwestern Ohio.

"That's not the point," Gabe said.

"Besides, Mom, he ain't the only one. Mandy Keim calls me Jew girl too, and she goes to our church. So does Brittany Augsburger and Johnny Schrock and Denise Livengood and—"

"What do you say to them, dear?"

"First I told them that I weren't, on account of Dad was only my sorta stepdad, but since my real dad—I mean what's their names up in Minnesota—don't even want me anymore, and youse two is gonna adopt me, I tell 'em I'm half Jewish, and so what?"

"Dis von makes me proud," Ida said.

"And if being proud wasn't against my religion," I said, "I'd put Grandma Ida's pride to shame with how much pride I feel."

And indeed, I was proud of Alison, although it broke my heart to hear her refer to her birth parents as "what's their names." That scoundrel—the one who stole my maidenhood under false pretenses—and his wife had actually petitioned the courts to have their parental bonds with Alison officially terminated. Their motive was to end the child-support checks they sent to me every month, which I faithfully deposited in Alison's college fund. Of course the judge didn't grant the Millers their wish directly, but he did sentence them both to six months in jail for child aban-donment and had the state declare them unfit parents, which amounted to the same thing as a parent-child annulment.

Gabe's response to Alison's answer was to get up and put his arms around her neck. "Just think, honey, in only two more months Mom and I will be able to legally adopt you."

Ida hoisted her bosoms onto the table so that she could lean forward as much as possible. "*Nu, bubbeleh,* den vill you be a Rosen, or a Yodel?"

"That's Yod*er*," I roared.

At that, Little Jacob decided his dinner was over and it was time to kvetch big-time. His sudden cry of distress was so loud that even I, the one who'd been holding him, was startled. It was almost as if he'd popped out of nowhere and yelled, "Boo." Naturally I whipped off the blankie that had been covering him, popped his dinner container back into its holster, and proceeded to burp the little fella.

Poor Ida turned white, then pink, then white, and then pink again, all in slow motion. Observing her reaction was a bit like watching a chromatically challenged lava lamp, except that lava lamps generally do not possess the power of speech.

"*Oy gevalt!*" she finally managed to say. "Und dis you do in front of your family?"

"Don't you eat in front of this family?"

"Yah, but—dis—dis mitt de breast, und in front of de child yet!"

"Don'tcha worry none, Grandma Ida," Alison said. "I seen this a million times, so I'm used to it now. And it ain't gonna per-vert me any, 'cause I'm already perverted. Ain't I, Mom?"

"*What?*"

"Don'tcha remember that at Cousin Freni's farm I seen that bull and a cow make themselves a calf?"

"Yes, dear. But Ida—"

"Und my poor little Gabeleh? You do such a ting in front of him?"

"Ma, get off her case," Gabe said, much to my surprise. "I'm a doctor; I think I can handle it."

"Besides," I said, perhaps a wee bit cruelly, "how do you think Little Jacob came to be?"

"Funny that you should bring up that subject," Alison said, "because I've been meaning to ask you about that."

"*Oy veys meer*," I said just as Little Jacob let out an enormous burp.

17

Alison merely wanted to know if there were parallels to be drawn between the mating cows and what humans did behind closed doors. She'd already concluded as much; she just wanted an adult to confirm it. My intent was to tell her that a loving, committed relationship was a lot different than livestock breeding, but I made the mistake of beginning my explanation with the word *yes*, which sent her gagging from the room. The next morning, as I drove her to school, she declared that she would never, ever have sex, not even if she lived to be a million years old, and if at some point she should decide she wanted a child, she would adopt one just like we did. Silently, I thanked the Good Lord for the amorous bull, and wisely, I said nothing.

Usually Alison rides the bus, which stops at the end of our driveway, but on this particular day I had an unscheduled parent-teacher meeting to attend. The victim of my visit was Merle Waggler, a soft, sloppy, but perpetually smiling young man who teaches Alison eighth-grade math and earth science. Merle is a lifelong member of Beechy Grove Mennonite Church and has been a member of the brotherhood ever since he married about ten years ago. Most important, he was near the top of my suspect list.

It may seem odd to save one of my biggest suspects for last, but I'd been out of practice for the length of Little Jacob's gestation, and I needed to get my size elevens wet again before jumping back in up to my neck. Besides, I've always found Merle's perpetual smile a bit off-putting. *I* know it's a smile because he's a Christian and attends my church; if I was a stranger, however, I would be sorely tempted to interpret his upturned lips as a smirk. Maybe it's because what goes on in his eyes simply doesn't match what comes out of his mouth on a good many occasions.

Alison used to adore Mr. Waggler until he started reading, in a loud voice, the class's math-test scores. He said that he did it to reward the good students and encourage the middling ones, but Alison believes, as do I, that he wasn't above humiliating the poor students. I don't think he did it to be mean (Alison does), but to shame his pupils into studying harder. I base my interpretation of his motive on the fact that shame was a huge motivator for me while I was in school. Not only was I "Yoder with the Odor," but because of one D on a spelling test (I was out with the flu the week the words were assigned), I was dubbed Dumbdalena for an entire semester—and *that* was by a teacher: Mrs. Regier.

At any rate, I found Merle Waggler in the teachers' lounge, in his usual sloppy attire, having a cup of coffee and chatting with a very pretty—and unnaturally blond—student teacher from over by Somerset. I was hoping that my unexpected appearance would put the fear of Magdalena in Merle, because he is a good ten years younger than me, if not more, but he merely smiled. Or smirked, depending on one's interpretation.

"Mmm," he intoned, as per his usual way of beginning to

speak. "Let me guess: she's held up a gas station, and you're on your way to bail her out of jail. You want me to know that I shouldn't delay class on her account."

The student teacher twittered while I raged silently—well, for all of five seconds. "*Excuse* me? Was that supposed to be funny, Merle?"

"Mmm, Magdalena, you must admit that your—ah, how shall I put this—protégée? Anyway, she has all the makings of a juvenile delinquent."

I couldn't believe my ears. This from a teacher who wore sweatshirts to school? Never mind that when he was in high school—I forget which year—Merle and a buddy were arrested for spray painting near obscenities on the bridge over Slave Creek. The only reason the judge dismissed their cases was because the boys had been clever enough to employ euphemisms instead of outright vulgar expressions. Personally, I find the use of innuendo just as offensive.

"She is not a juvenile delinquent!" I ejaculated angrily.

"Mmm, I didn't say she was; I said she had the *makings* of one. Really, Magdalena, you do jump to conclusions."

"At least I get my exercise—oops, that wasn't very nice of me. Sorry."

"Mmm, I'll take it as you meant it. So, what do you want?"

No beating around the bush for me. "Did you like Minerva J. Jay?"

"Did I *what*?"

"You dropped the *mmm*s."

"Huh?" He looked at me like I was the crazy woman I've sometimes been made out to be.

"You do say it a lot," the student teacher said, and then, realizing that she'd placed a fledgling foot in her mouth, made a sudden exit from the room.

"Back to Minerva, dear," I said. "Did she get on your last nerva?"

"You're so droll, Magdalena, that sometimes I forget to laugh. And yes, she did get on my nerves; she got on everyone's nerves. *Didn't* she? Can you honestly name one person in this town who liked her?"

"Reverend Richard Nixon—he of the church of thirty-two names. He probably liked her; he likes everybody."

"Yeah? Well, he doesn't like Roman Catholics; he told me that once himself."

"Just because of their religion?"

"Mmm, you got it. Anyway, now that your little survey is finished, I need to be getting to my homeroom; the bell is about to ring."

"Bells, shmells; the kids can wait. Let them throw paper wads like we used to do. You see, Merle, this isn't a survey. I'm investigating Minerva's murder, and you're one of the suspects."

Yes, the Germans came up with the word *schadenfreude*, but one must admit that it describes a very universal condition: that of taking pleasure in the misfortune of others—although a great many pious and/or enlightened folk will hotly deny they have ever felt this way. What I'm getting at is that Merle's smirk dried up like a rain puddle on a cloudless August day, as his tiny eyes flickered from side to side. After all, there were several other teachers in the lounge, and my accusation had not been delivered in a whisper.

"For Pete's sake," he hissed, "keep your voice down."

"All right. And there's no need to get your jockeys in a jumble if you cooperate."

"Do I even have a choice?"

"No."

The bell rang. As the other staff members filed out, you can be sure that every single one of them was staring at us. Several of them even collided with one another, which, in my opinion, served them right. I know, that's not the way a good Christian should be thinking, but I resolved to pray about my attitude just as soon as I had a moment to myself.

"Okay," Merle mumbled when the door finally closed, "but do you mind if we sit down first?"

"Not at all, dear."

Alas, I'd spoken too soon. Much to my surprise, I discovered that some teachers can be incredibly messy. Someone had been eating a pastry coated in powdered sugar, and that someone had apparently dropped said pastry on my chair. I only noticed this when I was adjusting my skirt, *after* I'd been seated. However, I doubt that this was the same clumsy person who had wiped peanut butter on the armrest; again a fact that I discovered *after* it had been transferred to my dress sleeves. I sighed dramatically as a way to let out steam.

"Hey, don't blame that on me too, Magdalena. I always eat over there at the table."

"I was merely emoting, dear—as is my wont under the circumstances. Now, just so we're clear: I expect your full cooperation in this investigation."

"By what authority do you act, Magdalena? Your Honor the mayor? Pretend policewoman? Head deaconess of Beechy Grove Mennonite Church? Richest woman in Hernia?"

"Why, you impudent little—well, man. See what you almost made me do? I don't normally call people names, you know."

"Mmm, but you do try to intimidate them; you can't deny that."

"When the shoe fits, dear, I wear it. And yes, this sensible black brogan with the eighteen-inch lace fits very well. That said, Chief Chris Ackerman, of the Hernia Police Department, has asked me to investigate this case on his behalf."

"Is that even legal?"

"Well, it certainly isn't illegal for me to ask questions. You are, of course, free to refuse to answer. Be fairly warned, however, that by doing so, you will cast further suspicion on yourself."

"You're basically saying that I have no choice but to submit to your grilling."

"Like a weenie on a green willow branch."

"That would be roasting."

"Not the way I do it. Now, spill; I want to know all about your run-ins with our town's least-liked personality."

"Mmm, well, I'd have to say that up until this morning, you and I have managed to avoid any direct confrontations."

"Very funny. Now, be a dear and hurry—wait just one Mennonite minute! You weren't kidding, were you?"

"Face it, Magdalena, if it wasn't for that pile of money you've made from fleecing tourists at your inn, we wouldn't even be having this conversation."

"I don't fleece these folks! These are very wealthy people who expect to pay through the nose for poor service and a good helping of attitude. After all, almost all of them enjoy traveling in Europe, and a good percentage of them adore Paris. And if you're insinuating that the ALPO—Amish Lifestyle Plan Option—that I offer these sophisticated travelers has somehow affected my interpersonal relationships, you're dead wrong. I have oodles of friends and a handsome husband to prove it."

"Mmm, whatever."

"You're trying to get my goat, aren't you? It's a ploy to distract me. Well, I have news for you. It's not going to work."

He jumped to his feet, and as he did so, his trademark smirk returned to his round, doughy face. "I've changed my mind; I won't be cooperating after all."

"*I beg your pardon?*"

"You might intimidate the others who volunteered to make pancakes that morning, but I'm *not* going to let you do that to me. So take your twenty questions, Magdalena, and put them—"

"How rude! I demand that you sit back down right now."

He started to walk away but stopped when he was halfway to the door. "Mmm, and one more thing—"

"If you're going to apologize, dear, then come back and do it right."

"Ha, you really are a comedienne. The next time you speak to me, it better be with a court order. Is that clear?"

I jumped to my size elevens, and had I been a Methodist or a Baptist, I might even have tackled Merle Waggler. But I was a mere Mennonite, a pacifist by breeding and disposition. When words failed me, I was as helpless as an Easter chick in the hands of a two-year-old. Still, even though he refused to cooperate with the interrogation, he couldn't very well ignore a mother's plea to put an end to the anti-Semitic taunts hurled at her child.

"You can ignore me, but you can't ignore the bullying that goes on in this school!"

I'm sure that Merle Waggler broke several laws of physics by turning on a dime. "*What* did you say?"

"Other children have been calling her 'Jew girl.' "

"Isn't she? I never see her in church with you."

"No, she isn't Jewish. Her adoptive father—well, soon to be, at any rate—is, but not her."

"Magdalena, what you've described is not bullying. Bullying is being called 'Pillsbury doughboy' and having your head stuck in the toilet while the other boys take turns flushing it. Bullying is being the last one chosen in gym, *every* single time, and being called 'girlie' because you have some breast development. And when we played dodgeball—we don't have mixed gym classes in Hernia, as you well know—all the boys ganged up on me, even my supposed friends. And where was the teacher? Standing right there with a wicked old grin on his face."

"And where are *you* when Alison gets teased?"

"Look, Magdalena, it's hardly the same. Those people have brought it on themselves."

"I can't believe I'm hearing this, and from a member of my church."

"Well, it's true. They're the ones who rejected Jesus, not us."

"For your information, not even my mother-in-law was around two thousand years ago."

"Perhaps you should read Matthew 27:25. The Jews who demanded Christ's crucifixion volunteered that His blood should be on their heads and on the heads of their children."

"Ah, but it says nothing about the children agreeing to that arrangement. But speaking of blood, do you enjoy a good blood sausage?"

"*Blutwurst?* Yes, of course; my mother was a German Mennonite."

"Ah, then you may do well to memorize Leviticus 17:10— nope, I take that back. According to that verse the Good Lord has already set His face against you, and cut you off from among His people."

"Mmm, perhaps some Sunday school teachers need to read their Bibles more, Magdalena. Are you forgetting that in the Book of Acts the apostle Peter has a vision in which the Lord tells him that all creatures are now—how shall I put this?—acceptable for human consumption."

"Well, I for one would certainly be cautious about questioning a voice heard in Peter's trance. On the other hand, in Leviticus 3:17, the Lord Himself, who has been speaking *directly* to Moses all along, has the following to say: 'This shall be a *perpetual* statute *throughout your generations* in all your dwell-ings: you shall eat neither fat nor blood.' The Good Lord is omniscient, Merle, and He could see all the way down the line to the apostle Peter, yet He didn't put an escape clause in that verse, did he?"

"That's because the verse you just quoted applies to Jews only."

"Peter was a Jew. You see, Merle, I was the Scripture-verse-memorization champion three years in a row at vacation Bible school. After that they made me ineligible; they said I was demor-alizing the other kids."

"Mmm, maybe you know your Scripture, Magdalena, but you obviously haven't been around those people very much. In college—"

"Well, I do know this, Merle: in Hernia the mayor is also the president of the school board."

He took two steps back as his face assumed the color of a brat-wurst, which is yet another German sausage. "Is that a threat?"

"Heavens, no; I was merely stating a fact. And I shall be stat-ing this same fact when I speak to your principal in a few min-utes. Of course, I will also remind him that we already have two applications for eighth-grade math teachers for next year and that your contract is up in June."

"Mmm, you wouldn't dare."

"On the other hand, getting a new teacher is akin to buying a pig in a poke, no matter how well we screen him or her; appli-cants are not above lying, or getting their references to lie. But I already know what kind of pig you are. And if I need to, I know just where to poke you—it's called a salary freeze."

"Hey, I'll make the kids stop harassing her."

It may have been childish on my part, but I prefer to view the fact that I swept past him to the door as a power move. "See that you do, Merle Waggler. Oh, and by the way, when you come to church Sunday, bear in mind that you'll be worshipping one of my husband's people; one of *those* people."

"Huh?"

"Think about it, dear."

18

On the way back to the inn to feed my sweet Baby Bumpkin, I decided to make an unscheduled stop at Susannah's house. This was a dangerous move on my part: dangerous, that is, for my psyche. My sister is as unpredictable as a Super Bowl game, plus she has a master's degree from Adolescence State University.

Once I found her hanging by her knees from a trapeze in her living room. She said she'd read somewhere that Australians were the smartest people on the planet, and that since their brains were "upside down," she wanted hers to be oriented that way as well. I told her that made sense, and then I sat down and waited until her knees gave out—all of two minutes later. Fortunately, my reactions were quick that day and I was able to catch her before she broke her neck.

When our parents died, squished as they were between the milk tanker and the semitrailer carrying state-of-the-art running shoes, they left us the farm on which I later established the PennDutch Inn. My sister is a full partner in this endeavor, although she's never lifted a manicured finger to do as much as fold a towel or mail a brochure. One might reasonably ask why I haven't tried to buy her out, or otherwise exclude her from the huge profits I've managed to make over the years.

The answer is twofold: first, Susannah is a free spirit who doesn't just march to the beat of a different drummer; she has an entire college band in her head—and, I'm ashamed to add, at times in the past they were sometimes found in her bed as well. Second, even though our parents lied to me by not disclosing my adoption, I promised them I would always look after my sister. On her own, my sister could not survive. Of course, I'm not a total idiot; Susannah's fortune is in a trust until she proves herself responsible. In the meantime she receives an allowance that is sufficient for her needs, but not so generous that it encourages her to lead a life of flagrant debauchery.

A little circumspect debauchery might even be a necessary requirement for maintaining one's sanity for those folks who live in Foxcroft, our only, and incongruously, named subdivision. There the houses are cookie-cutter images of one another, the paint colors vary only slightly, and the foundation shrubs differ only in the amounts of foliage their respective owners elect to leave before they tire of playing with their electric shears. It is understandable, then—just not excusable—if a little spanky along with the hanky-panky is seen as a morale booster. This, of course, brings me back to poor Susannah, who, now that her murdering husband is out of the picture, has been lonelier than a cat at the Westminster Dog Show.

They say that water seeks its own level; therefore, I should not have been surprised when a nun with a very morose expression opened Susannah's door. The woman's face was as pale as my cellulite, and her gray eyes appeared almost translucent.

"Yes," she said. "May I help you?"

"Uh—isn't this 907 Red Fox Lane?"

"It is."

"I'm here to see Susannah."

"She isn't receiving visitors."

"I'm not a visitor; I'm her sister."

"Ah, so you must be the bossy one they call Magdalena."

"Indeed I am— Wait a minute! Bossy? Says *who*?"

"Says me." The nun started to close the door, and might have gotten away with it had I not noticed that beneath her surplice there was a surplus of activity. In fact, to the uninitiated it might have appeared as if the nun's bosoms were running from side to side, pausing every now and then to leap outward, as if to strike me. But the clincher was the attendant vocalizing. Real bosoms seldom growl, and in my experience never, ever bark.

"You're not a nun," I said calmly. "You're Susannah."

"No, I'm not."

At this point the leaping, snarling bosom emitted an odor so foul that its origin was incontestable. "Calm down, Shnookums," my sister cooed as she peered down into the recesses of her habit. "It's only your auntie-poo."

"I'm not that thing's auntie, dear," I said, "and I'm certainly nobody's poo." I gently pushed my way inside. A second later I wished I'd kept on driving. "Susannah! What on earth have you done with all your stuff?"

"Really, Mags, you know good wordsmiths eschew the word *stuff*."

"Stuff and nonsense! All your things, for crying out loud! Where is your furniture—although you'd think that would take a plural verb—and the rest of your bric-a-brac?"

"Which is just a fancy word for *crap*."

"Susannah, what happened? Were you robbed?"

My sister's high-pitched laugh set the mutt in her Maiden-form to howling, which in turn set my teeth on edge. I have nothing against dogs, but the rat-size pooch that prowls her bra is undeserving of the moniker. Should I ever find myself alone in a room with him, and me with a frying pan in one hand, I'd conk myself up the side of the head to put myself out of my misery until help could arrive.

"Please," I begged.

"Oh, all right."

She reached down her habit and withdrew a two-pound beast, half of which was sphincter, the other half teeth. "Now, run along, sweetie, to your beddy-bye and take your morning nappy-poo. Mommy will be there in a minute to tuck you in."

The hideous thing snarled and snapped at me for good measure and then trotted off, nails clicking on hardwood floors, as bid, into Susannah's boudoir. I waited until I was sure the coast was clear before speaking my mind.

"How old is that thing?"

"Mags, I keep telling you, he's not a *thing*; he's a pure-blooded, prize-winning, stud-quality Russian terrier. But to answer your question, he'll be eight in June."

Endeavoring always to be kind, I tried not to smile. "So what's he got left—two, maybe three more years? I mean, what a shame."

"More like eight or nine. Usually the smaller the dog, the longer they live."

"Like I said, what a shame." I swallowed hard; disappointment can be as difficult to get down as Granny Yoder's rhubarb pie. "So tell me, what's with the empty house?"

"I sold everything. You're kinda stingy, Mags, and I wanted a new vehicle."

"A *vehicle*? What exactly does that mean?"

"It's an old school bus. I'm having it painted black with white lettering. It will be delivered tomorrow."

"What lettering?"

"The name of my order." She fingered a cross that appeared to be carved from a bar of soap and which hung from her neck on a length of white cotton clothesline.

I felt the need to sit down. "Do you still have kitchen furniture?"

She shook her head, causing her wimple to rustle. "We can sit on my bed. It's the only thing left."

I pictured the college band doing more than sitting on Susannah's bed. "No, thanks; I'm good. Okay, spill. What order?"

"It's a religious order, silly—only it's not exactly religious on account of I'm not religious. I'm calling it Sisters of Perpetual Apathy—SOPA is the acronym. That's why I'm wearing this cross. Our motto is 'We care about nothing, so leave us the heck alone.' I might leave off that last part, though, because it could be a turnoff to potential postulants. Then again, why should I care?"

I had a short-lived vision of me slapping Susannah on both checks, knocking some sense into her, as it were, and then us hugging and crying, and vice versa, but at the same time I knew it was all a senseless fantasy. Once she has her mind made up, there's nothing you can do about it but wait it out. Really, it's hopeless.

In the meantime, however, a sister has a right to know a few things. "Susannah, who is this 'we' that you mentioned? Aren't you the only member of the Sisters of Perpetual Apathy?"

"You see just how little you believe in me?"

I shrugged. "Why should that matter?"

"For your information, Mrs. Mayor, Mrs. I've-Got-a-Doctor-for-a-Husband, Mrs. I've-Got-the-Perfect-Baby, there are fifteen other nuns in my order. There's Sister Despair, Sister Disgruntled, Sister Disenchanted, Sister Disingenuous—"

"Wait a minute! You're serious?"

"No, I'm Mother Dispirited."

My knees shook, my head swirled, and giant hands were ringing my stomach like a dishrag, and all because I knew now, without a doubt, that she was indeed as serious as a preacher on Judgment Day. This was exactly the kind of thing my baby sister would do if she ever found herself desperate and disconsolate.

I lowered my body to the floor. "Let me guess, dear. Is there a Sister Disconsolate?"

"Yes, how did you know?"

"A Sister Desperate?"

"Mags, how did you know?"

"Just a guess. Where did you find these women—if you don't mind me asking?"

"They're former Melvinites who have seen the light—more accurately, that there isn't any. Just shades of gray. Gray and beige."

Of course, why hadn't I thought of that? The Melvinites were members of a wacky cult who literally worshipped Melvin Stoltzfus, the convicted murderer, who also happened to be Susannah's ex-husband. The proof of their religion lay in their so-called holy book, the Book of Melvin, which declared itself to be true. Come on, give me a break.

"Look, Susannah, we all feel discouraged from time to time."

My sister held her long slender hands in the air, palms outward. "Not me! Sister Discouraged might be the prettiest one of us all, but this isn't *that* kind of a group—not that there's anything wrong with it."

"But that's not what I meant!"

Of course she wasn't listening at that point. "There's too much pain in this world, Mags. War without end; that's what Bush gave us. And when we pass that on to Little Jacob's generation, it will be along with a national debt so high that—never mind, there's no point in even getting upset about it. Or global warming. Or hunger, poverty, injustice—or anything. You know why? Because we can't do anything to fix any of those problems. It's all too late."

"What's your solution, then? Should we all just lie down and die?"

No matter how hard I try, I'll never be able to sigh like my little sister. "Honestly, Mags, don't you listen to a word I say? We're going to travel around the country—maybe even the world—and preach the Gospel of Despair."

"The *what*?"

"Instead of giving the people false hope, like the establishment has been doing for thousands of years, we're going to tell it like it is. Like it *really* is. You see, when people have hope, they also hope that someone else will do the work for them. But when they believe that their backs are truly against the wall, that's when they come out fighting."

"Yes, but we finally have a large segment of the population excited about a presidential election, one of historic significance. That qualifies as real hope to me."

"It won't last more than two years, just like Sister Discontent predicts."

I nodded just to keep the peace. "Well, sis, I've got to be running. I just stopped on my way home from the school. But I'm sure glad I caught you. When are you leaving?"

"Tomorrow."

"That soon?"

"As soon as the bus arrives. We have an apathy rally scheduled in Cleveland at six p.m."

"But who's to care if you're a no-show, right?"

"Very funny, Mags. Sister Distemper handles our bookings, and she's the least mellow of all of us. But hey, don't worry, we'll make it a point to stop by the PennDutch first and say good-bye. I have to see my nephew before I go."

I struggled to my feet. "Right. And would you have stopped by if I hadn't come here today?"

"Of course, silly. Now you're being paranoid."

"Reasonable people have always been called that. Tell me, doesn't Sister Distemper's name sort of depart from the rule?"

"Yeah, kind of. But she was bitten by a mean dog once, and she gets crabby if you don't call her that."

"Speaking of the little beast, are you taking him with?"

"Of course! Sister Disengage—she's the one who made all our habits—is sewing him a tiny robe, because I'm giving him the title—"

"Rabbi Rabies? No, wait, that would be the wrong religion. Okay, I got it now; Friar Yuck. No? Then how about Brother Bottom-Sniffer?"

"Out, Mags, out!"

"Okay. There's no need to be snippy, Sister Mother. I'll still be seeing you tomorrow, right?"

"Out," she shrilled, but the push she gave me was surprisingly gentle.

Although it's nobody's business but my own, I could tell by the pressure in my twin feeders that it was time to hustle my bustle back to the fruit of my bloomers. But since I was already "oot and aboot," as our Canadian friends are wont to say—and the Zug twins originally hail from Manitoba—what harm could I possibly do anyone by a spontaneous ten-minute drop-in?

19

Not even the twins' mother can tell them apart. If the rumors
are true, their wives can't either, but I don't want to go there.
Dr. Nolan, himself a twin, and a twenty-nine-year veteran of the
Ohio Twins Days Festival, once said that the Zug brothers are the
most identical twins he's ever seen. If it wasn't for the fact that
he'd seen them both at the same time, he would have sworn they
were the same person. Dr. Nolan is free to swear because, like
Susannah, he is a lapsed Presbyterian.

"Hmm," I wondered aloud, "are the Sisters of Perpetual Apathy permitted to swear?"

"I'll let you know," a voice from on high said.

At the moment I was engaged in this heavenly conversation,
I was standing on the Zugs' front porch, my finger poised to ring
the doorbell. As I've been fooled by what I've *thought* was the
Good Lord's voice before, I looked carefully around me. Except
for three Adirondack rocking chairs, a rickety wicker table sporting a pot of fake, and faded, violets, the covered porch was empty.
It was quite possible, then, that, finally, after all these years of

faithfulness, I really was hearing the dulcet tones of my deity. After all, if Balaam's ass could speak, why couldn't Magdalena Portulaca Yoder Rosen hear God's voice?

"Hallelujah," I cried joyously. "At last my prayers have been answered!"

"This obviously pleases you, Magdalena."

"You betcha—only I don't bet, so I shouldn't have said that. I don't know what came over me—uh, yes, I do: it was the Devil. It had to be; that's the only explanation, because I've never said that word before. I swear I haven't!" I couldn't believe what I'd just said. To demonstrate my horror, I slapped myself so hard that, had my head not been connected by some pretty stubborn tissues, it might well have ended up in the Zug brothers' yard.

"Magdalena," the Good Lord said softly, "are you all right?"

"I'm fine and dandy. Actually, I'm finer than that: I'm as fine as frogs' hair. That's a joke, You know, because frogs don't really have hair. Of course You know all that, on account of You know everything, and that's why I'm all in a dither, because now that I've finally, and I do mean *finally*—not that I'm kvetching, mind You—have a chance to ask You questions, I'm more nervous than a long-tailed cat on a porch full of rocking chairs. Come to think of it, kind of like this porch."

"Questions? What sort?"

Despite the fact that my feeders were full, and I really needed to be hoofing it home, I wasn't about to pass up the opportunity to pump the Good Lord for the answers to some of the questions I'd been saving up in my mind ever since I was six years old.

"Well, I'll start with Adam and Eve's firstborn: Cain. The Bible says that after he slew his brother, Abel, he went to land of Nod, where he married and built a city. Whom did he marry? And where did all the people come from who populated his city?"

"That's a fairly easy question. Cain married—"

"Ah, but see here, if You're going to say his sister, which, by the way, isn't mentioned in Genesis, then what about all the laws against incest that come slightly later in Leviticus? Take chapter 20, verse 17, for example."

"Why are you quoting Scripture to me?"

"Silly me! It was You who dictated the Bible to begin with."

"Forgive me, Magdalena, but you're really beginning to annoy me with this nonsense."

"*Nonsense?* Don't tell me the Episcopalians are right and that You merely *inspired* the writers—not that so much inspiring would be an easy thing, I'm sure."

The Good Lord sighed mightily. "Just tell me why you came here, because I need to get back to work."

"But I only got to ask one question."

"Then perhaps you should take your questions to someone else."

"Oh, I get it. I'm being tested like Job, aren't I? This is a contest between You and Satan, isn't it?" I slid off the rocker to my knees. "Oh, please, I beseech Thee, cover me not in boils, and take not from me my firstborn."

"That does it, eh; I've had enough."

I closed my eyes tightly, bracing myself for the divine wrath. If my punishment was to become a pillar of salt, then I hoped Gabe had the good sense to put me in the north pasture so that my two cows could get in a good lick at me now and then. If I was to be smitten with leprosy—or would that be *smited*? Somehow *smote* didn't sound correct in the conditional tense. Heavens to Betsy, I didn't even know how to conjugate *smite,* and here I was about to meet my Maker face-to-face. And not under the best of circumstances.

I heard a thud on the porch somewhere in front of me. "Magdalena, what are you doing?"

"Bracing myself whilst bemoaning my poor command of archaic constructs. Of course, You can read my thoughts, so why am I even bothering to say this aloud? Come to think of it, since You can read my thoughts, why did You ask—oops, I'm not being cheeky. Honest. Just plain ole curiosity."

"Magdalena, have you seen a doctor lately?"

"Just Little Jacob's pediatrician."

"I was thinking more of a psychiatrist." Heavens to Murgatroid. The Good Lord was indeed sounding like an Episcopalian. Perhaps it wasn't even Him I was conversing with. To be on the safe side, I opened one eye.

"It's you!" I shrieked, and jumped to my feet.

It wasn't the Good Lord I'd seen, but one of the Zug brothers. The poor man shrieked as well, staggered backward, and fell off the porch into some Japanese yew bushes.

I recovered sooner than he did and extended a long, skinny arm to pull him back up. However, he needlessly and rudely rejected my offer of help. He might even have said some very uncharitable things that shocked my tender ears.

"Well, I never!" I said, and plopped my patooty right back in the rocking chair.

The Zug twin clawed his way to a standing position but remained in the bush. "You're absolutely nuts, eh? You know that?"

"Put me on an ice cream sundae and call me delightful. Listen, dear, I may be nuts, but I'm not sacrilegious. I don't hang out on rooftops pretending to be God."

"I wasn't pretending anything. I was replacing some worn-out shingles, and then suddenly you start yammering away."

"Yammering? They say that in Canada as well? Look, what just happened was—well, it was unintended. So you can't tell anyone, *comprende*? Anyway, I came to ask you and your brother a few questions about the morning Minerva J. Jay died."

"Oh, that." The Zug twin clambered up on the porch and plopped his narrow patooty into the adjacent Adirondack. "We knew that the States has a murder rate that is three times what it is back home, but who knew that a little speck like Hernia would turn out to be one of the most dangerous places on the planet?"

"*Murder?* Who said anything about that?"

"Give me a break, Magdalena. Your reputation as an amateur Mennonite sleuth is common knowledge throughout the Mennonite communities of Manitoba."

"No way, José!"

"But to be honest, so are your eccentricities, eh."

"I am not eccentric!"

"I believe *weird* is the word most often used—although of course you have your staunch defenders, eh."

"I do, eh?"

"Veritable Magdalena Yoder Fan Clubs. There are two in Winnipeg alone, eh. One of them even has a fanzine."

"A *what*-zine?"

"A fan magazine. I believe it's called *Magdalena Gumshoe*."

There is no sin that Satan loves more than pride. That's because he can plant a little seed in your mind and water it with flattery, and the next thing you know it spreads like the kudzu vine that they say is taking over the South.

"Do you think I could find a copy of this fanzine online?"

The Zug twin frowned. "Uh—sorry, I misspoke; I don't remember the name of any of the fanzines."

You see? And I should have known better because one of the first Bible verses I memorized was Proverbs 16:18: "Pride goes before destruction and a haughty spirit before a fall."

I hung my head in shame. "Well, I guess I deserved that—sort of."

"No, there really is a magazine called *Magdalena Gumshoe*, and it does star you, but it's a comic book."

"You mean like Donald Duck?"

"Like who?"

"The duck with no pants on."

"Yeah, I think I've read one of those. But these are grown-up comics and, I must say, the artist has done a good job of portraying you. But surely you know all this. I mean, didn't they ask your permission? Surely you're getting royalties of some sort, eh."

A comic book featuring *moi*? How cool was that? Now, that would send Mama spinning in her grave so fast she could supply at least half the country with electricity, thereby reducing our dependency on foreign oil, and freeing us up to put the screws to Saudi Arabia to treat their women as equals. However, if the comic book (could there possibly even be a series?) contained sex, or gratuitous violence, I'd have to put the kibosh on it. After all, I am a peaceful woman by heritage and practice, and my message is one of loving kindness.

"Do you have a copy?"

"No, but I used to. First edition too, eh. I could probably sell it now for a mint. But you know, you can find just about anything on Amazon or eBay."

"Too true! Toodles, dear," I said and, like a superhero, practically, flew off the porch in my haste to return home.

"Vanity of vanities, all is vanity." Thus said the preacher in the Book of Ecclesiastes. It was a verse that I knew by heart but hadn't taken to heart, foolish woman that I was.

What the Zug twin failed to mention is that *Magdalena Gumshoe* was the product of his imagination and, as such, was not available for purchase over the Internet. I didn't want to believe this at first, but after shaking my computer and whacking my keyboard against the wall, I finally listened to Gabe and did a search from his laptop. The results were the same. Then, with naught left to lose, and possibly a two-dimensional caricature to gain, I called the acquaintance of an acquaintance up in Winnipeg and asked her if she'd ever heard of the comic books starring yours truly.

"We Manitoba Mennonites don't read a lot of comics, eh," she said.

"Is that a *no*?"

"Yes, that's a *no*, eh. But I have heard of you. You're that eccentric woman who owns the bed-and-breakfast, where folks have to pay an enormous sum just to be abused."

"That's me, all right! But no *Magdalena Gumshoe* comic books, eh?"

"Are you making fun of my speech, Miss Yoder?"

"Absolutely. You people would too, if you spoke normal like we do."

"Good-bye, Miss Yoder." The woman had the temerity to hang up on me.

Next I called the first cousin of a second cousin once removed in that fair city, followed by the third cousin of a double fifth cousin twice removed. And then a comic book and collectibles shop. All of the above stated unequivocally that they had never heard of *Magdalena Gumshoe*, and one of the women I contacted went so far as to say that if she ever did come across some copies she'd buy them all up and burn them just to spite me.

Needless to say, I felt both angry and relieved. At least I didn't have to worry about getting the publisher to correct any misinformation contained in the comic, or to go through the hassle of trying to get him or her to pay me. On the other hand, it was a major letdown; the Zug twin had carried a practical joke way too far—if indeed he'd even meant it in the spirit of fun.

Suppose he'd meant it purely as a distraction? Eh? If so, his ploy had certainly worked. I'd taken off like a bat out of Hades in search of my fictional self, having totally dropped the subject of Miss Jay like an oven rack of hot potatoes. Ding, dang, dong! I didn't even know which Zug twin I'd been bamboozled by, so I couldn't throw a proper hissy fit without confirming what everyone from Hernia to Winnipeg already thought about me: in a bag of cashews and raisins, I was *not* the dried, wrinkled grapes.

"Woe is unto me," I cried, suddenly feeling the weight of the world pressing down on my thin, though rather comely, shoulders.

The phone rang. And rang. And rang some more.

"Isn't anybody going to get that?" I hollered. "Yes!" I may have finally snapped into the receiver. "What on earth is it?"

"Magdalena," a soft voice said. "I need to speak to you at once."

20

Luscious Lemon Pancakes

No collection of pancake recipes would be complete without this one, and no other lemon pancake could be quite as delicious. The recipe is adapted from Marion Cunningham's *The Breakfast Book* (Knopf, 1987).

3 large eggs, separated
¼ cup unbleached all-purpose flour
¾ cup low-fat cottage cheese
4 tablespoons (½ stick) unsalted butter, melted
2 tablespoons sugar
¼ teaspoon salt
1 tablespoon grated lemon zest

Confectioners' sugar and mixed fruit (sliced strawberries, blueberries, and raspberries) or warm maple syrup

1. In a large bowl, combine the egg yolks, flour, cottage cheese, butter, sugar, salt, and lemon zest. In a separate bowl, beat the

egg whites until soft peaks form. Carefully fold the beaten whites into the batter just until blended.

2. Heat a large nonstick griddle or skillet over medium heat until hot enough to sizzle a drop of water. Brush with a thin film of vegetable oil, or spray with nonstick cooking spray. For each pancake, pour a scant ¼ cup batter onto the griddle or into the skillet. Adjust the heat to medium-low. Cook until the tops are covered with small bubbles and the bottoms are lightly browned. Carefully turn and lightly brown the other side. These cook quickly. Repeat with the remaining batter.

3. Serve with confectioners' sugar, accompanied by sliced fruit or warm maple syrup.

MAKES ABOUT TWELVE 3-INCH PANCAKES.

21

I agreed to meet Chief Ackerman in Settlers' Cemetery atop Stucky Ridge. This is where Mama and Papa are buried, along with their forebears, and where I plan to have my weary bones laid to rest someday as well. As the name suggests, this graveyard contains the remains of Hernia's original European founders. It is reserved for their descendents only and, of course, their spouses.

The fact that I'm adopted doesn't change my status one whit vis-à-vis burial rights, because the Stoltzfuses, my biological parents, were also both descended from founders. Besides, although both families are currently Mennonite, both arrived in this country as Amish in the early 1700s. As a result, our bloodlines are so intertwined that if I skin my knee, it is my cousin who moans in pain.

Stucky Ridge is the highest point in Bedford County, even higher than Buffalo Mountain. Fortunately, not all of the land was dedicated to the dead. In addition to the cemetery, there is a picnic area overlooking Lovers' Leap, and a patch of woods where oversexed teenagers come to grope each other on Saturday nights.

I almost lost my life when Melvin the Maniac Mantis, who, it turned out, was a full sibling, as well as my brother-in-law, pushed me over the edge of Lovers' Leap. Thank heaven for my sturdy Christian underwear, which caught on a tree branch and kept me from plunging to my death. Had I been wearing a thong, I'd have taken up residence next to Mama and Papa long before Little Jacob could be born.

And speaking of the little fella, since I'd never taken him up there, and it was turning out to be a nice warm afternoon, I decided to introduce him to some of the Yoder clan. I started with Granny Yoder's headstone.

"Here's your great-grandson, Little Jacob," I said, minding my manners. (Forty years ago in Miss Entz's citizenship class I learned that one must always introduce the lady first, especially if she's older.)

"And this is your great-granny Yoder," I said. "You may have seen her standing imperiously on the stairs back at the inn. As my friend Abigail Timberlake Washburn from Charleston says, Granny Yoder is an Apparition American. Of course, we people of faith are not supposed to believe in such nonsense, and most of us don't, but that's because most of us haven't come face-to-face with any incontrovertible evidence. I'm telling you, though, once you encounter an Apparition American, it's all over but the whimpering."

Little Jacob whimpered.

"Please forgive him," I said to Granny Yoder's headstone. "He's awfully young. And you must admit you are a bit scary, what with that lemon-sucking scowl and those three eight-inch hairs growing from the mole on your left cheek. Really, Granny, even I am—I mean *would* be—scared of you if I was his age."

"Magdalena."

I jumped clear out of my brogans when the hand, as light as a biscuit, rested on my shoulder. "Aaaaaaaaaaaaaaaah!"

"Waaaaaaaaaaaaaaaaah!" Little Jacob wailed.

"Shi—ta—ke mushrooms!" Chief Ackerman exclaimed, his face every bit as white as Granny's the last time I saw her in the flesh.

The three of us gasped, panted, and hollered for several minutes. Finally the chief and I settled down on a stone bench facing Buffalo Mountain. I asked him if it was okay to nurse Little Jacob for a bit, as that was the quickest way to shut him up.

"Fine by me," he said. "I'm from California, remember? Besides, my mom nursed me a lot longer than most other mothers nurse their babies. I think it's a beautiful thing."

I turned away until Little Jacob was covered with a light cotton blanket. Then, before we got down to police business, I just had to ask one personal question.

"How long is a *lot* longer?"

"Let's put it this way: she stopped the day I said, 'I like the pink bra better.' "

I shuddered. "Well, I stop the day he bites. Okay, young Chris, what is so urgent? And tell me, why so secretive that we can't discuss it in your office?"

"All right, second question first, and the answer is: Sam."

"Smarmy pseudo-cousin Sam from Sam Yoder's Corner Market, the one who mid-husbanded this bundle of joy?"

"That's the one. Magdalena, you are aware of how much he likes to gossip, aren't you?"

"Was Menno Simons Mennonite?"

"Huh?"

"Yeah, that was sort of a trick question, since Mennonites are the followers of Menno Simons, and he couldn't very well be a follower of himself. Anyway, of course I'm aware of Sam's wagging tongue. That's the only reason I go in there: to get the scoop."

"Well, Sam already knows about your—uh—visits, let's say,

to the Brotherhood volunteers on pancake day, including your front porch chat with the Big Guy Himself this morning."

"*What?* The Zug twin already ratted me out?"

"I must say, Magdalena, that your vocabulary is not what I expected of a Mennonite housewife before I moved to Hernia."

"Nor should it be after you leave, because I am iconoclastic, a classic icon, if you will—not that I'm bragging, mind you. We have an old saying here: 'Scratch your arm at Sam's store, and you'll be dead by the time you get home.' "

"Meaning?"

"That even before cell phones were invented, gossip had a way of traveling faster here than a race car, and that the stories were invariably blown to almost unrecognizable proportions if they came by way of Sam's."

"Is he malicious?"

"Bored. And horny—oops, pardon my Bulgarian."

"Your Bulgarian?"

"Why should the French get all the credit for talking dirty? There have to be at least some Bulgarians who are vulgarians, not to be confused with the Vulgar Latin, of course."

"Or with the very rude Cuban I dated two years ago. At any rate, Magdalena, it has crossed my mind that—well, this is going to sound paranoid, I'm sure—that your telephone might be bugged."

It felt like ice water was being poured down the back of my dress. "Is that why you asked me to meet you here?"

He nodded. "It was a spur-of-the-moment thing. But I was already up here, and I've been watching carefully. We *are* alone."

"Where are you parked?"

"Where else?"

"Ah, the woods. If only those woods could speak—on second thought, I'd have to cover my ears and run away."

The chief laughed. "How do you think I feel on Saturday nights, playing nanny to a bunch of repressed kids who are finally out of their parents' sight? You could cut the pheromones up here with a knife."

"Back to my phone. Why do you think it might be bugged? Does it show up on some kind of machine?"

"No, I've got to admit that it's just a hunch. But you're a veritable clearinghouse of information, Magdalena. I know that if *I* was going to commit a crime of this magnitude in Hernia, I'd tap your phone."

The chills down my spine were gone. "Well, I don't feel that. Maybe it's *your* phone that's bugged. Have you checked? I mean taken it apart completely, etcetera? That's such a handy word, isn't it?"

As he shook his head, he colored considerably. "I did a quick sweep. Frankly, Magdalena, I'm overworked. That's another thing I need to talk to you about: we need at least two more officers in the department. I can't work twenty-four seven."

"But we're an itsy-bitsy traditional community, for crying out loud. Besides the Saturday-night crowd up here, what else do you have on your plate?"

The young whippersnapper had the temerity to laugh. "Good one! Let's see. This morning Patricia Maron poured bleach on Margaret Cornwall's mint patch, so it wouldn't spread like it did last year and contaminate her phlox bed. I thought one or both were going to have heart attacks, they were so mad."

"Patty's a Baptist from Punxsutawney and Marge is a Methodist from Scranton."

"That explains it?"

"Uh—maybe not entirely. And yes, I know, Nixon was a Quaker, but you know what I mean."

"Not exactly. Anyway, yesterday Delphina Wilder thought

she had an intruder in her basement, and she did, but it turned out to be a possum."

"Delphina is from suburban New Jersey and has Lutheran forebears."

"Magdalena, you sound disturbingly prejudiced."

"*Moi?* I assure you that's simply not so. But just look around you, dear. In the old days, as far as the eyes could see, this was Amish and Mennonite territory. The Plain People, we called ourselves. Now most of the Mennonites have gone fancy—except for Beechy Grove—and the Amish are beginning to sell their farms to outsiders because they can get cheaper land, and more of it, down south. I'm just saying that there is something to be said for having a homogeneous population."

"I once dated a brilliant gay man, but to be absolutely frank, I prefer them more on the dumb side. Anyway, my point is that there is a whole lot more to this job than one person can handle. Were I to—uh—not sign up for another year, you'd be hard put to replace me."

"That sounds like a threat."

The poor man is without guile, so he looked me straight in the eyes. "I'm sorry. It is. What else can I say?"

"Okay already, get those calf eyes off me before I cave in and double your salary as well."

"As well as a deputy?"

"Just the deputy. Now, look away, ding-dang it."

"I can't, because I'm giving you *the look*."

"Forsooth, dear, that's what I'm objecting to—although it's getting a mite tiresome trying to get the point across."

The chief rolled his expressive peepers up before training them off my beady little pair. "I forget that you don't watch TV. That means you haven't seen *the look* Larry David dishes out on *Curb Your Enthusiasm*."

I checked the nursing blanket and saw that my modesty was still intact. One other possibility sprang to mind.

"I don't have any boogers hanging out, do I?"

"No—do I? See, Magdalena? You always get me off track. I'm giving you *the look* because of the key you swiped from my desk. And don't even try to deny it, because that will just waste both of our time, and I have to go talk some sense into old Tom Arnold before he shoots Connie Betz's dog. And here I thought you were supposed to be a peaceful people."

"Tom is Church of God, originally from Akron, and you have to admit that Connie's dog makes an incredible amount of racket every day at sundown. So, how did you know it was me who borrowed that key?"

Chris sucked air through his flawless teeth in a gesture of genuine concern. "You're going to hate this."

"Oh, don't be silly. *I* am a native Hernian, a Mennonite born and bred, although not bred to a Mennonite, as I am not a cow or any other sort of animal."

"When I went over to Sam's to get the cream for your tea, I found him staring at you through a pair of binoculars."

I leaped to my feet with so much force that my suckling babe—if I may use such a provocative term—was dislodged. As a result, Little Jacob went from being an unobtrusive third party to the center of attention. Come to think of it, the ensuing din might have been my saving grace, because I actually called Sam a doo-doo head—maybe even several times. Never in my life have I sunk to such a low level of vitriolic verbiage. Potty Mouth should have been my middle name, not Portulaca.

It took a good ten minutes to calm everyone down, and some of us were still less calm than others. "Just wait until I get my hands around his scrawny neck," I said through gritted teeth.

22

"I thought you were a pacifist," Chief Chris Ackerman said.

"Indeed I am, but these are extenuating circumstances, are they not?"

"So you get to pick and choose? Honestly, Magdalena, you sound just like everyone else; I'm really disappointed."

"But I'm only human!" I don't mean to be immodest, but my cry of distress rang out over the surrounding valleys of the southern Alleghenies like the rumble of approaching thunder.

"Be careful, Magdalena; that eerie sound you're making might wake the dead."

"Then, boy, are we in for a lot of trouble. It might surprise you to learn that not everyone buried here—those that knew me, I mean—found me to be as delightful as you originally did." I emitted more distressing sounds for good measure.

"Oh, all right, I'll give you what you want: I still find you delightful. Compared to most Hernians, you're a breath of fresh air."

"Thank you. Now tell me, why aren't you angry that I took the key?"

"Because I trust your instincts, Miss Yoder. I figured that if you thought it was important enough to swipe, then it must have been. By the way, I have to say that it was very clever of you to spontaneously substitute one of your own keys for the one Minerva left me. As you might have guessed, I didn't discover the switch until I got all the way out there to the Land of the Weird and Godforsaken Sinkholes. In order to gain access to Miss Jay's house, I had to get both a court order and a locksmith, and they were a waste of time and money; you won't find anything useful to the investigation there."

"Perhaps this breath of fresh air will see things through fresh eyes."

"Like I said; you're delightful."

I sighed heavily. "Alas and alack, our seven suspects don't share your sentiments."

"They hate your guts?"

"You could have the decency to sound surprised. Besides, I'm not sure they all do, as I spoke to only one Zug twin."

"Right, but unless we can figure out which one is which, I think we should treat them as one person. Nonetheless, what are your impressions of them?"

I waited while, off to my left, in the woods, a mourning dove sounded its plaintive coo. "I'll start with George Hooley," I said. "Did you know he was gay?"

Chief Ackerman put both hands on his hips in mock surprise. "Say it ain't so!"

"Of course you did; everyone does. Still, somehow Minerva managed to blackmail him. At least that's what he claims."

The chief scribbled on his pad. "That's serious stuff. Can you get proof?"

"I'll try. But I don't think George did it. Murdering someone requires a mind that is able to think outside the box, and George is stuck in a rut so deep he can hear Laotian voices at the bottom."

"Not Mandarin?"

"George isn't straight, remember? When he digs a hole, it doesn't go down to China. As for James Neufenbakker, he may have been a Sunday school teacher—*my* Sunday school teacher—but that man's got a temper worthy of a Bush."

"Is that a straight euphemism?"

"No! I meant George Bush. Anyway, James—or Jimmy, as I call him—practically chased me off his porch. He also called Minerva a trollop."

"Hmm, do you think that means he slept with her?"

"Chris, dear, is that what you call your—uh, paramours?"

"My what?"

"Lovers," I said reluctantly, "but my, how I hate that word. It's just so—well, so accepting of the whole notion of sex without the bondage of holy matrimony."

The chief shook his impossibly handsome head. "First of all, I don't call my lovers *trollops*—although I have called a few of them *sluts*. And second, while I believe you meant to say the holy *bonds* of matrimony, I think I prefer your slip of the tongue. And third, I was suggesting that Mr. Neufenbakker's strong negative reaction might be a decoy to keep us from discovering an ongoing physical or emotional relationship with our victim. Such affairs are often hard to end satisfactorily, and sometimes one or both parties suffer deeply."

"Dr. Chris Ackerman, I presume," I said, unable to keep all my sarcasm at bay.

"Well, I did take freshman psychology at the junior college before I joined the police academy," Chief Chris said proudly.

More power to him; better a half-wit than a dimwit, I always say. Still, we had a lot more ground to cover. I laid little Jacob over my shoulder and gently patted his back.

"Gwerrp."

"Good boy." I continued to pat lightly. "Frankie Schwartzen-truber, however, really does have a reason to be upset with Minerva. That woman hit on her husband."

"That old battle-ax is married?"

"*Was* is the operative word. Decades ago. Frankie has a long memory, but like they say, there is no statute of limitations on crimes of passion."

"Who says that?"

I may have swallowed hard, but I didn't look away. "Well, *somebody* has to start those sayings, so why can't it be me?"

Young Chris smiled. "I figured as much. Go on."

"There's not much else to say. I tried to talk to Merle Waggler, and although he admitted he didn't like Minerva, he and I— Look, the man's an anti-Semite, and I kind of got into it with him."

"You fought with him?"

"We argued. At school. But it was on behalf of Alison, who was being teased, so it was completely justified."

"What about Elias Whitmore?"

"He's a real hottie, isn't he?"

"*Excuse* me?"

"You know, really cute. Good-looking. Isn't that the lingo these days?"

"Magdalena, I'm a police officer, and you're a married woman assisting me on the case. We can't use language like that." He glanced around as if to make sure that no one had heard us—except maybe for the mourning dove in the woods, and two sparrows hopping between the headstones twenty feet away.

"Sorry. I don't know what came over me; it was like a hot flash of Presbyterianism. Anyway, that kid is so popular. His house is like an ashram or something—but Christian, of course. See that brown square there, poking above the trees on Buffalo Mountain? About an inch from the end?"

"Yeah, I think so."

"That's his rooftop porch. You can see all the way to Maryland from there. Anyway, despite being a Christian guru, Elias really hated Minerva J. Jay. He blames her for his father's death."

Chris rubbed his hands together. "Now we're getting somewhere."

"Maybe. Elias's father was a drunk who tried to walk the straight and narrow path a number of times—at least to hear him tell it—but each time, Minerva pushed him off. Supposedly she thought she could get her hands on his fortune easier that way. Oh, and Elias volunteered the fact that Minerva was poisoned. You didn't mention that to him, did you?"

"Absolutely not. Very interesting. What about the Zug twins?"

"I have failed," I wailed.

"Your wailing is really getting to be annoying—if I may say so."

"You may, but now I'm annoyed. It's not like I go through a verb-selection process when I emote and then come up empty-handed. Wailing happens to be my signature vocalization."

"The *Zugs*," he said through clenched teeth.

"Oh, all right. Those Zugs! Rather, I should say *that* Zug! He weaseled out of my grilling by appealing to my vanity."

"There's nothing wrong with taking the easy way out, so long as it's effective."

"Whose side are you on anyway?"

"Uh—yours, of course. Although I guess strictly speaking I'm on the side of Lady Justice. Hmm, interesting that she's a lady, isn't it?" He rubbed his face with hands that were better tended to than mine will ever be. "Hey, speaking of ladies, we may not be able to tell the twins apart, but their wives look nothing alike. Why don't you try talking to them? Maybe invite them over to tea?"

"Tea? I'm not Agatha Christie, for Pete's sake; this isn't an English cozy. Besides, I hardly know them."

"Don't they go to your church?"

"That's the thing. The Zug twins are Mennonite by birth and joined Beechy Grove as soon as they moved here from Canada, but, like me, they are unequally yoked."

"I don't get it. Is that some kind of egg thing?"

I reined in my smile. The chief is a lapsed atheist, a man raised without faith, but he is now at least open to exploring the options. Still, when one is talking to him it is easy to forget that biblical references, which pepper everyday speech in Hernia, are as foreign to him as tofu is to Amish cooking.

"It's what happens when you hitch an ox and a donkey to the same plow. Take the Babester and me: he's the bull and I'm the ass, and spiritually speaking it's not a good match. The Zug twins also married outside the Mennonite fold. One is a Pentecostal—I think—and attends the church with thirty-two words in its name, and the other is a nothing. At any rate, neither of them ever shows up at Beechy Grove for services, although they do come for potlucks and anything that basically involves food."

"So you have met them."

I sighed. "Okay, I'll invite them to lunch at the Sausage Barn and put the screws to them there."

"When?"

"I'll call this evening, but I can't guarantee I'll even be able to get through. The man who invented caller ID—and it had to be a man—will have his own special place in you-know-where."

"Why don't you slip a note under their door on your way home this afternoon, suggesting lunch tomorrow? Say, noon at the Barn?"

"Noon," I snapped. Let's face it, it's hard to be pleasant when someone half your age is micromanaging your avocation.

꩜

Yes, a retired husband can be a big help, and so can a mother-in-law. Ditto for a daughter and a housekeeping cousin. But only yours truly was equipped to feed a growing boy in the middle of the night, after which said boy refused to go back to sleep. As a result, *I* got as much sleep as a polygamist on a ten-minute honeymoon.

The next morning I was dead on my feet, and right after a six a.m. feeding (Little Jacob promptly fell asleep), I went straight back to bed, an act that is just as much a sin in my culture as the aforementioned polygamy.

Just once before I die I would like to spend an entire day lolly-gagging about on the sofa eating chocolate bonbons. I might even watch a television show. I've heard that *Oprah* and *The View* are both worth seeing, but since I'll have only this one day in which to commit the second-worst sin, that of sloth, I should probably do some consulting first. Maybe even look at a few clips from the shows before I decide. You can be sure, however, that I will *not* be watching *Ellen*, as I'm already in enough trouble with the Good Lord without adding dancing, the worst of all sins, to my litany.

Now, where was I? Oh yes, after a couple of hours I woke up, groggy and grainy eyed, because the little one was crying to be changed.

"Gabe," I called sweetly.

After I'd added several decibels and tone changes, my dearly beloved finally appeared in the bedroom door. "Hon, can you make this quick? The Yankees are playing the Red Sox."

I glanced at the bedside clock. "It's only ten in the morning."

"Yeah, I know, but since you don't allow TVs in the house, I'm watching it on my cell phone from a disk I downloaded. The game was actually yesterday."

"That's nice, dear. Your son—that's the infant in the crib next to me—needs changing today. Would you be a darling and do it this time?"

"Poopy or pee?"

Poopy? Gabriel Rosen is a medical doctor, for crying out loud. A cardiologist and well-known surgeon.

"Number two, I think. Does it matter?"

"Ah, hon, you know I can't handle the stink of really messy diapers; it's just not in me."

"This is your son," I growled, "the fruit of your loins, flesh of your flesh, blood of your blood, and *poop of your poop*. So put on your big-boy pants and deal with it." I smiled sweetly to soften my words.

Without another word, Gabe picked up his son, but he held him at arm's length during the entire changing process. "There, you happy now?" he said when he was done.

I didn't know if he was speaking to me or Little Jacob, so I murmured soft obscenities. "Ding, dang, dong, ding."

"What was that, Magdalena?"

To be truthful, my response would have been a lie. Fortunately, I was stopped by the presence of a nun standing in my bedroom door.

"Susannah?" I asked through my veil of grogginess.

"I'm Mother Dispirited, remember?"

I pulled myself to a sitting position. "Oh, right. And I'm Sister Disturbed; I'm disturbed that you're still going through with this apathy thing."

Susannah shrugged. "Really, Mags, you're not supposed to care. Anyway, I'm here to say good-bye to my favorite nephew."

"You have only one, dear."

"He's still my favorite. And Sister Disaster has come to say good-bye to her son."

"What? But there aren't any men here."

"Thanks," Gabe said drily as he handed Little Jacob to his sister-in-law.

Susannah, who adores her nephew almost as much as she does the loathsome cur that nestles in her Maidenform, took my baby with the utmost delight. It would embarrass me to no end to repeat the gaga-doo-doo baby talk she inflicted on the boy when she wasn't attempting to smother him to death with kisses. Meanwhile, my question went unanswered.

"Can I take him out to show him to the sisters?" she finally asked.

"Yes, but you have to promise first that you won't kidnap him and turn him into a monk—or a monkette—or whatever the word is for a tiny male person of your unorthodox persuasion."

"How about mon*key*?" Susannah said, and then skipped off giggling with my life's one achievement in her arms.

It was only when Susannah was gone that Gabe and I noticed the very stout nun standing just inside our bedroom door, to the left and in front of the closet. This sister was so short, and had such an enormous chest, that her habit made her body look square. As for her face—let me say with all Christian charity that with her hair pulled back and tucked under her wimple, she might well have passed for a geriatric gorilla. A lemon-sucking geriatric gorilla.

So alarmed was I that I leaped from the bed and into Gabe's arms. "These are private quarters," I eventually managed to gasp. Gabe, of course, had said nothing.

23

———◆◆◆———

"*Nu?* So I come to say good-bye to my son. Do you mind?"

I did a double take. Then a triple.

"Ida? Is that *you*?"

"Don't be silly, hon," my darling said. "This woman's a nun."

"My name is Sister Disaster," the homely woman in the religious garb said.

"Ida," I said, "it *is* you, and you *can't* be a nun, because you're Jewish!"

"*Ma?*" I'd told Gabe the night before about Susannah and the Sisters of Perpetual Apathy, but he'd been pretty uninterested in the whole thing. "Sounds just like your sister," he'd said. Apparently now that the wimple was on a different head, it was another story.

"I think we need to talk," I said calmly. "Gabe, dear, hoist her up on the bed, so we can at least be eye to collarbone with her."

Although he doesn't think well under duress, the Babester can sometimes take direction. Thank heaven he did now. With Ida jammed between the two of us, and three feet off the ground (mine is the SUV of king-size beds), I felt that we had at least some control in what was otherwise a totally insane situation.

"Now, dear," I began, "you do realize that Susannah—aka Mother Dispirited—is wearing a cross around her neck. I know, it's just a soap cross, and if she showers with it on, it won't be long before it's not a cross at all. But my point is that this mother and sisters gig is a Christian, not a Jewish, thing."

"*Oy gevalt!*" Gabe said suddenly and clapped both hands to his head. "Ma, you didn't convert, did you?"

At that Ida tugged on a cheap chain that disappeared down the neckline of her habit and retrieved a startlingly large wooden star of David. "Dis vas supposed to be on de outside, ya? But I dress in a hurry."

"So you're still Jewish?" I said.

"Ya, und I see dat you are still meshugah. Of course I didn't convert. De Sisters of Apathy dun't care about your religion; all dey care about is dat you shouldn't care anymore. Give up, und give in. Dat is our message. Vee vill all lose in de end, so vhy vorry?"

"But, Ma, that's fatalistic. That's just giving up. And what is it that makes your life so darn hard that you feel like this?"

"*Vhat* you say? Look around you, Gabeleh. Vhere are vee? In de shticks, dat's vhere. Und I am living alone in a big house all de vay across de road. Vhat kind of life is dis, I ask you?"

"What kind of life do you want, Ma?"

"She wants to be living with you in New York City," I said. "She wants to play mahjong every afternoon and talk about her son the doctor. Oh yes, and she'd like to keep Little Jacob with her and leave me behind."

Sister Disaster wasn't so apathetic that she could restrain from punching my ribs with her elbow. "I vould only play mah-jong five days a veek!"

"Sorry, hon," Gabe said, reaching around her to pat my back. "I thought that in time she'd learn to love you as much as I do."

"Sometimes I think she does," I said.

The Babester didn't have the courtesy to respond to that. "Ma, why do you call yourself Sister Disaster? That's such an awful name."

"Because I am a disaster, yah? First, I vas unable to make you happy in New York. If I had been, vee vouldn't be here. Dat is a fact. Und now, I am not able to fit into dis litle family dat you have made."

"Ma, that's simply not true; you fit in just fine. Alison utterly adores you. Even Freni has learned to tolerate you."

"Ya? But vhat about dis von?" The cubically shaped pseudo-nun jabbed a thumb in my direction.

"Hon," Gabe said, turning to me, "tell Ma that you love her too."

Even though I heard the pleading in his voice, and I have been known to stretch the truth upon occasion (they were all justified occasions, I assure you), I could not bring myself to flat-out lie this time. And yes, I'm well aware that in Matthew 5:44 Jesus commanded us to love our enemies. I accept that as gospel, but at the same time, may I respectfully submit that the Lord did not have a mother-in-law? There, that's all I have to say on the subject.

"I'm sure you love her very much, dear," I said sweetly.

"Dere, you see?"

"Hon," Gabe said in his most pleading of tones, "you've got to help me out here."

"I love you," I said. Okay, perhaps I mumbled the words. At any rate, what I didn't add is that I meant those words in the spiritual, God-wants-me-to-do-it sense, not in the warm, fuzzy sort of way.

"*See*, Ma?"

Ida shook her head so vigorously that I suffered a wimple burn on my left arm. "Ha! She dun't mean it. Anyvay, it is too litle, too late. I have decided dat de Sisters of Perpetual Apathy is de only vay for me now. I must renounce all my emotions. Or else I explode, ya?"

Sometimes the Devil, who is always standing just over my left shoulder, and who must have received the wimple burn as well, commandeers my tongue. That's the only way I can explain what came out of my mouth next.

"Isn't it curious," my lips said, "that she was able to pronounce the name of this bogus religious order without the slightest trace of an accent?"

"Mags," Gabe said sharply, "you're only making things worse. I'd rather you didn't say anything at all."

"You're telling me to shut up?"

"Your words, not mine."

"In that case, I'll hie my heinie out to this bus full of hopeless hinnies and rescue my little one from an imitation Mother in gray gabardine garb—pardon the alliteration."

It was a bizarre sight to say the least. There truly was a bus full of women dressed in nun's habits and, judging by the expressions on their faces, they were the most phlegmatic folk I'd seen in a month of Puritan Sundays. They may as well have been carved out of the same soap as their neck ornaments.

Although I don't watch movies on principle, many years ago, when I was but an errant youth, I did drive all the way into Pittsburgh, where I sneaked into a theater and watched *The Sound of Music* (just so you know, I have long since repented of that sin). The point I am trying to make is that the pseudo-sisters aboard

Susannah's "vehicle" weren't anything like Julie Andrews. Even the stern nuns, who disapproved of Maria running in the abbey, would have been more fun than this bunch.

I scanned their bland faces, which, for the most part, looked alike to me. Oh, there were a couple of women young enough to be sort of pretty even under these circumstances, and one was an older lady whose mannish features and coarse skin were somewhat unsettling, but on average it was hard to distinguish one woman from another. No doubt the uniforms—I mean the habits—were partly to blame. Devoid of makeup, and with their hair pulled back and hidden behind gray veils, the women of Hernia were proof positive that we were, at our core, a plain people.

After extracting the fruit of my bloomers from his aunt's loving arms, I sorrowfully bid her good-bye. I even went so far as to hug her, taking care, of course, to keep both my baby and my bosoms from touching her surplice.

"Is the rat still in there?" I said.

"His name is Shnookums, Mags, and he has a good-bye present for you."

I reared back like a mare with a burr under her saddle. "No thanks, dear."

"Please, Mags. If not for him, then do it for me. It will mean so much." Mother Dispirited was no longer speaking in a monotone, but in her little-girl voice, the one guaranteed to take me back to days when I was her guardian and primary friend.

"All right," I said.

"Thanks." Susannah reached under her surplice and, from the surplus room not occupied by Shnookums, removed a small framed picture.

"This is for you to remember us by."

I stared at a snapshot that had been taken at a Christmas party. And at my sister's house at that, even though I hadn't been invited. Susannah was posed in front of her tree, proudly holding the mangy mongrel, which was decked out as an elf, replete with enormous velvet ears and green boots. In the background were the faces of familiar people—folks who obviously rated higher than I did on the invitation scale.

"What am I on, the B list?"

"Mags, you don't approve of Christmas parties that don't stick strictly to the religious theme. I was playing Mrs. Santa Claus, for Pete's sake."

"And who was the fat man himself?"

"Our old Sunday school teacher, Mr. Neufenbakker."

Yup, that was him all right, half hidden by the tree. I'd recognize those splayed feet anywhere.

"You could have at least asked me if I wanted to come," I said.

"You've just validated my new religion, sis," Susannah said, sounding dangerously excited. "If you were a Sister of Perpetual Apathy, you wouldn't care if you'd been slighted."

"So I was *slighted*?"

"Bye, sis, I have to go!" With that, my baby sister, the one whom my parents entrusted me to take care of before they were tragically squished to death beneath a Pennsylvania mountain, climbed into the driver's seat of an old school bus and drove away with thirty or so of our town's most pathetic—I mean apathetic—citizens.

As sad as it was to see Susannah drive off with a bus full of nuns, at least none of them were holding babies—or headed for a cliff, for that matter. I knew from experience that my baby sister would eventually tire of this game and come slinking back to Hernia, because despite all her bravado and brazenly worldly ways, she would never be able to shake what was at her core: inbred Mennonite guilt. But there was something sinister about her departure as well. It wasn't anything in particular; I couldn't place a well-shaped finger on it. Then again, it felt like a cold stone at the bottom of my stomach, and few of my digits are that long.

Therefore, I was almost grateful when Gabe threw a hissy fit over his mother's chosen vocation. At first he ranted and raved about the absurdity of a homegrown religion called the Sisters of Perpetual Apathy. Something like that could only happen in a novel, he said. Then, since Susannah couldn't hear his diatribes, he began to vent at me.

"It *is* your fault," he said. "Ma was right. If you'd been nicer to her, this wouldn't have happened."

Little Jacob could sense the angry vibes and began to squirm, so I patted him gently. "Shush," I whispered to the wee one. I raised my voice only slightly to address Gabe. "I don't want to fight in front of the b-a-b-y."

"The *baby*? You have to spell it? He doesn't understand what we're saying!"

"I think he does."

"That's ridiculous. I'm a doctor, hon. I know these things."

"And I'm a mother; *that* trumps a doctor." I said it softly, but my son could still feel the tension; he began to whimper.

"He's saying he doesn't agree with you."

I rubbed my baby's back as I twisted my torso from side to side. The fact that I said nothing at that point was the absolute most annoying thing I could have done to Gabe.

"Okay, be that way," he said after several minutes had passed and Little Jacob was almost asleep. "But you know what? I'm not putting up with this *Huafa mischt* any longer."

Huafa mischt? You see what happens when you teach your Jewish husband the Amish word for horse manure? *Oy veys meer,* but one can rue the day that one strives to be linguistically inclusive. Better we should all stew in the *cholent* of our own upbringing, if you ask me.

"So what are you threatening this time?" Perhaps I was egging him on just a wee bit, but there is a lot more babe (as in *baby*) in the Babester than I had ever imagined back in the days when my reproductive clock was ticking louder than Freni's windup oven timer.

Gabe ran perfectly manicured fingers through a head of still dark, thick hair. "No threats, just facts. I'm moving back across the road to my own farm."

"Your *own* farm? Don't we own everything together?"

"Apparently not. You seem to think our son is exclusively yours."

"He's not a possession, for goodness' sake. All I was saying is that I think it's harmful—"

"Tell that to my back," Gabe said, and stalked off.

"Well *that's* really mature," I shouted after him.

24

"Ach!" Freni said, her dark eyes widening behind her bottle-thick lenses. "So now the divorce, yah?"

"*Divorce?*"

"For the English the rate is fifty percent, I think."

"But I'm not just any old English," I protested. "I'm a Mennonite whose ancestors were Amish for hundreds of years."

"Yah, but Gabe is English, and he is fifty percent of your marriage." She paused in her dough kneading and inched closer so that her flour-speckled bosoms were uncomfortably close to mine. Then she twisted what little neck she had upward and trained those beady eyes on mine. "But I think maybe your husband was already married—metamorphically speaking."

"Uh—I'm not quite sure what you mean, dear."

"I mean that he is married to his mama, of course. Just not in the physical way."

"Oh! You meant *metaphorically*!"

"Yah, that is what I said. Magdalena, the Bible says that no man can serve two masters. This is the same for families; a man must choose to put his wife before his mother. That is what God wants."

"Does this apply to your Jonathan and his wife, Barbara?"

Despite her stubby legs, Freni managed to leap back about a yard. "But that woman is from Iowa! And so tall!"

"Who happens to be a doting wife and a wonderful mother to your three grandchildren. Freni, you might wish that Barbara would go back to her family's farm, like Gabe did to his farm, but in that case she'd take the triplets with her."

"Ach! So now I say no more," Freni said, and went back to punching dough.

If I didn't believe that the Babester would calm down and see the error of his ways by suppertime, I would have followed him across the road to the other farm, the one he calls *his*, and—well, I would have come up with something. But I didn't need to go that far with my thinking, because a doctor wouldn't cut off his nose to spite his face. Okay, so maybe a plastic surgeon at a narcissists' convention might do that so he could reattach it and garner some business, but then his motive wouldn't be to spite his face. At any rate, you get my point.

Confident that my marriage would be mended by din-din, I buckled Little Jacob into his car seat, and off we headed to the Sausage Barn for my business lunch. I had yet to hear back from the Zug women, but I took them both to be the type to just show up, rather than respond courteously to my invitation. A free lunch is a free lunch, but good manners are a thing of the past.

Certainly the owner and hostess of the Sausage Barn, Wanda Hemphopple, seemed to be expecting me.

"In the future, Magdalena, kindly make reservations for a party of this size."

"At the moment, it's me and the baby, or did a Zug woman or two show up?"

"Harrumph. And just when I thought we were getting to be friends."

"I thought so too. Tell me, Wanda, what have I done to offend you now? And just so you know, I fully intended to retrieve that sausage link that I dropped down your beehive at the pancake breakfast, but then Minerva keeled over dead and—"

"You *what*?" Wanda doubled over at the waist and shook her head vigorously. Out of the volcanic cone of a hairdo fell a fork, a book of matches, three toothpicks, and a button, but no sausage link.

"I was just kidding, dear. Really, Wanda, you might want to shampoo that thing occasionally. Aren't you afraid of rats?"

"Magdalena, how could you? And after what you did to me in high school." Then I really did drop a wiener down her do, and it stayed there until it got ripe enough to draw attention to itself.

"I was mere kid then, a child of seventeen. Besides, I've apologized a million times. Now, may we skip to the part where you effusively admire my baby, whom you haven't seen since his little—um—thing was ritually made even smaller."

Wanda flipped the perilous pile of filthy hair back into a skyward position and glanced at the cutest baby ever to render a human body practically in twain. Little Jacob was wide awake and even smiled at the restaurateur—then again, he may have been merely passing gas beneath the privacy of his blanket. Either way, the effect was the same.

"As I live and breathe, Magdalena, this *is* the cutest baby I have ever seen! He looks exactly like his father."

"Thanks."

"I was being sincere, by the way—on both counts. Say, what's the deal with the Sisters of Appetite?"

"You mean Sisters of Apathy," I said.

"I meant what I said. If you think Minerva ate a lot, these ladies would have given her a run for her money—except that would be *your* money, given that Susannah said lunch was on you."

"They were *here*?"

Wanda is a keen practitioner of schadenfreude. She nodded happily, causing the tower of vermin atop her head to teeter perilously.

"You bet your bippy," she said.

"When?"

"They left not more then five minutes ago. What a strange bunch. One of them sounded just like your mother-in-law."

"It was; Ida Rosen is now Sister Disaster."

"Wow. But hey, wouldn't that make her your sister-in-law as well?"

"Probably. Now, if you'll excuse me, dear, my dogs are barking, so I'd like to sit down."

"Dogs? I don't allow animals in here, Magdalena! Not even that rat of Susannah's—or Mother Disturbed, or whatever it is she calls herself."

"It's just an expression; it means my feet hurt."

"Okay, okay, you don't need to be so grouchy."

"I'm not being grouchy," I may have snapped. Honestly, nothing makes me crabbier than being accused of being irritable in the first place. It's unfair, and I hate injustice, plain and simple. It's not a character fault and I don't need to apologize for the fact that I sometimes have the right to be annoyed.

"I put youse in the Oak Dining Room on account of there's so many of youse," Wanda said, and without a trace of sarcasm.

With Little Jacob's carrier slung over one arm I trotted along behind the hostess with the mostest—hairdo, that is. The Sausage

Barn has two special meeting rooms, the Oak and the Sycamore, and I've eaten in both plenty of times, but never by myself. Oh well, as long as I got fed, who cared.

❦

I have been blessed with healthy gums and strong enamel. Were that not the case, my dentures would surely have cracked when my jawbone hit the floor. As it was, my chin took quite a beating and I had to set Little Jacob on the nearest table while I stooped to pick up that errant part of my anatomy.

"Well I'll be dippety-doodled and hornswaggled," I eventually gasped.

"What did she say?" the Zug wife demanded. "Is that American?"

"It's Magdalena trying to speak southern," Frankie snarled. "We don't all speak that way, including the southerners."

I stared at my entire list of suspects. Even the smug mug of Alison's math teacher, Merle Waggler, was represented. What had he done, called in sick? And at the taxpayer's expense! Perhaps it really *was* time to look for his replacement.

But if one cannot help being taken by surprise now and then, it is best to keep an arsenal of snappy rejoinders ever at one's disposal. I pulled just such a zinger from my verbal quiver and took aim at the handsome Elias Whitmore.

"How's the BUM business, dear?"

"Now, I recognize filthy American innuendo when I hear it," the Zug wife said.

"Actually, dear," an unidentified Zug twin said, "it stands for Beiler's Udder Massage, and it's a cream that you rub on a cow to keep the milking machine from chafing."

"Hmm," I said. "Might I assume that you are to be paired with the wife who just spoke?"

"You might," said the other twin, "on account of my wife just ran off with your sister and her traveling circus."

"Indeed? I must say, that bus has engendered a good deal of fuss."

"That's not even remotely funny," my former Sunday school teacher, the ailing James Neufenbakker, said. "Magdalena, your sister is a pagan."

"As is the runaway Zug spouse, dear."

"She has a name," her husband said hotly. "It's Annabelle."

"Why, even that name has pagan undertones, given that it was the name of the tragic character in Edgar Allen Poe's 'Annabelle Lee.' "

"I've always liked that poem," George Hooley said.

"Aren't these short hours, even for a banker?" I asked. Without waiting for a reply, I returned to the woman from Winnipeg. "For your information, dear, Edgar Allan Poe married his thirteen-year-old cousin. *That* makes him a certified heathen in my book."

"Ha," scoffed Merle Waggler, "that just goes to show what little you know; a pagan and a heathen are hardly the same thing."

"You tell her, Merle," said Frankie Schwartzentruber. "Honestly, Magdalena, sometimes you're just too big for your bloomers."

"Why does everyone have to pick on me?" I whined.

"Stop that as well," Frankie snapped. "I like you better with a backbone."

"Let her dangle," Merle said. "It serves her right."

"You see? Besides, spineless people don't dangle; they slump."

"People, *please*," the handsome Elias said, "can we just get this over with?"

"Yes, let's," I said. "Wait just one greasy, sugar-coated, Sausage Barn minute! Get *what* over with?"

"Well," said Wanda, bursting into the room, "are we ready to order?"

"Absolutely," George said. He pursed his lips several times like a goldfish kissing its reflection on the side of its bowl. "But first, what exactly is the Dieter's Surprise?"

Wanda chuckled uneasily. "Oh, that. Ya see, I had me one too many of those big-city tourists in here, with their highfalutin ways."

"Is *that* an American word?"

"To the apple core," I said. "So what surprise do you spring on them, Wanda?"

"Fried ice and doughnut holes."

"But that's nothing but water and air," the Zug wife cried.

Wanda nodded proudly. "But that's nothing. Magdalena charges her guests extra for the privilege of doing chores."

"You don't!"

"They should both be ashamed of themselves," the handsome Elias Whitmore said, "and just so you know, neither of those practices is indicative of the way most Americans conduct business."

"Some of us weren't born with silver spoons in our mouths," Wanda said.

The young man colored. "Just so you know, I may have inherited BUM from my family, but the BUM Wrap is my own creation. 'For the udder bag that's soft and pliable overnight,' " he sang, keeping time on the table with the blunt end of one of Wanda's forks, which, by the way, was anything *but* silver.

"That's a catchy tune," Merle said. "Are there more lyrics?"

"What?"

"I think that's sarcasm, dear," I said. Then again, I couldn't be sure.

Wanda pulled a stubby pencil—by the looks of it swiped from

a miniature golf course—from the base of her beehive. "Okay, folks, enough chitter-chattering. I have a new fry cook today who's just itching for some splattering. There, you see, I'm a poet *and* I know it."

"Forget it, Wanda," James Neufenbakker wheezed as he laid his menu on the table. "There's not a one of us going to order until we've set Magdalena straight."

25

Ginger, Carrot, and Sesame Pancakes

Grated carrots, sesame seeds, and ground ginger give these small pancakes their distinctively Asian taste. They are perfect finger food with drinks before dinner or served as a side dish with grilled soy-marinated seafood or chicken. Once the ingredients are prepared, the pancakes go together and fry up very quickly. For the full flavor treatment, make sure to serve them with the Thai Dipping Sauce.

2 tablespoons sesame seeds
3 cups shredded carrots (about three medium)
½ cup finely chopped scallions
2 tablespoons grated fresh ginger
1 garlic clove, crushed through a press
¼ cup cracker meal
2 large eggs, lightly beaten
1 teaspoon salt
Vegetable oil

Thai Dipping Sauce (recipe follows)

1. Toast the sesame seeds in a dry skillet over low heat, stirring until golden, about 2 minutes.

2. Combine the carrots, scallions, ginger, and garlic in a large bowl; stir to blend. Add the cracker meal, eggs, sesame seeds, and salt; stir to blend.

3. Heat ½ inch oil in a medium skillet until hot enough to sizzle a crust of bread. Add the batter by rounded tablespoons and fry, turning once, until browned on both sides. Repeat with the remaining batter.

4. Serve warm with Thai Dipping Sauce.

YIELD: MAKES ABOUT 20 BITE-SIZE PANCAKES.

Thai Dipping Sauce: Combine ¼ cup soy sauce, ¼ cup fish sauce, ¼ cup fresh lime juice, ¼ cup hot water, 2 tablespoons sugar, 2 tablespoons thinly sliced hot chili pepper, and 1 minced garlic clove in a small bowl. Serve at room temperature.

26

Why was I *not* surprised? Not that they should gang up on me—that was to be expected—but at the folly of humankind in general. What fools those mortals be that try to hold out against Wanda's cooking. Throw in my stubbornness, and it's about as effective as trying to instill moral values in a lost generation by burning one tube top at a time. After all, six of their number were male, three of whom were under forty and had the metabolism of tapeworms.

"We can eat, or you folks can lecture me," I said, looking at Wanda. "*Or*, if you're really clever, you can lecture me *while* you eat. I recommend the cheese omelet with extra-sharp cheddar, a rasher of bacon—now, that's a funny word, isn't it—hash browns, toast with marmalade, a stack of hotcakes, but forget the fruit plate. Wanda's idea of fresh fruit means that she drained syrup from the can this morning. *Extra fresh* means that it was packed in light syrup."

"How's the oatmeal?" the Zug wife asked.

Frankie Schwartzentruber, who, despite her fearsome visage, is really a kind Christian woman, howled with laughter.

Even George Hooley, who could have gotten a job injecting citric acid into lemons, forced a grin.

"It's an urban legend," Wanda said. "Don't listen to them."

"Wanda's right," I said. "The story about her oatmeal being used to plaster the inside of the Allegheny Tunnel is simply not true, and I ought to know. Now, let's get down to business: which one of you killed Minerva J. Jay? Who amongst you had the strongest motive?"

After that it was harder to get rid of Wanda than it was to get rid of head lice in a fifth-grade classroom. The promise of all the money in the world couldn't begin to compare with the amount and quality of gossip she hoped to pass on to her customers. You could almost see the woman grow roots that cracked right through the linoleum-covered cement floor, eventually connecting her to a mighty banyan tree on the outskirts of Kuala Lumpur.

Frankie Schwartzentruber was the first quisling in the bunch. "Elias Whitmore did it; *he's* the one with the strongest motive."

"*What?*" Elias demanded. "She's crazy!"

I pretended to glower over horn-rimmed reading glasses. Dismissive looks are always more effective when delivered over black plastic frames, don't you agree?

"Elias is right, dear," I said. "Your statement does put your sanity in doubt."

"And why is that?" Frankie said passionately. "Everyone knows how much he detested Minerva."

"Yes," I said calmly, "but you all hated her. What I meant is that it's highly improbable that anyone, especially a woman of your dotage, would just come right out and call Elias handsome to his face. One might think such a thing, but one doesn't say it."

"What on earth are you blathering about, Magdalena? I said no such thing! *You*, however, just did."

"Oops. Perhaps my internal dialogue could use a wee bit of editing."

"Minerva tried to blackmail me," George said, taking me quite by surprise.

I nodded encouragingly. "Go on, dear."

"She accused me of having an affair with my secretary."

"*And?*"

"I confessed, of course. That's the only thing an honorable man can do when confronted with the evidence. You can expect me to be making a public confession at church this Sunday, Magdalena."

"Was the secretary named Steve?"

"Magdalena, that's just cruel," the Zug twins said in unison.

"But George told me—"

"She's always been this way," James Neufenbakker said. "Ever since she was a little girl. I used to say that if there was one child in Hernia who was going to end up on the wrong side of the law, it would be Magdalena."

"Is it any wonder she can't keep a man?" Wanda wondered aloud.

Suddenly I felt sick, and I had yet to eat a single bite of the three basic Mennonite food groups: fat, sugar, and starch. "*What?*"

"Oh, come on," Wanda said, and pointed a badly maintained fingernail at my minuscule, but arguably beating heart. "Everyone in Hernia knows that Dr. Rosen walked out on you this morning, except for Widow Hastings, who is deaf and dumb—and by that I mean literally less intelligent than a hunk of salt pork."

When no one objected, I stamped a size eleven down as hard as I could without permanently injuring myself. Having done it many times before, I seem to know just how far to go.

"That was so mean! If I had said that, you folks would be all over me like grease on one of Wanda's menus."

"That's because we know you're mean-spirited, Magdalena," Frankie said. "Wanda, on the other hand, doesn't have a mean bone in her body."

"Yes, she does," the Zug wife said. "What else would you call that Dieter's Surprise?"

"They're only tourists," Frankie hissed.

"Yes, but they could have been Canadians."

Elias Whitmore sprang to his feet, and in the process knocked his chair backward to the floor. His rage made him more than handsome; it made him downright sexy—of course, in a Christian, older-married-lady, younger-unmarried-youth-leader, not-adulterous sort of way.

"And *that* would have made it all right?" he shouted.

"Simmer down, young fella," James snapped.

"Don't you tell me what to do," Elias shouted, still caught up in his righteous rage. "I organized this intervention so that we could talk some sense into Magdalena, but I almost didn't invite you. Do you know why? Because you can be a rude old coot, that's why."

My ears burned with indignation. "An intervention? Is that what this is supposed to be? For *what*? I have no addictions except for hot chocolate and ladyfingers."

"It's to stop you from picking on the brotherhood volunteers," Frankie said.

But Elias wasn't through with his tirade. Turning to George Hooley, he began wagging his finger, à la Bill Clinton.

"You, sir," he said, "are no longer going to be my banker. I have to trust *my* banker."

Merle Waggler snickered.

"Which brings me to you, Merle. I put up with you only because we're commanded to love one another. If it was a personality contest, Magdalena would win hands down every time."

I patted my bun, flattered to the hilt, as a strange stirring swept through my . . .

"Loins," Wanda said, apropos the prospect of a dwindling profit. "I have several nice pork loins slow roasting in the kitchen; it doesn't have to be breakfast."

"Stuff your pork loins, Wanda," Elias said. "Maybe I'll come back for dinner." Then he stomped out, no doubt ruing his decision to join forces with Frankie Iscariot Schwartzentruber and the not-so-merry band from the brotherhood.

"Just so you people know," I said, "I've already spoken privately to each and every one of you, and each of you has what would appear to be ample motive to have done away with the quite ample Minerva."

"That's an out-and-out lie," one of the Zug twins said. "You spoke to my brother, not me."

"And I didn't tell you anything," the other one said.

"But it's not fair! You have no business looking so much alike. What are you going to do, pray tell, if one of you makes it to the Pearly Gates, and the other twin ends up at the opposite place—"

"St. Louis International Airport, Concourse A?" the Zug wife asked.

"Something like that," I said, "only not quite as bad, from what I hear. Anyway, what if your destinations are switched? At least one of you is going to have to do some mighty fast talking."

"Oh, they're not that hard to tell apart," the Zug wife said. "*Trust* me."

The twin closest to her sat bolt upright, like he'd just plonked his patooty on a tack. "What is *that* supposed to mean?"

"Once just for fun—never mind, darling. Perhaps this isn't the right time and place, eh?"

"The Concourse A it isn't!" the Zug twin shouted. With that

he clambered to his feet and stumbled from the room, blinded as he was by tears. A few stunned seconds later he was followed by his cuckolded brother and the intentionally adulterous woman from Manitoba.

I say *intentionally* here, because one must always take care to differentiate between an inadvertent adulteress from Hernia and a wanton bed hopper from a thriving metropolis as large as Winnipeg. Yes, I had the wool pulled over my eyes by Aaron Miller, but the Zug wife, no doubt, pulled a colorfast, hypoallergenic poly-wool blend over two sets of Zug peepers and thus deserved every minute she'd spent in the St. Louis International Airport.

"Well, I certainly didn't see that coming," Frankie said as soon as the coast was clear.

Wanda, true to form, was busy taking notes on her order pad. "Leave it to Magdalena to clear out a room," she mumbled.

I glanced around in mock surprise. "And yet I still hear voices. Unless someone tells me right now what you guys hoped to accomplish by this ambush, I'm going to continue swinging my wrecking ball until not a single one of you remains standing. Wanda, in your case, that would apply to the Ruti Tooti Faux-Fruiti Pineapple Upside-down Muffin recipe you swiped from Freni."

"You wouldn't!"

"Start with one package of blueberry muffins from Pat's IGA—"

George Hooley slipped an expensive-looking pen from the breast pocket of his three-piece gray suit and was writing every word down on his paper napkin.

"Stop!" Wanda cried.

She lunged at me, no doubt hoping to clamp a spidery hand across my lovely, loquacious lips (I say that with all modesty). Unfortunately for her, I sidestepped her charge, sending her sprawling headlong into Merle Waggler's chair. One would think that a man of Merle's girth would have been able to anchor said chair and remain in a sitting position, but apparently he was like my favorite candy bar—"fluffy, not stuffy."

It happened so fast that I barely had time to enjoy it, even in retrospect. The sight of Wanda and Merle tangled in a melee of waving arms and legs and a wobbling beehive was nothing short of a balm for my aching heart. Of course I repented of this sin, but to be absolutely honest, I did so a bit later in the day. After all, schadenfreude, like a cup of good homemade cocoa (served with ladyfingers for dipping), is to be savored.

Predictably, Wanda was beyond livid and would have called the sheriff, had I not threatened to reveal more of the recipe. As for Merle, his pants somehow split in the fracas, revealing a bit more than he'd intended, such as that some men wear neither briefs nor boxer shorts. As a result I got a bird's-eye view of what one might describe—if one were using a vegetable metaphor—as two tiny peas and a baby carrot. Even Little Jacob, it seemed, was better equipped than the smirking, smart-mouthed Merle.

I tried to avert my gaze, but it was like trying not to notice the huge booger half out of your minister's nose when he greets you on Sunday morning. (At least I only stared at Reverend Amstutz; it was Mama who unintentionally called him Reverend Booger to his face, and then refused to go to church for the next six weeks because she was so embarrassed.) At any rate, Merle's full disclosure sent him fleeing from the room as soon as he assessed the situation, which wasn't soon enough for anyone else.

"Well, that certainly explains his Napoleon complex," Frankie declared as the door swung shut behind her compatriot.

"That does it, Magdalena," James Neufenbakker said as he struggled to his feet. "You absolutely humiliated that man. Shame on you; you are a disgrace to the Mennonite community. I am going to start a petition asking to have you removed as head deaconess."

"*What?* You can't do that!"

"Watch me." He began shuffling for the door.

"But I didn't do anything except dodge a menopausal missile; the pants split on their own accord."

"You pushed me," Wanda huffed. She'd dropped her order pad and pencil so that both hands could be free to shore up the Hemphopple tower of pestilence.

Had I come alone, I could have risked the prospect of her beehive actually collapsing. But I had Little Jacob's health to consider. Twenty years of unwashed hair threatened to be every bit as lethal as Chernobyl or Three Mile Island.

"Toodleoo, dears," I said as I scooped up my precious in his car seat.

"You can't leave now!" Frankie screeched.

I scurried to the door, but I had to wait until James shuffled through before I could plant one foot firmly outside. "Frankie, I only invited the Zug wives here for lunch. As far as I am concerned, the rest of you are all interlopers and, as such, have interfered in a semiofficial investigation. Believe me, this is all going down in my report."

Frankie had lived too long to be intimidated. "What we're trying to tell you, you dunderhead, is that you're barking up the wrong tree. Yes, we may all have our reasons for not having liked Minerva J. Jay, but why limit your investigation to the members of the brotherhood?"

I was flummoxed. "What in tarnation is a dunderhead?"

"It means you're a dunce. And according to *Merriam-Webster's Collegiate Dictionary*, it's been an English word since 1625."

One has to admire a woman with a head for facts, no matter how annoying she is. "Frankie, even a dunce like *moi* has to conclude that it had to be an inside job; no one else had access to the batter."

"Yes, they did."

"*Excuse* me?"

"Who was it who objected to putting port-a-johns in the north corner of the parking lot?"

"But renting them would have eaten into our profits."

"So instead we let people come through the kitchen on their way to the restroom."

"Only if they *really* had to go. Those were the strict instructions I gave you."

"Little children always wait until the last minute, so they always have to *really* go. As for adults drinking coffee, and those with incontinence issues—"

"Okay, I get the picture. But surely they were shepherded right through without any dawdling."

"You were there, Magdalena, serving pancakes out front. You saw how many people there were. That breakfast was a much bigger success this year than any of us had anticipated. And if you thought it was busy on your end, you should have spent more time in the kitchen. If someone had to walk through to get to the restroom, we didn't have time to stop what we were doing and escort them."

I nodded reluctantly. We'd actually made a killing on breakfast, no pun intended. The mixes were generic and had been about to expire, so I was able to pick them up for a song at Pat's IGA in Bedford. I mean that literally. When I saw the dates on the boxes, I took them up to Pat and began to sing the opening aria by Aida from the opera by that name (it is something the Babester has forced me to listen to after you-know-what). At any rate, my singing voice has been compared to a cross between nails on a chalkboard and a basset hound in heat. Pat gave me not only three cartons of pancake mix, but as much generic syrup as I wanted as well.

"You see," George said—reminding me that he was present—"Minerva's killer could have been *anybody*. It could even have been the Baptist minister. He was there that morning, and he once called her the Whore of Babylon."

"He did? When?"

George's eyes darted from side to side, as if checking for spies that might have sneaked soundlessly into the room during that split second when our attention was diverted to Merle and his cloven britches. "I shouldn't be saying this, so consider it confidential, please. All of you, please. Reverend Brimstone is one of my clients—I mean, my *bank's* clients. At any rate, we were talking once about people we know in Hernia, and Minerva's name came up. Has anybody checked to see if Reverend Brimstone is still in town?"

"He was at Little Jacob's bris," I said. "I felt obligated to invite him since he's one of the town's leaders, being a clergyman and all."

"He's definitely still around," Frankie said. "I ran into his wife at Sam Yoder's Corner Market over the weekend. Did you know that they actually buy those canned snails that Sam sells? Escar*guts* I think they're called."

"Close enough, dear."

"Besides, if the Brimstones had left town, we'd have heard plenty. Those Baptists are not a quiet bunch."

"Wow," I said. Wanda seemed to have her tower of terror under control now, so I stepped back into the room—but just for a second. "I guess that does change things a bit. Rest assured I will expand my investigation commensurate with the information I have gleaned from this most productive, but hardly digestible, lunch. Perhaps next time we will actually eat."

That said, it was time to make like a stocking in a briar patch. And run I did, for I had just experienced an epiphany of sorts.

27

I was starving by then, and Freni had taken off for the rest of the day, so what was a nursing mother to do? Perhaps drive the two miles up to the turnpike and hit the plethora of fast-food restaurants that have brought splashes of bold color and bright lights to our otherwise boring landscape of farms, forests, and small towns? While a triple cheeseburger and a large chocolate shake were rather tempting, it was doubtful the young staff at any of these establishments would be willing, or able, to deliver wise counsel along with my meal. Therefore, a home-cooked meal and the ear of an old coot were definitely worth the ten-mile drive to the far side of Hernia.

As usual, Doc Shafor and Old Blue, his bloodhound, were waiting for me at the end of his long drive. Doc is an octogenarian with the libido of an eighteen-year-old, and Old Blue is the canine equivalent of a man in his nineties, but whose sexual interest was nipped in the bud, so to speak, when she was just a pup.

"What took you so long?" Doc asked. That's what he says every time I show up unannounced. "Lunch is getting cold."

"How did you know I was coming?" That is my usual patter.

"Old Blue here could smell you coming the second your mind turned to it. Of course, she's a mite confused by the baby. Do you mind if she gets a better whiff?"

I bent down and let the old girl, who is almost totally blind, snuffle her big black nose all over my son. Little Jacob, who was wide awake, gurgled with apparent glee. Although I love animals of all kinds—I once carried a pussy in my bra—I draw the line at slobber. Just as a string of drool was about to detach from the ancient pooch, I yanked up the car seat.

"Well, what's for lunch?"

"Not so fast," Doc said. "I want to get a gander at your son." He peered at Little Jacob almost as intently as Old Blue had sniffed him. But since Doc is nearsighted, it seemed to be a bit much. My son, however, seemed rather pleased by the intense scrutiny and smiled broadly.

"Everything is still there," I said. "So far there've been no recalls—knock on wood."

"I was trying to determine whom he looks like. I'm betting that he'll grow up to be the spitting image of his daddy."

Half of me was elated, the other half disappointed. "Why do you say that?"

"His eyes have already turned a nice rich brown, and what little hair he has is coming in dark as well. But I can see that he has your personality; the kid's got moxie. I have a special feeling about this one, Magdalena. Take it from an old geezer like me: your son is going places."

"Is this, like, a prophecy?"

"Let's call it a feeling. Hey, what do you think of Susannah running off with a bus full of nuns?"

"They aren't really nuns, and they ran off with her."

"The Eternal Sisters of Pariah—sheesh, what a name."

"It's the Sisters of Perpetual Apathy," I said, "and by the way, your ex-sweetie has joined them."

"Which one?"

It was a fair question. Doc remained celibate for the first fifteen years following the death of his wife. In the last five years, however, he has courted just about every single female in Bedford County between the ages of eighteen and 108. The latter literally died on him when he foolishly (they could have been arrested for jumping there!) took her tandem bungee jumping off the New River Gorge Bridge.

"I'm talking about Ida Rosen," I said. "My mother-in-law."

"No kidding!"

"I don't have an imagination, Doc. I couldn't possibly have made this up."

"Do they have to take a vow of celibacy?"

"Think about it, Doc. My sister, Susannah, is in charge."

"Oh, yeah. Shoot, I should have asked to go along—maybe as the bus driver."

"Doc, remember that these are women who've dedicated themselves to apathy. Seducing them wouldn't be nearly as fun as you think."

"I could handle that; I've slept with Englishwomen before."

"TMI!"

"What's that mean again?"

"Too much information. Doc, how's your head?" Doc had been critically brutalized about the time I found out I was pregnant. His assailant was Melvin Stoltzfus, who once was our former chief of police but now is an escaped murderer. It was at Doc's house that I confronted the menacing mantis (he really does resemble one), and that I also learned that the despicable man was my biological brother. This, of course, makes him the uncle of the world's sweetest, most attractive baby boy.

"I'm doing just fine, girl. It's Old Blue you should be worrying about. This morning a chipmunk ran within six inches of her nose and she kept on sleeping."

"Maybe her dreams were too good for her to want to wake up. I've had that happen to me."

"Let's hope. I don't know what I'll do when the time comes—" His voice cracked.

"I'll be there, Doc; we'll get through it."

"You're a good friend, Magdalena."

"Tell that to my enemies, will you?"

"Well, you know what they say."

"No, what do they say, Doc?"

"That a life lived without accruing any enemies was not a life worth living."

"Really? I haven't heard that one before. Speaking of enemies, Doc, I'd like to ask you a question, but it's kind of sensitive."

"Don't listen to those women's libbers, Magdalena; Viagra is really your friend."

"Doc! It isn't about sex! It's about Melvin. As far as the authorities know—well, they *don't* seem to know anything about his whereabouts. *Nada*. Zip. Not one thing. He could still be in Hernia, hiding out in someone's barn, or he could be in Timbuktu. Aren't you afraid living out here on the edge of town all alone?"

"I'm not alone; I've got Old Blue, remember?"

"No offense, Doc, but she's a senior citizen as well."

"And so was Moses when he led the Exodus. And Abraham when he became the father of a great nation. What's your point?"

"Nothing, I guess."

"I've always said you were a reasonable woman, Magdalena."

We continued to walk in companionable silence to the house.

Sure enough, the table was set for two, but since I know that he still sets it for his deceased wife, Belinda, I didn't put too much truck in Old Blue's ability to predict the arrival of guests. Still, there was enough food to feed two Mennonites—or two buckeyes of any faith—or four cradle Episcopalians from New England.

I lunched on a hot roast beef sandwich with mashed potatoes and homemade gravy. On the side Doc served some green beans he'd canned the previous summer, as well as a carrot and raisin slaw, and pickled beets. For dessert he cut me a slab of the world's densest butter pound cake, over which he spooned fresh strawberries, which he claimed had been flown into Pittsburgh all the way up from Chile.

When I was stuffed to the gills he told me to belch, which I did, and then he served me a cup of hot chocolate with ladyfingers on the side. "Now, tell me why you're here," he said.

"What do you mean? To see how you are, of course. You're my friend."

"Yes, but I'm also a dirty old man who hits on you every time you set foot on my property. Plus, I know a story when I hear it."

"Okay." I slurped loudly with forced languidness and then settled back in my chair, my left hand resting on Little Jacob's chest. The dear baby had fallen asleep again; I'd fed him lunch just before I sat down to eat my own meal. "It's this: the Babester has left me, and I'm having one St. Louis Airport—Concourse A—of a time trying to figure out who killed Minerva J. Jay."

Doc shook his head. "I see you've been there as well."

"Not me; one of the Zug wives. Anyway, Doc, I'm at the end of my rope, and it's about to break."

"First things first. What's this about that rich young doctor of yours leaving the most desirable woman in all of Hernia? When did *that* happen?"

"This morning! His mother's conversion into a devotee of

apathy was apparently the last straw. That—and he thinks I'm being controlling when it comes to you-know-who."

"He's right on that score," Doc said sternly. "A man *should* be in charge of his own genitalia."

"*What?*"

He shook his head again. "And really, don't you think that now you're a married woman you should move past cute names like *you-know-who*? Belinda and I—"

"TMI to the max!" I cried, clamping my hands over my ears. "And anyway, I was referring to Little Jacob; that's *who* the Babester thinks I have control over."

"Hmm, he may be right on that score too. Some folks, I hear, can't even agree on how to change a diaper. Here, let me give you a little test." Doc reached over and tossed my napkin back into my lap. "Let's pretend for a moment that that's a diaper. Show me how you'd fold that."

I stared at the square of white cotton-poly cloth. "To be honest, Doc, I wouldn't, because I use disposables."

"Well, how would you fold *them*?"

"You don't fold them, Doc. They come preshaped with little tucks all around the leg holes for a snug fit so that nothing seeps out. And one doesn't use pins anymore; the diapers self-fasten."

Doc rubbed the snow-white stubble on his chin. "Dang, I guess I'm further behind the times than I thought. And since I'm obviously not the genius I'd like to think I am at relationships, perhaps we should move on to the subject of Miss Jay. Now, there was a woman who could make a train jump its tracks."

"*Excuse* me?"

"I hate to speak ill of the dead, Magdalena, but Minerva J. Jay was Jezebel, Delilah, and Mata Hari rolled up in one very large package. I'm ashamed to say that no heterosexual man could possibly have resisted her."

"You don't mean—you *do* mean! Doc, how *could* you?"

"It was years ago, Magdalena. I was a much younger man, maybe just in my mid-sixties. I was still practicing veterinary medicine. At any rate, she brings in this stray kitten that's been hanging around her garbage can. The poor thing has a broken leg that needs to be set, and even though large farm animals are my specialty, I do it. She asks me how much, and I say five dollars, on account of I don't know what else to charge for something I've rarely, if ever, done. Then she notices I have a huge pile of paperwork in my so-called office and volunteers to help out—just for an hour or two on weekends."

"I don't remember that!" I could practically feel my blue eyes turn the color of Irish moss.

"Don't get your knickers in a knot, Magdalena; it didn't last long. She thought she noticed a bit of laxness in the way I reported my taxes and she threatened to go to the IRS."

"Unless what?"

"Unless we did the mattress mambo, as you so quaintly put it."

"You didn't! I mean, how could you possibly perform the bedroom bossa nova with someone who was trying to blackmail you?"

Doc recoiled in genuine surprise. "I'm a man, Magdalena. More important, I'm a mortal—unlike *someone* in this room."

I sighed. "Sorry. That really wasn't any of my business. Anyway, Doc, Minerva was killed by a lethal combination of legal medications that somehow got into her bloodstream via our pancakes. Since only seven members of the Beechy Grove Mennonite Church Brotherhood were stationed in the kitchen that day, it stands to reason that one of them is responsible. Right?"

He nodded slowly. "Were the drugs altered in any way by heat? I mean, is there any chance Minerva downed them herself?"

"No, they were in fact cooked in the pancake batter."

"And nobody else had access to the kitchen?"

"The volunteer servers pretty much stayed in the fellowship hall and the platters were passed back and forth through the door. This saved a lot of bumping into one another. However, we did allow quick passage through the kitchen to those who were desperate to use the restrooms."

"Well, then I'd say—"

"But Doc, my kitchen volunteers were too busy mixing batter, frying, and flipping to have put up with anyone coming close enough to drop anything in those big aluminum bowls."

"In that case, I'd have to say—"

"But they think I'm being unfair, that I'm not widening the investigation enough. So they scheduled an intervention lunch! Can you believe that? Meanwhile, I thought I was going there to put the screws to the Zug wives, since I can't seem to make heads nor tails of their husbands."

"Where was the intervention?"

"Wanda Hemphopple's Sausage Barn. Just before I came here."

"So you'd already eaten. I knew that lactating animals had increased appetites, but—"

"No, I didn't eat; the whole thing was a bust. Literally. You see, Merle Waggler split his pants. Unfortunately, he goes about without skivvies, so were all able to see that it would be more appropriate if he was named Wiggler, rather than Waggler. Other than that, it was a waste of time."

Doc chuckled briefly. "Who called this meeting?"

"Apparently the handsome young Elias Whitmore."

"Pardon me? What did you say?"

"What do you mean?"

"You called this young fellow handsome."

"I most certainly did not!"

"I may be losing some of my hearing, Magdalena, but I'm getting better at reading lips. Besides, you look practically smitten with him."

"What a silly thing to say!"

"Yeah, well I've got a bad feeling about this kid; I've never liked him."

"How come?"

"That house of his up on Buffalo Mountain, for one thing."

"But it's beautiful!"

"It's crap." Doc was at liberty to cuss, having freed himself from all religious strictures the day he joined the Marines back in the Civil War—or whenever that was.

"What's wrong with it?"

"*Wrong* with it? For one thing, it ruins the view from on top of Stucky Ridge. You're not supposed to be able to see any houses on top of the mountain from up there. Nada. Not a one. And then there's the noise. All that Holy Roller Christian rock music that kid plays, and the car lights bobbing back and forth. You can't tell me there aren't drugs being bought and sold."

"You're equating Christian rock with drugs?"

"Uh—well, no. But face it, Magdalena, these young people today have the morals of alley cats."

"Meow?"

"Touché. But I still think this kid's bad news, and if he's the one who organized the so-called intervention, then I say focus your investigation on him. He's trying to divert your attention away from the fact that he's the one who murdered Minerva J. Jay."

"Maybe you're right."

"Aren't I always?"

"Doc, if I recall correctly, you predicted that a moon landing would lead to the moon veering out of orbit, and that it would most probably head to Earth and kill us all within two years."

"Yeah, but 'one swallow doth not a summer make.' William Wordsworth, by the way."

"Yes, but he was misquoting Aristotle, who said 'one swallow does not make a spring'—of course not in English."

Doc grunted. "And you wonder why I find you so dang attractive. Now's your chance, Magdalena. Get rid of that interloper from out of state, then marry me. With your looks and brains, and my life experience—the world would be our oyster."

"You wouldn't need oysters, Doc—not with your libido. And in any case, I couldn't keep up. You were born into the wrong culture; you should be living someplace where you could have a harem."

"Hmm, maybe I'll look into that. More pound cake and strawberries?"

"Thanks, but no. If I'm going to put the screws to Elias this afternoon, I need to get home and feed Little Jacob."

"You can feed him here if you like."

"Doc, he's nursing. Feeding him here would be like waving a flank steak in front of a lion."

Doc sighed. "Perhaps you have a point."

I jumped up and gave him a kiss on top of his hoary, horny head. Immediately after that I scooped up the joy of my life and skedaddled while the going was good. I knew from experience that Doc would refuse help with the dishes, and that me lingering any longer would simply be torture for the man with the iron willy.

There is no satisfactory way to explain marital separation to a child. Alison, as was her right, jumped to conclusions, just as quickly as I tend to do. Although I view my sudden leaps as a form of exercise, and thus defend them vigorously, I felt responsible for Alison's frame of mind. Especially since she came down on my side of the finish line.

"I'm never going to forgive him," she said.

"You *what*?"

"How can I? He didn't just walk away from ya, Mom; he walked away from me too. And my baby brother."

"But I'm sure that wasn't his intent; he just needed to get away from me for a while. He'll be back to see you two all the time. Or you can go over there."

"Yeah? Then why didn't he come to school and tell me that?"

"Because it just happened this morning. He hasn't had time to think it through."

"Ya always defend him, Mom. Ya know that?"

"Well, maybe that's because he's a good man."

"Then how come ya treat him like a baby?"

"I most certainly do not!"

Alison has shot up in the last year, so that now at five foot seven, while still as thin as a rotisserie spit, she can do a decent job of looking me in the eye. Her eyes, by the way, are a light Caribbean blue. One of my guests once described them as the color of a Paraiba tourmaline. When she trains those eyes on you, you realize that it's not a matter of *if* you'll get around to seeing things her way, but *when*.

"Mom, ya do so treat him like a baby! Ya make fun of him because Grandma Ida cuts his meat for him."

"Yes, but isn't that justifiable? I mean, a grown man! That's just ridiculous."

"Yeah, but ya shouldn't do it in public; that's the thing."

"I don't do it in public."

"Ya did that time at the church supper when all youse ladies was talking about your pet peas."

"The word is *peeves*, dear— Wait a minute, you *heard* that?"

"Mom, the way ya were mocking Grandma Ida and her accent, the whole church heard ya."

I slapped the offending mouth in question. "Oops. I guess I got carried away."

"Yeah, well maybe she deserves it now, because I'm mad at her too."

"Yes, I can imagine how hurt I would be if my grandmother hadn't said good-bye to me." The truth is that I would have been immensely relieved if Grandma Yoder had not paid any attention to me when I was Alison's age. The woman had passed on when I was just nine, and although her bones lay moldering in the grave atop Stucky Ridge, her controlling spirit had yet to budge an inch outside the parlor where she allegedly gave up her ghost. I couldn't even run through that room without feeling Grandma's icy talons digging into my shoulders and hearing her ravenlike voice cawing in my ears.

"It ain't me, Mom, that I'm mad for. I'm fourteen, so I'm all growed up. I'm mad on account of Little Jacob. He ain't never going to know what having a grandma is like—well, except for Freni. But she ain't our grandma, 'cause she's some kind of a cousin."

My heart overflowed with love for the girl I had taken in. Instead of focusing on herself, as could well have been expected, her concern was for the baby, even though he was still not legally her brother. And given the sad state of my marriage, Little Jacob might never officially be her sibling.

"You're darn tooting," I said.

"Wow, Mom, ya just swore!"

"Just this once. And just to show you that I agree with you; you *are* all *growed* up."

"Mom, the word is really *grown*; I hope ya know that. I just say *growed* to get a rise out of ya. But anyway, since I am an adult and everything, can I go out tonight with Ronny Dietrich?"

"That high school boy on the basketball team? The one whose hands hang down past his knees?"

"Yeah, but he's, like, only a sophomore, on account of he flunked two times in junior high."

It's conversations like these with Alison that can take a reasonable woman, such as me, zooming from Point A to Point Z in a split second. "You're not even allowed to date!"

"But ya just agreed that I was an adult. Adults can do what they want, can't they? Besides, I've decided that I'm Jewish, and when Jewish girls turn twelve, they become adults in the eyes of the community."

"Give it up, Alison. Even if you were allowed to date, which you're *not*, I wouldn't let you date someone that much older, and even if I did, which I *won't*, it wouldn't be Ronny Dietrich. Not after what he did at the Fifty-Second Annual Hernia Daze Picnic last summer."

"Youse old ladies didn't really think that was lemonade, did ya?"

"Mrs. Hurley almost had a heart attack after swallowing some."

"No offense, Mom, but Mrs. Hurley was a witch—and I mean that with a *B*."

"Don't you dare talk like that in front of your brother!"

You see how our conversations seem to ricochet from one subject to another? Before we knew it, we were arguing over how much bare midriff was the maximum amount any self-respecting girl (either Mennonite or Jewish) could wear to school (my answer was none), and the evening just seemed to slip away.

I slept fitfully until about two o'clock, when the need to

micturate and some exceptionally bright moonlight rescued me from a string of mildly unpleasant dreams. In them Susannah, working in cahoots with Ida, had managed to physically re-strain me—tying me up with old toaster cords—and forced me to convert to Apatheism. Needless to say, it was not a religion I embraced wholeheartedly. I was even ambivalent about my habit, which unlike those of the other sisters, was puke green. Strangely, Little Jacob was not in the dream, nor was the Babe-ster. At any rate, I was just about to take my final vows of pov-erty, temperance, and irrelevancy, when the need to pee roused me—thank heaven.

Finally, at about ten o'clock, when both children appeared to be down for the count, I slipped outside into the cold night air. From my vantage point on the front porch, I could look through the still, leafless trees, across the road and Miller's Pond, and see the distant lights of the farmhouse across the way. Somewhere in that house my beloved ached for me—or not.

Or *not*? How could such a thought even pop into my mind?

"Get behind me, Satan!" I said.

Immediately the phone rang.

"Oh, no, you don't," I said. "You're not fooling me; I know exactly who you are."

But instead of switching over to message mode after five rings, that instrument of evil kept at it: over and over again. Un-less I hustled my bustle back in and answered the ding-dong thing, the cherubic Little Jacob and annoyingly adolescent Alison were both going to be awakened, and then the rest of the night was for sure going to be ruined. I wouldn't be able to get a single page of reading done, not even the charming southern mysteries of Carolyn Hart, the chocolate-coated tales of Joanna Carl, or the exotic world of Manhattan as delineated by Selma Eichler.

Seeing that I had no choice but to let Lucifer have it with both lungs, I virtually flew back into the house and snatched up the nearest phone. "It's not funny, you idiot!"

"Uh—"

"By the way, is it hot enough for you?" I slammed the receiver down, shaking with anger and trepidation. After all, it's not every day that one yells so directly at the Big S, and Heaven only knows what torments he's capable of enacting as earthly revenge.

Within two seconds the horrible machine that Alexander Graham Bell invented rang again.

"Miss Yoder, don't hang—"

The Devil sounded maddeningly familiar. But since deception is what he does best, that wasn't too surprising.

"I'd tell you where to go, except you're already there," I cried. "So, with all due respect—oops, there isn't any—get thee to the St. Louis Airport, Concourse A." Again I slammed the receiver into its cradle.

They say that the third time is a charm. I won't agree in this case, but at least by then I thought to turn off the ringer, if need be, rather than smash my phone or rip the cord from the wall. As for simply unplugging the jack, what kind of satisfaction would there be in that?

"Look, you asp," I screeched into the receiver, "you two-headed son of a viper—"

"Elias Whitmore is dead."

28

"You're going to kill him just to get back at me? Well, I have news for you, buster; even if you do, the Lord will still claim his soul. Elias Whitmore is a bona fide born-again Christian."

"No offense, Miss Yoder, but have you ever considered seeing a shrink? Sometimes you make less sense than a single copper penny."

"Good one, Chief—*Chief*, is that you?"

"Of course. Who did you think it was?"

"Not the Devil—I mean, how silly do you think I am? Magdalena Cuckoo Yoder is not really my name, despite any rumors you may have heard."

"Miss Yoder, please quit babbling, and just listen for a change."

"Will do, buckaroo—er, Chief—not that anyone really says *er*, except in works of fiction."

"Did you hear me say that Elias Whitmore is dead?"

That's when his words first sank in. "*Dead* dead, as in *really* dead?"

"Totally dead. Can't get any deader. As a matter of fact, I want you to come up here and take a look before the sheriff gets here."

"Where are you?"

"Halfway up Buffalo Mountain, on Zigler Bend Road at the second turnaround."

"I'll be right there, dear."

Don't get me wrong; I don't enjoy looking at dead bodies—or corpses, if you prefer—but I do find them rather interesting. What fascinates me is how *un*lifelike the empty human shell is, even just a second after death. There isn't a mortuary beautician in the world capable of making human remains really appear as if the deceased is merely sleeping. The truth is, either we are corpses or we aren't, and the transformation is instantaneous.

All of Hernia seemed to be asleep, making the swirling red light atop Chief Ackerman's squad car all the more startling. I pulled over as soon as I found some shoulder and walked up the rest of the way. The last fifty yards I had a flashlight shining in my face.

"What are you trying to do, dear, blind me?"

"Why did you stop so far down the road?"

"I didn't want to inadvertently drive over any evidence. Where is he?"

"You're going to need to steel yourself, Miss Yoder. This isn't pretty."

"I've seen ugly before."

"Not like this. You might even vomit—like I did."

"Please be a mensch and don't let me step in that."

"What?"

"Just tell me where to walk."

The chief took my elbow and gently led me toward the outer

edge of the turnaround. The clearing is a semicircle carved into the woods and is meant not so much as a second chance for fearful or fickle drivers, as a place to pull over in emergencies, such as failing brakes. The surface of the turnaround is flat and smooth, chiseled out of solid bedrock, but it is surrounded by a low stone wall that defines its boundaries and gives at least the illusion of safety.

Halfway to the perimeter I stopped on my own. "Oh no, his car went through the wall and over the edge. How awful! What do you think happened? Did he fall asleep?"

"He didn't go over," the Chief said.

"Oh. But his car did, right?"

"No. His car is still up at his house."

"Then I don't get it."

"That damage was most probably done by a steamroller."

"Elias was driving a steamroller? But why? Aren't they used to flatten things—like dirt and freshly laid asphalt?"

"Elias wasn't *driving* it. Magdalena, look straight ahead and on the ground. Look carefully. And I'm here to brace you."

"Okay, but all I see is black rock and some wet, dark mud, and some rags—oh, my Land o' Goshen!" I started to sway like a young pine in a late March wind.

"Easy there, Miss Yoder. Take a deep breath. Remember, I've got you. You're not going to fall."

"But I am going to hurl!"

"I thought as much."

And retch I did. However, young Chris Ackerman is a gentleman and even offered me his shirt upon which to wipe my face when I was quite through. His mother should be very proud of him, even though he has stolen from her the "right to be a grandmother," and she has had to change churches twice in order not to hear sermons preached against her son.

"That—that was Elias?" I finally was able to gasp.

"Yes. As you saw, he's been squished flatter than a pancake. What's left of him could fit in a pizza box—if you folded him several times."

"So the steamroller responsible for this continued on over the side of the mountain?"

"Actually, no. Whoever lugged it up the mountain hauled it back down again."

"Chief, how'd you find out about this?"

"Mitzi Kramer's beagle wouldn't shut up until she took him inside."

Mitzi is even older than Doc Shafor and has kept a succession of outdoor dogs ever since 1963, when, she claims, she caught Sasquatch—or his Pennsylvania equivalent—peeping in her bedroom window. Unfortunately for Mitzi's neighbors Hernia's sound ordinances don't apply to Buffalo Mountain. The old woman doesn't know how lucky she is that we are basically good folk and would rather simmer with resentment than harm an animal just because it has an inconsiderate owner.

I stared openmouthed at Elias's flattened remains long enough to catch a nightjar. "Good golly, Miss Molly," I said.

"Forgive me, Miss Yoder, but you're turning into a real potty mouth. You weren't that way when I first moved here, and I kind of liked that better."

"Maybe it's been all of your negative California jives."

"I think you mean *vibes*—then again, with you I'm never sure. Anyway, the sheriff's bringing his own dogs. But unless whoever did this to poor Elias drove the steamroller back down the mountain, I don't expect the dogs to contribute much except for more noise. Shoot, I can hear the sheriff's siren now."

"Talk about being a potty mouth; that's merely vowel substitution."

"Pardon me?"

"Never mind. Hand me your flashlight, please."

The chief was loath to do so, but since *loath* is such an underused word these days, one couldn't begrudge that emotion. At any rate, I took the torch—as they say across the pond—and quickly swept the edge of the clearing for clues. Forsooth, I stayed as far away as I could from the flattened remains of the young but no longer quite so handsome Elias Whitmore. In fact, I wasn't even tempted to glance his way.

Okay, so maybe I was tempted a wee bit, but as we all know, it's not the act of temptation that counts, but whether or not we succumb to it. The fallen angel on my left shoulder was making a good case for taking a quick second look. After all, she said, I was unlikely to get another opportunity such as this. How many people had ever seen a human pancake? she asked. And didn't I realize that my observations might be of scientific interest?

Meanwhile, the good angel on my right shoulder was practically shouting in my ear words to the opposite effect. Elias deserved respect, whereas my desire to take a second gander was merely morbid curiosity. I am happy to say that in the end my good angel and my gag reflex won out, and I truthfully averted my eyes as much as possible.

Of course, the aforementioned is all metaphorical, except for the flatness of poor Elias, which cannot be exaggerated. Neither can my sense of vertigo when I looked down at the unbroken tree canopy far below. I staggered backward, nearly stepped on Elias, and then fled screaming to the far side of the turnaround where it abuts the road. In seconds Chris was at my side.

"You all right?"

"Of course not! I almost stepped—thank the Good Lord I didn't. But it's so awful."

"Miss Yoder, I've never seen you like this. You're known for your sharp wit. To be honest, this new side of you really freaks me out."

"But I *am* freaked-out!"

"So am I. But don't you think a little of your macabre humor might make this a bit more bearable for both of us? At the very least, give me a good dose of your famous sarcasm. And, if you have to scrape the bottom of the barrel, I'll take just plain old-fashioned criticism."

"Hmm. Was *all right* one word or two?"

"Beats me."

"Purists and older grammarians would have your head on a paper platter if you made it one word, but common usage will eventually change that. I read recently that even some copy editors permit the use of *alright* these days. I made it two words in the first instance for old time's sake, but one word just now."

"You're really weird, Miss Yoder. Are you *sure* you're not a closet Californian?"

"Like I said before, anything's possible. Besides, it worked. I'm feeling much calmer, and here's the sheriff now."

As much as I'd wanted to stay until someone from the sheriff's team had rappelled down the slope and tramped around a bit, I had to get back to the children. Before leaving, I'd wheeled Little Jacob's crib into Alison's room and positioned it next to the head of her bed. Upon returning I found Alison sprawled out under the crib on the floor, with the baby asleep on her stomach. A sheet had been draped over the crib to form a tent.

I lifted my son back into his crib, and then shook my daughter gently. "Alison, I'm back."

She opened one eye. "Yeah, I can see that."

"Don't you want to get back into bed, dear?"

"Nah, maybe later. I'm kinda comfortable right now. What gives, Mom? Where'd you go?"

Her eye closed, and, thinking she was asleep again, I started backing from the room. "Sweet dreams," I mouthed, and blew them both air kisses.

"Ain't'cha gonna answer?"

I sat on the bed and rested my chin in my cupped hands. "There was sort of an accident up on Buffalo Mountain; Elias Whitmore is dead."

"Ya mean that really cute guy from your church?"

"Yes."

"Who killed him, Mom? How?"

"What do you mean?"

"Ya said 'sort of an accident.' That's Mom talk for it weren't no accident, so I want the details."

I swallowed hard. "I'm afraid that it's privileged information, dear."

"And that's Mom talk for 'you're too young to hear all them gross details, yet you're old enough to take care of your little brother while I traipse off and investigate me a murder.' "

"*Traipse?* Since when do fourteen-year-olds use that word? And if you don't mind me saying so, Alison, your grammar is terrible."

"When they have ya for a mom, and yes, I do mind; you're trying to change the subject, and ya know it."

My sigh of resignation blew candles out as far away as Susannah's apathy vigil in Cleveland (I was informed later that the rally had been canceled for lack of interest). "Elias was flattened by a steamroller up on the second turnaround on Buffalo Mountain. It was not a pretty sight."

"Cool.

"*Excuse* me?"

"I didn't mean it in a bad way, Mom. It's just that if you're gonna be dead—uh, I don't know how I meant it, 'cause it ain't gonna sound right, no matter what I say. But remember that I'm just a kid, and I seen a lot of them horror movies before I came here."

"Saw."

"I seen those too. The *Texas Chainsaw Massacre*—"

"Not that. You *saw* the movies. You didn't *seen* them."

"Of course I didn't *seen* them. Who the heck talks like *that*?"

"*Oy vey!*"

"I was just trying to say that to a kid, being squished is way more cool than just dying of old age, or something boring like that."

"My parents were squished."

"Cool—I mean, ouch! I'm sorry."

"Alison, what are you doing *under* your brother's crib?"

"It's comfortable down here."

"It *is*? But you hate the floor; when you have sleepovers—"

"Okay, if I tell ya, will ya promise ya won't get mad?"

"Did you wet your bed? That's all right, dear—two words, of course—although you have been reminded a million times that the last thing you should do before retiring for the night is use the little girls' room."

"Ya see, Mom, you're already mad, ain't ya, and I ain't even had a chance ta tell ya."

I prayed silently for patience and understanding. This is my least answered prayer. Then again, it is, perhaps, the one into which I put the least amount of effort.

"I'm not mad, dear. Nor am I angry. I'm tired, and in the mood for an *I told you so*. But I'll try to hold back now, I promise."

Alison can tell when I'm calling on divine help, and sometimes she even tries to cooperate. "Ya know that picture ya have on your dresser of that mean old woman?"

"Grandma Yoder?"

"Yeah. Well, she was here."

"A cold cliché just ran up my spine," I said.

"What?"

"A chill. You saw a ghost."

"What else is new?"

"You've seen her before?"

"Lots of times. That old lady—I mean Great-Granny Yoder—is all the time coming in here and checking on me. She gets really mad if I don't put away my stuff. And sheesh, you should see how much she hangs around Little Jacob." She rolled out from under the crib and sat facing me cross-legged. "Ain't ya seen her, Mom?"

"I have, but not for a long time. Not since I discovered that the Yoders weren't my birth parents."

"Yeah, but aren't your *real* parents the ones who raise ya?"

I smiled. "That's right, they are. I've sort of been forgetting that in my case."

"There ain't such a thing as *sorta*, Mom; that's what you're always saying ta me. Either something is, or it ain't."

"From the mouths of babes, dear."

"Hey! I ain't no baby!"

"That's for sure; you're a very wise teenager—when you're not trying to date. So anyway, do you find that hiding under a tent works?"

"Oh, it ain't the tent so much; it's that lavender bath junk I sprinkled on top. I read in some book that ghosts don't like lavender, so they plant it around castles on that account."

"I thought something smelled good."

"Ya ain't mad that I used it?"

"Alison, I don't have mad cow disease—or rabies. Do I fly off the handle at everything?"

She shrugged. "Pretty much, but ya ain't too bad, Mom. Ya ain't never hit me like Lindsey Taylor's mom. Lindsey's always covering up for her, but I seen the bruises. Making excuses, ya know."

I jumped to my feet. "That's terrible! We have to do something about that."

Alison jumped to her feet as well. "But Lindsey will get in a lot of trouble; her mom will just hit her harder. And Lindsey will hate me."

"It sounds as if they both need help. If I notify the right people, Lindsey's mother can get counseling—in fact, they can both get counseling—and in the meantime, Lindsey can be put in a protective environment where she won't be abused."

"Ya mean like an orphanage?"

"No. I happen to know a family—the Kreiders—who've been approved as foster parents, and they're the kindest people I know. They've also raised seven children of their own. Why don't I ask them how to go about this? They can tell me who else to call."

"Ya mean it? Ya'd do this for Lindsey, even though ya don't know her?"

"But I know you, and I love you."

Although I am not Alison's biological mother, thanks to the genetic web that the Amish, and those Mennonites descended from them, inherit, the child and I are fifth cousins six different ways, and only once removed. Math has never been my forte; nonetheless, by my reckoning, if you divide the five into the six, you get the number one, plus a remainder. Drop the remainder to make up for the *once removed*, and Alison and I are, in effect, first cousins. Thus what happened next was practically off the charts in its remarkableness.

Simultaneously Alison and I threw ourselves into each other's arms. Whereas we should have repelled each other like black-

and-white Scottie magnets, we maintained a loving hug position for almost thirty seconds, without so much as a back slap. Of course it was emotionally exhausting, and we were both panting by the time we mutually agreed to disengage.

"Just so ya know," my teenager said, "I don't usually go in for all this mushy stuff, on account of its too weird and all."

"Yeah, like, really," I said.

"Mom! *That* was weird too."

"Sorry." I yawned. "Well, dear, if you'll excuse me, I'm going to push this little feller's crib back into my room and topple into bed. It'll be time to get up and get you off to the bus before you know it."

"Ya know, I think I could get myself ready for school; I am capable of fixing my own cold cereal."

"Yes, but on mornings when Freni's not here, I make you cinnamon toast as well."

My beautiful pseudo- but almost-daughter rolled her eyes. "Ya toast the bread, ya butter it, and then ya sprinkle cinnamon and sugar on it. Duh. How hard is that? It ain't like ya gotta follow a recipe."

The promise of more than two hours of sleep was too tempting to pass up. "Thanks, dear." And despite Alison's loud protests, I kissed her on the top of her head.

I didn't get to sleep in as late as my body would have liked. After just one hour Little Jacob woke up and demanded to be fed. I was able to coax him back to sleep, but approximately three hours later my telephone rang a thousand and one times. I didn't exactly count the rings, but they were woven into the fabric of my dreams.

"Scheherazade speaking," I said when I at last picked up. "I'm fresh out of stories."

"Miss Yoder, I'm sorry to disturb you so early, but I need your woman's intuition."

"Which is worth two facts from a man."

"Miss Yoder, are you listening?"

"I don't have the energy to do anything else, dear."

"The sheriff just called. He said that a small steamroller—suitable for home landscaping—was checked out from Rent-a-Dent. That's the home supply store all the way over by Somerset. The individual renting it paid cash in advance for two days' use of the roller, but supplied their own flatbed truck on which to haul it. Although that too may have been rented—but from somewhere else."

My heart sank as a lightbulb went off in my sleep-deprived brain. "Does the clerk remember this individual?"

"Unfortunately that clerk started vacation today. He's on a flight to Cancún, Mexico, as we speak; his flight left Pittsburgh at two thirty this morning. Apparently it was a last-minute deal. Tell me, Miss Yoder, what are the odds?"

"I believe it's called synchronicity—it's not compatible with my belief system, and ergo does not really exist, but I must say it does seem to happen with astonishing frequency."

"You're truly a puzzle, Miss Yoder."

"I'll take that as a compliment, dear. So tell me, what exactly is it you need from me?"

"To be honest, just about everything at the moment: a warm shoulder, a tender heart, a sympathetic ear—oh, catfish, that didn't come out right."

"Then give it another shot. I am, if anything, the epitome of patience."

To his credit, he barely snickered. "No argument there, Miss Yoder. And just so you know, the longer I live here, the deeper my understanding is of what an invaluable resource you are—a veritable font of information, as they say."

"No one your age says that, Chief. And while you may certainly continue to butter me up, perhaps we should defer that most pleasant of activities to another time. What say we cut to the chase now and tell me what this huge favor is, before *I* decide to book a flight to Cancún. I have no interest in the beaches, mind you, but I've always been fascinated by the Mayan civilization."

"Uh—ahm—uh—"

"Spit it out, dear. I probably have less than fifty Christmases left."

"Well, remember how we originally discussed that once I moved to Pennsylvania my personal life would remain just that?"

"And so it has. If I wanted to dredge up dirt on someone's sex life, there are plenty of heterosexuals hereabout I could go after. For instance, there is Miss I-Can't-Be-Bothered-with-Drapes even though she plays the organ for the Baptist church, and then there's our local representative, Congressman Narrow-Stance Buckley—"

"Miss Yoder! I've been arrested!"

29

"You've *what*?"

"It was in order to keep our agreement, you see. Last night, after I wrapped up my part of the crime scene investigation, I felt so revved up that I drove into Pittsburgh and— Shoot, there's no way to say it other than to just say it, I guess."

"Then say it, for crying out loud. What did you do? Rob a bank? Because that's what I'd do if I was really revved up and I thought I wouldn't— Oops, I didn't just say that, did I?"

"Being funny is not going to help me. I was arrested for trying to pick up an undercover officer outside a gay bar."

"Oh, my stars! You mean to say that there really are such places as gay bars? Good heavens, what won't they think of next!"

"I hate to break the news to you, Miss Yoder, but gay bars are hardly a new phenomenon."

Ever the practical sort, my mind had skipped ahead a step or two. "Chief, do you need a good lawyer? And is bail going to be an issue?"

"No. Kevin—that's this guy whom I met in the clinker, and

that's his term for it, not mine—has a roommate who's a civil rights attorney. But if you'll recall, my contract with the municipality of Hernia has a morals contract, which I signed, stating that my employment would be terminated immediately if I was ever arrested. For *anything*."

"Surely it reads *conviction*."

"No. Besides, I've been giving this some thought, and I really do want to quit police work. Let's face it, Miss Yoder. You're a far better policeman than I've ever been."

"I'll choose to take that as a compliment, dear. What will you do instead? Where will you go?"

"I have a cousin in San Francisco who owns a designer pet store. She's been working for years on breeding a strain of guppy so small that a dozen of them can swim comfortably inside a water-filled bra. One's own body heat would supply the warmth that these tropical fish need, and every time the wearer raises and lowers her arms—presumably the market is women—a miniature pump delivers oxygen into the twin chambers of this wearable tank. True, it's a gimmick, but some gimmicks have a way of really catching on, you know? Doris plans to market this as the Flaunt Your Fins Bra, and if she can get even just one member of the Chinese Olympic swim team to endorse it, we'll have it made in the shade."

"Hmm. Well I hope she has better luck than Cousin Horatio did with the Chihuahua-size lap horses he bred in the 1970s. Everyone thought that his Hold Your Horses marketing scheme was brilliant too, but there was just one caveat."

"What was that, Miss Yoder?"

"Have you ever seen a male horse, Chief?"

"Of course I have. I've been living in Hernia, remember?"

"Well, not all the new owners thought that holding an aroused horse, no matter how tiny, was to their liking."

"Oh."

"Chief, what happens now to your Minerva J. Jay case?"

"I have no more case—and neither do you. Do you hear me, Miss Yoder?"

"We do seem to have a bad connection."

"I'm serious, Magdalena."

"So now, finally, you call me by my first name? What if I object?"

"You could try firing me."

"Touché."

"Well, good luck with the case, even though it seems hopeless. But if anyone can solve it, it's you. That key switch was nothing short of brilliant."

"It was rather clever of me, wasn't it?"

"You're just a bag of tricks, Miss Yoder. You sure you're not a gay man in drag?"

"Pretty sure. Why? Is that a compliment?"

"Only of the highest caliber. Listen, if it's all right with you, I'll be spending the next couple of days in Pittsburgh, and then I'll be back to clear out my office and pack up my house—unless you want me out of the office sooner."

"Take your time, dear. Cheerio, tut-tut, and all that sort of rot." I paused long enough to swallow a lump the size of one of Freni's dumplings. "Oh, by the way, some of us are going to miss you."

"Ditto, Magdalena."

Then I did what comes naturally and hung up the phone.

Clad only in his black silk pajama bottoms, the Babester opened the door languidly. My, what a devilishly handsome creature he was. Had I not just recently passed a watermelon on the floor of Sam Yoder's Corner Market, I might have jumped his bones, thereby initiating the reproductive process all over again. Speaking only on my own behalf, the most effective birth control in the world is birth.

"Hi, hon, come on in."

"Just like that? No preamble? No preconditions?"

"Mi casa es su casa."

"Chili con carne is about all the Spanish I can muster at this hour of the morning—well, or anytime, for that matter. Will I have to have Little Jacob deprogrammed at a later date?"

Gabe laughed and reached for his son. "My house is your house. And it's his house too. I think he can live with that."

"Okay, who took my husband's crabby mechanism and replaced it with this disgustingly cheerful mood? Is there a chickadee hiding behind the couch?"

"A *what*?"

"I know, strictly speaking a chickadee is a species of bird, but isn't *bird* cockney slang for woman?"

"No chickadee, or chick, or bird of any kind; I'm just happy to see you."

I tried desperately to maintain eye contact. "So you are. Listen, I was wondering if you could do me a favor."

"Anything. You know that."

"I *do*?"

"If I can."

"Could you please watch my—*our*—son for the morning?"

"That's a favor? Come on, hon, that's not a favor; that's Heaven."

I handed him the bag at my feet. "Here's all the diapers you'll need, and several onesies, and I've expressed two bottles—that device really isn't too bad in a *pinch*, ha-ha—but since I just fed him, I should be back in plenty of time to see that he doesn't starve—even though he may sound that way."

"Looks like you've covered all the bases— Hey, wait just one Yoder minute. This means that you're about to do something crazy, doesn't it?"

"I'm always doing crazy things. Ask anyone in town."

"Hon, look, I know you well enough to realize that there's no stopping you. So please be careful!"

"Aren't I always?"

"No, you're not; but you are very, very lucky. This time be careful, as well as lucky."

Little Jacob gurgled and burbled similar sentiments.

"There, you see? Do you think I'd take any unnecessary risks with this little guy to come home to?"

"You've got me."

"Sure, it's probably just gas, but mark my words— *What* did you say?"

"Darling, I've been a donkey's patooty—as you'd so quaintly put it. I've been acting like a spoiled mama's boy, not the man that I know myself to be. Can you forgive me?"

"Well, I—"

"You don't have to give me an answer now. Please just don't write me off entirely until you've given me a chance to prove that I can step up to the plate."

I sighed. "Don't take this as a compliment, but you look like you're already about to swing—maybe even hit a home run—not that I would notice such a thing at a time like this."

"Does that mean what I think it does?"

"It means that I'm in a hurry and that we'll talk later. Toodleoo." I started to flee.

"Mags—"

"I don't even have a minute, and the doctor says I shouldn't even think about it for another month."

"I just got off the phone with Ma."

"And now let's add another month."

"She says she's never been happier. That makes me very happy too, so I can't thank you enough for what you did."

"What did I do?"

"You know, making her so miserable that she ran off and became Sister Disgusting—or whatever her name is."

"*Excuse* me?"

"Ma says that the rally in Cleveland was a bust because nobody cared enough to show up, so Susannah booked them all into a motel—two to a room. Ma's roommate was this woman who had to spend more time shaving than Ma, which really made her feel good."

"Your mother shaves?"

"Sixty percent of American women are unhappy with the amount of their facial or body hair; she is not in the minority."

"In that case I am glad to have been of assistance."

"Oh, she said to give you her love and to tell you that she is praying that you achieve a blasé state of mind."

"I would say *how sweet*, but I lack the motivation to do even that."

As I leaned forward to give Little Jacob a parting kiss, I smelled the Babester's manly scent. My knees went weak, and my heart began to pound, but worst of all, I thought I might throw myself into his arms and crush Little Jacob—so powerful were those pheromones wafting to me on that gentle late April breeze. Gabriel Rosen was a Greek god (albeit a Hebrew man) in a body of steel, and I was a Mennonite magnet, completely powerless over my corpuscles of clay, if you'll pardon the mixed metaphor of a hormonally challenged woman.

There was only one thing in the world that could have prevented me from abandoning my mission right then and there.

Unfortunately for Minerva J. Jay's killer—and Elias Whitmore's, I might add—my cell phone rang.

Is it possible that when the Rapture comes, half the folks will not hear the trumpets of glory because their ears will be glued to their cell phones? Far be it from me to speak on behalf of the Lord, but I don't think there will be cell phones in Heaven, in which case a good many folks may well ask for a transfer down to the St. Louis Airport, Concourse A. And yet as critical as I am of others being addicted to this horrible Pavlovian device, I am all but powerless to resist when its ringtone beckons me to answer.

"Hello?"

"Magdalena, where are you? I need you right away." More was said, but I didn't catch it all. The speaker was quite possibly a woman, but she, or he, was whispering so softly that even a rabbit would have had trouble hearing all that was said.

"I was about to throw myself into my husband's arms," I said, "and possibly even do unseemly things in front of our firstborn. To whom am I speaking, by the way?"

Gabe reached for me, but I stepped adroitly away. "It's not too late, hon," he said.

"We'll talk later," I said to him, and mashed my cell phone hard against my ear. "If you don't tell me who this is, I'm hanging up."

"This is *Agnes Mishler*, for crying out loud! I'm your best friend."

"Oh. So you are. Look, Agnes, dear, this is not a good time to give you the recipe for chicken walnut salad—"

"This isn't about a recipe, Magdalena; it's about Wanda Hemphopple."

"Just consider the source, dear, and let her remarks—whatever they were—slide off you like rain from a greased duck."

"Oh no, she didn't say anything bad about me. But she's here, and she says that she knows who killed Elias Whitmore. Is he really dead, Magdalena?"

I grew up with the knowledge that the Hernia grapevine was somehow quicker than the telephone, but even I was stunned. "That's impossible. He was killed just last night. *Late* last night."

"Squashed to death with a steamroller, right?"

"Slap me up side of the head and call me Debbie Sue!"

"What?"

"Never mind; I just always wanted to say that. What else did Wanda tell you?"

"That's it, except that she needed to use the little girls' room."

"Agnes, I keep telling you that you're *not* a little girl, so using that expression is demeaning. Do you think that the president of the United States visits the 'little boys' room'?"

"You're digressing, Magdalena. You're fiddling on your soapbox while Rome burns."

"Touché for the mixed cliché. What is Wanda doing now?"

"I offered her some coffee and a store-bought cinnamon roll, but she's very agitated. She keeps pacing the kitchen. And every now and then she looks this way—into the living room. That's why I'm having to whisper."

"I'll be right over," I said. "Have your uncles entertain her, if you must, but whatever you do, keep her there."

Although Agnes lives in the country, and on the opposite side of Hernia, thanks to some creative driving, I was there much quicker than one might think, if one were to go by the posted speed limits.

30

Wheat Germ and Buttermilk Cakes with Peach and Cinnamon Maple Topping

1½ cups unbleached all-purpose flour
½ cup wheat germ
2 tablespoons sugar
1 teaspoon salt
½ teaspoon ground cinnamon
½ teaspoon baking soda
1¾ cups buttermilk, or more as needed
4 tablespoons (½ stick) unsalted butter, melted
1 large egg

Cinnamon Maple Topping (recipe follows)

1. Combine the flour, wheat germ, sugar, salt, and cinnamon in a large bowl. Sieve the baking soda into the flour mixture. Stir to blend.

2. In a separate bowl, whisk the 1¾ cups buttermilk with the butter and egg until blended. Add to the flour mixture and stir just

until blended. If the batter thickens too much while standing, stir in a little more buttermilk, about 1 tablespoon at a time, to thin slightly.

3. Heat a large nonstick griddle or skillet over medium heat until hot enough to sizzle a drop of water. Brush on a thin film of vegetable oil, or spray with nonstick cooking spray. For each pancake, pour ¼ cup batter onto the griddle or into the skillet. Adjust the heat to medium-low. Cook until the tops are covered with small bubbles and the bottoms are lightly browned. Carefully turn and cook the other side until lightly browned. Repeat with the remaining batter.

4. Serve the pancakes warm with the warm topping.

MAKES ABOUT TWELVE 4-INCH PANCAKES.

Cinnamon Maple Topping: Melt 1 tablespoon unsalted butter in a medium skillet over medium-low heat. Peel and cut 2 large peaches into thin wedges. Add the peaches to the butter and cook, stirring, to coat and heat through. Sprinkle with 1 tablespoon fresh lemon juice and ½ teaspoon ground cinnamon. Stir to coat. Add ½ cup maple syrup, or more, to taste, and stir to blend. Gently heat. Do not boil.

31

Agnes Mishler would love to live in town, but she feels responsible for her two elderly uncles. *They* have to live in the country; after all, the Mishler brothers are nudists who spend a great deal of time outside playing badminton, horseshoes, and shuffleboard. Even on this relatively balmy late April morning, I could tell at a glance that neither man had converted to the Jewish faith since last I'd seen them.

I waved at the uncles as I zoomed past them, and then I abruptly squealed to a stop in front of Agnes's back door. The uncles fled like a pair of wild albino chimpanzees, but Wanda and Agnes struggled to be the first to reach me. Wanda, being a good deal thinner—and meaner, I might add—made it through the kitchen door first.

"Don't listen to a word she says, Magdalena. I don't know anything about this case; I was just going on a hunch. Don't you have a saying about that?"

"Hunching is not good for your back," I said. "If you don't believe me, just ask that fellow at Notre Dame."

"Remind me to laugh, Magdalena. Honestly, I don't know why people say you're such a wit."

"They do? Well, if so, they're wrong by half."

By then Agnes had squeezed through her own kitchen door and caught enough breath to speak. "Tell her everything, Wanda, just like you told me."

When Wanda recoils, her beehive hairdo shoots like a launched rocket ship. "Nobody—and I mean *nobody*—tells Wanda Hemp-hopple what to do."

"Fine, then I'll tell her myself. You see, Magdalena, Wanda here has been having an affair with—"

"I was having a late cup of coffee after closing hours when Chief Ackerman happened to stop by."

"What time was that?" I interjected.

"Three—maybe three thirty. Anyway, he looked really tired, and like he could use some coffee as well, so I let him in. That's when he told me about Elias Whitmore and the steamroller."

"Just like that? He's a policeman, for crying out loud; he can't be spilling the beans to civilians."

"And what are you, Magdalena, an officer of the law?"

"There's something dripping from your chin, Wanda. Here, let me give you a tissue."

She actually reached for it, but Agnes intervened at the last second. "She's being sarcastic as well. Ladies, we're wasting precious time. Wanda, tell her what else happened so that we can get on with it."

Wanda sighed like a teenager when asked to clean up her room. "Okay, just don't be so pushy. Anyway, it didn't exactly happen just like that. Maybe I fudged just a little. But he did come in for coffee, and he was asking questions, like had I seen anything unusual drive by, on account of the Sausage Barn sits right on the main road into Hernia. And I said that as a matter of fact, I had. When I was locking up the garbage cans after closing—you gotta do that, or else the raccoons will get in—I heard kind of a roar, and I looked up, and there was this flatbed with a steamroller on it, just flying by."

"Did you get a good look at the driver?"

"Only a glimpse. He was wearing a hat—like a baseball cap. And he was real short. Or maybe he was slumping. So even if he'd been driving slowly, there wouldn't have been anything to see."

"What time was this? I need to know *exactly*."

"Sometime between eleven thirty and twelve."

"And then after you told the Chief what you saw, he told you about Elias?"

"Not right away. First he had a good cry in booth eight. Then I served him a piece of cinnamon apple pie à la mode, and then he told me about Mr. Whitmore. He said it would be on the news anyway the next day, so what was the point of holding back? Nice boy, that chief. If I was ten years younger—no, make that fifteen—"

"You're married, Wanda, and Chris bats for a different team. Besides, aren't you having an affair?"

"Oh, right, my affair with Mr. Sudoku. Unlike Miss Fecund at forty-eight, here, I'm already going through menopause, and I'm only forty-seven. A lot of nights I have trouble sleeping, so I sit up and amuse myself with Sudoku. I've gotten really hooked."

"You're seeing a Japanese gentleman?"

"Why, Magdalena, you sound almost jealous."

"Curious, that's all. Where did you meet this gentleman?"

Wanda and Agnes both laughed. I could tell that it was at my expense, so I decided to laugh along with them. In fact, I may have outdone them, because not only did I get several dogs to howl, but the Bontragers' donkey began to bray.

"That ass has always had a thing for me," I said.

"He's probably smarter than you," Wanda said. "Sudoku isn't a person; it's a type of puzzle. Sort of like a crossword, but with numbers."

"Oh, *that*," I said. "I've seen those books for sale at Pat's IGA. Why didn't you just say so?"

"*Ladies*," Agnes hissed, "let's get back to Mr. Whitmore's murder."

"Indeed," I said. "But frankly, Agnes, I fail to see why you called me over. I already knew that a steamroller was involved, and since Wanda couldn't identify the driver of the flatbed . . ." I let my voice trail off.

"The driver was a woman," Wanda snarled.

"Aha! Now we're getting somewhere; my ellipse was eclipsed by an assertion! On what do you base that, Wanda?"

"Because what I didn't tell you was that I barely made it to the garbage cans in time. There was a family of raccoons crossing the road, single file, just as that flatbed roared by. They were all in the opposite lane by then, except for the last little cub. Whoever was driving that flatbed swerved just the tiniest bit, to keep from hitting it. A woman would have done that."

Agnes gasped. "Wanda, now I'm surprised. That's very sexist of you. Are you saying a man *would* have hit the cub?"

"No, I'm only saying that a woman would *not* have hit it. We're nurturers. Why, even Magdalena has a maternal side."

"Let me get this straight," I said. "Do you really believe that a woman, on her way to squash a man with a steamroller, would swerve to avoid hitting a raccoon?"

"It was a baby. It was cute. And it's called compartmentalization, Miss Smarty Pants. Besides, she screamed something out the window as well. It was a woman's voice, so there!"

"Agnes," I said, "aren't there times when you just want to take Wanda and shake some sense into her?"

"Boy, I'll say. Wanda, did you recognize the voice?"

"No. Don't you think I would have told you that?"

And then just like that, I had all the pieces to the puzzle. "Ladies—and naked gents hovering in the distance—I must bid adieu, for duty calls."

"What?" Wanda said. "You know I don't speak Spanish."

Despite her size, Agnes could move with lightning speed, and she managed to grab my arm before I could hoof it back to my car. "Not so fast, Magdalena. You're on to something, and we demand to know to what."

"Yeah," Wanda said. "After what you put us through last time, we have a right to know."

"More than that," Agnes said, gripping my arm even tighter, "we have a right to come along."

"And what exactly do you mean?" I said.

"We were your Ethel Mertzes in your last shenanigans: when you hoisted your mother-in-law onto a cow and sent it crashing off through the woods. You put our lives on the line that night— chasing down an armed couple—but I must say, it was the single most thrilling thing that ever happened to me."

"Who is Ethel Mertz?" I asked, and quite reasonably, I may add. My parents, Old Order Mennonites both, never watched a single television program in their lives. I, however, have yielded to temptation and viewed a few of the older comedies, the one referenced among them. I must say, however, that the finest show ever produced was *Green Acres*.

"Uh, Magdalena," Wanda grunted, "you're helplessly conservative. There's no sin in watching old TV shows such as *I Love Lucy*."

"That wouldn't be Luci*fer*, would it?"

"She's trying to stall," Agnes said. "If she can succeed in making you blow your stack, then maybe you won't want to come with her."

"Ha! In that case she's out of luck. I bought that book *The Impatient Person's Guide to Meditation* back when it made the *New York Times* bestseller list, and I read most of it. I can become very tranquil if I set my mind to it."

"Then for the love of scrapple," Agnes panted, "set your mind to it now."

"Ohmmmmmmmmm."

Life's many twists and turns are supposed to be what keeps it interesting, but a *peaceful* Wanda? Now, that takes the cake! This I had to see.

"Okay," I said, "but I can't guarantee your safety, and you have to do exactly as I order."

"Listen here, Magdalena. I don't take orders!"

"Yes, she does." Agnes let go of my arm and enclosed Wanda in her bulk. "Say it again, Wanda. Ohmmmmmmmmm."

Wanda's eyes narrowed but she complied, and so we three musketless dears set off to catch a killer.

Just as I thought, there was a cab with an attached flatbed trailer parked in the turnaround in front of Minerva J. Jay's house. Not being the total fool that some folks think I am, as soon as I caught a glimpse of this, I backed up for a good quarter of a mile.

"What gives?" Wanda demanded. "Are you losing your nerve?"

"No, dear, although you seem to have lost your *ohm-niscience.*"

"They were two-minute exercises, Magdalena, and there were only three in the book. It took us a lot longer than that to get all the way out here. Where *are* we, by the way?"

"Thousand Caves Retirement Village," Agnes said. "I brought my uncles out here to look at plots. Minerva assured them that there would be a nudist section, but they chickened out. You see, Uncle Remus is afraid of gaping holes."

"That's nice, dear. Okay, everyone out."

"*Out?*" They both sounded terrified.

"We can't sneak up on them in a car, ladies, can we?"

"No," Agnes said, "but we can call the sheriff."

"We can tell him that there's a flatbed truck out here, so what? You don't see a steamroller, do you? We need to get close enough to get some hard evidence. Besides, you can't get cell phone reception here; I've tried once before."

"Do you have a gun?" Wanda said.

"No! I'm a proper Mennonite, for goodness' sake, not a liberal one, like you." Oops, perhaps I had gone too far. Wanda belongs to the First Mennonite Church, not Beechy Grove, and they are indeed a different breed, but they are still ostensibly pacifist.

"Magdalena has her keen mind," Agnes said loyally.

"Ha," Wanda snorted. "If she's so smart, then why did she marry a bigamist?"

I took a deep breath and composed what I believed to be a beatific smile. "Wanda, dear, if you're afraid, then by all means remain in the car. Just don't play the radio, because we can't come back to a dead battery. If you get really bored, there's last year's *Farmer's Almanac* under the passenger-side front seat. Be sure to lock the doors, of course, and whatever you do, don't open the door if you hear something scraping against it. They say that the tourist from Harrisburg died of a heart attack, but what the paper didn't mention was the hook that was found hanging from the door handle." I flashed her my beatific smile again.

"Don't be ridiculous; of course I'm coming. You're going to need my brain to make yours a whole wit. But first, don't you have to use the bushes?"

I glanced around. "For what?"

"To relieve yourself, dummy. Isn't that what you were grimacing about?"

"Why, I never!"

"You do too; you always look constipated."

"Why, so help me, Wanda, I'm going to huff, and then I'll puff—"

"Stop it," Agnes hissed. "Both of you. You're getting louder by the second." She paused just long enough to catch a breath. "Look! Over there to the left. Isn't that smoke? And I hear something; something other than yinz excessive chatter. It sounds kind of like an engine. You don't suppose she—or he—could have hidden the bulldozer underground, do you?"

"The smoke is coming out of a flat expanse of rock," Wanda snapped. "You're starting to sound as crazy as Magdalena."

"Au contraire," I cried. "Agnes, you're on to something!"

32

Wanda was every bit as much afraid of gaping holes as was Agnes's nude uncle, Uncle Remus. Although she'd lived her entire life within an easy drive of Thousand Caves Road, and the weird limestone formations, she'd never even been tempted to mosey on out and take a peek, not even during the height of the development scandal. Once, when Wanda was a junior in high school, her parents dragged her on a family vacation to Mammoth Cave National Park in Kentucky. A terrified Wanda took only a couple of steps outside the car, threw up, and then spent the rest of the day sobbing in the backseat.

A control freak with a phobia is not a pleasant creature. Although she refused, at first, to set foot off the road, neither would she consent to being left behind. Wanda mumbled and grumbled, and uttered some words that even a liberal Mennonite had no business knowing.

Meanwhile, Agnes moved like a hound to the scent. Of course the trail of a rumbling, smoke-belching steamroller is not exactly hard to follow, even if it has been dumped in a large sinkhole.

About ten yards from the cavernous opening, Wanda stopped abruptly. "I'm not going any farther."

"Fine," I said. "Just wait here."

We were in an open area of flat, smooth limestone that crowned the rise of a low hill. The only trees were stunted pines that grew in places where, eons ago, eddies of water had carved out pockets, which were now filled with soil, but drought and infestation of foreign beetles had killed more than half of the pines, eventually turning them into bleached skeletons. With a sigh of relief Wanda sat shakily on one of these fallen trunks that had long since shed its bark.

Agnes, however, was as unstoppable as a bulldozer. Had I grabbed one of her pants legs (the poor misguided soul is a Methodist) and hung on tightly, I could have gotten a free ride. As it was, I had to trot to keep up, and I weigh a full one hundred pounds less than she does.

Still, the woman has to be admired. She didn't stop until she was standing on the rim of the abyss, staring down into the blackness, from whence came the sound and the smell of a crashed bulldozer. But then, instead of recoiling due to a bout of dizziness (like any normal woman), Agnes got down on her knees and peered into Satan's domain. Clearly, she was a woman possessed.

"Magdalena, come quick!"

"Don't rush me; I'm coming as fast as I can."

"But somebody's down there."

"What? *Who?*"

Agnes wouldn't say another word until I dropped to all fours beside her. "Look, Magdalena; what do you see?"

"An upside-down bulldozer with smoke pouring out of the engine."

"Not that, silly. There, to the left."

"Oh *that*: that's Frankie Schwartzentruber, our one female member of the Beechy Grove Mennonite Church Brotherhood."

"You don't seem surprised to see her!"

"I'm not; in fact, she's why we came out here. I just didn't expect to find her holed up in a—allow me to say it, please—a hole."

"Wasn't she the one who drove the bulldozer over that young, and extraordinarily handsome, Elias Whitmore?"

"Indeed." I reared back just enough to cup my hands to my mouth. "Oh, Frankie! Frankie, dear."

Although the roar of the bulldozer's engine drowned any echo, I was nonetheless heard, and the murderess looked up for the first time. It was obvious from where we knelt that the sink-hole extended a couple of feet beneath the ground, at least on one side, but Frankie did not seem interested in hiding. Instead she waved her arms and jumped up and down.

"It looks like she's glad to see us," Agnes declared happily.

"Can you hear what she's saying?"

Agnes cocked her head. "She's saying 'It will blow.' "

"Does a bulldozer have a whistle, Magdalena? I would have thought it had a horn."

It took a few seconds for my thoughts to catch up with my cranium. "Oh, my stars," I croaked. "She means the engine is going to explode; it must be leaking fuel."

"In that case, Frankie should climb out of that hole."

For a fraction of a millisecond I wanted to push Agnes *into* the hole for stating something so obvious. Instead, I took a deep breath and shouted down to Frankie.

"How can we help?"

"Don't be a dolt, Magdalena; I need a rope."

I gazed at the walls of the sinkhole. They were almost as

smooth as the Babester's chest that time he waxed it as a joke and got a terrible rash for the effort. There was one narrow ledge, a calcified swirl of limestone that began almost directly below us and followed the curve of the wall, widening as it descended, until it melded with the floor. An ancient whirlpool (not more than five thousand years old, of course) had carved this sinkhole and left an impression that looked for all the world like a giant scoop of soft-serve ice cream. Well, then again, we nursing mothers can never get too much to eat.

"Frankie," I bellowed, "can you climb up on that shelf?"

"It's too narrow! I keep falling off."

"You need something to steady yourself with."

"I need a ding-dang rope!"

"With language that blue, dear, you'll not being having a white Christmas next year."

"Magdalena, you're the biggest boob to ever walk the earth. If you don't shut up and get me out of here, we're all going to blow."

"Okay, but there's no need to get nasty. Where can I find some rope? In your truck?"

"Like I said, you're an idiot," she screamed. "It's going to blow any second. I need some rope *now*!"

"Let's take off our clothes," Agnes said calmly, "and tie them together in a knot chain. I saw that once in a movie."

"Did it work?" I said.

"Yes, until one of the sleeves ripped, and the hero plunged to his death."

"This is impossible, then. We'll just have to wait until help comes." I do have one foot in the twenty-first century; maybe one hand as well. I was wearing my cell phone in a flowered pouch dangling from my dress belt, and as I spoke I got it out and speed-dialed 911, even though I knew it was hopeless.

"I already tried that," Agnes said. "You were right; there's no service out here. This place is like the Twilight Zone."

Meanwhile, Frankie's cries for help were getting louder and more desperate. Something had to be done, even if it was drastic and full of risks.

"Oh, Lord," I prayed aloud, "give me clarity of vision and the wisdom of Solomon." I paused to tuck a wayward strand of hair back behind a clip. "If a clothes rope is the way to go—" The annoying strand slipped right out, forcing me to pause again.

"If you don't quit fussing with your hair," Agnes said, "any answer to your prayer will be a moot point."

Hair! That was it! Does not the Lord work in mysterious ways?

"Agnes," I cried, "how strong is human hair?"

"That depends on the human. There are many types, you know; straight, curly, fine, thick, black, blond—"

This was no time to update the encyclopedia. I raced back to Wanda. The restaurateur was lying in a heap, her face buried in her arms, and panting like a woman in the advanced stages of labor. Clearly she needed a project to take her mind off herself.

"Wanda, how long is your hair?"

"What?" she gasped.

"Your hair, dear. This is a matter of life and death. If you undid that beautiful mound, how long would your hair extend?"

She looked at me, color creeping back into her cheeks as her suspicions rose. "It's twelve feet, three inches," she hissed. "What about it?"

Agnes caught up with me. "How do you feel about saving somebody's life?"

As Wanda's head swiveled, her enormous bun teetered precariously. "Whose life? How?"

"Frankie Swartzentruber is down that sinkhole," I said. "The only way for her to get out is to climb up a very narrow ledge with nothing to hold on to. We—*she* needs you to let down your long hair so that she can keep her balance."

"Like Rapunzel," Agnes said.

"*What?*" Wanda snapped. "You want her to climb up my hair?"

"Absolutely not, dear," I said soothingly. "She merely needs to steady herself."

"In a pig's eye!"

"Wanda, *please*," Agnes pled. "Surely you don't want her to die."

"What about Magdalena's hair? How long is it?"

"Eighteen inches, tops," I said quickly. "I cut it when I was pregnant."

"Well, too bad, then, because I'm not going to have someone yanking on my hair. And FYI, I don't even like Frankie Schwartzentruber."

I opened my mouth to give Wanda a piece of my mind, but a sequence of misfired synapses contributed to an "aha moment" that got me sidetracked on a more productive tangent. It occurred to me that there is only one thing that can change a Hemphopple mind, once it's been made up, and that is flattery.

"Wanda, dear," I said, "how would you like to become a famous hero?"

"Cut the crap, Yoder. I know what you're trying to do."

"Yes, save a life. And do you know how many people are saved each year by a beautiful woman who lets her hair down into a limestone washout?"

"None, I bet. So what? I'm still not doing it."

"Not even to be on the *Today* show? Take it from me, dear, Matt Lauer is one long, tall drink of water."

"You don't even watch TV, Magdalena."

"He stayed at the inn once." It was only a small lie; I'm sure that he had once stayed at *some* inn, *some*where in the world. "As for Meredith Vieira; she's not my brand of tea, but if she was, I'd drink a full pot, and then some."

"Do you really think they'd have me on?"

Agnes threw herself into the game. "If not them, then *Good Morning America*. I bet they'd put you on the evening entertainment shows too. And of course you'd be all over the national news and in every newspaper."

"How would you feel about *People* magazine doing a spread?" I said. "I'm sure you could convince them to do several shots showing the Sausage Barn. But oh, my stars, then you'd be rich, and not everyone is cut out to be wealthy; not everyone can handle things the way I can."

Wanda's eyes blazed. "You think you're special, don't you?"

"Well, you have to admit; I haven't let my staggeringly large fortune change my standard of living a great deal. Sure, I drove that sinfully red BMW, but that was for a very short time. With the exception of Big Bertha, my whirlpool bath with more heads than Medusa's snake, I really haven't splurged at all. I still live in the same old farmhouse—well, a facsimile thereof—dress the same, and eat the same food. One might say that I live the lifestyle of 'old money,' rather than that of the nouveaux riches. It's quite an art, you know.' "

"And you think I can't do that?" Wanda was on her feet and had begun tearing out her hairpins. "Magdalena, I can out-rich you any day of the week."

"Show that stuck-up Goody Two-Shoes," Agnes hissed. She was, perhaps, getting too good at this game.

Wanda had no patience for us now. They say that love conquers all, but I do believe that greed and its lesser brother, envy, are both more powerful. Wanda and I have competed since we

were both in pigtails, and now that we wore buns, she was deter-
mined to prove that hers was made of steel. Despite her fear of
gaping apertures, my nemesis ran for the sinkhole, and we practically had to tackle her to keep her from going over the edge.

Once at the edge of the abyss, rather than giving us a hard
time, she merely closed her eyes and instructed us to each grab a
foot and to hold on tight. That said, she unloosed the final pins,
and hair that had not been freed from its mooring in three, maybe
four, decades cascaded like a waterfall into the chasm below.
Unfortunately—and I had expected this—Wanda's inverted
crown of glory did not quite reach the grasping hands of Frankie
Schwartzentruber.

"We'll have to lower you by your ankles," I shouted over the
roar of the engine.

"What if we drop her?" Agnes said. In all fairness, she had to
speak loudly to be heard over the roar of the engine and Frankie's
scream.

"I heard that," Wanda shouted.

"We won't drop you," I shouted back. "Because then how
would Frankie get out?"

"Ha-ha, very funny. That woman's a murderess. And just
so you know, I wear panties with the days of the week embroi-
dered on them; my mother-in-law made them for me last year for
Christmas. I even wear them on the correct days, except that for
some strange reason she forgot to include a pair for Thursday. So
that's when I go au naturel."

"That's nice, dear," I bellowed impatiently. I wasn't about to
get my brains blown out over a prolonged discussion on cute lin-
gerie. "You ready? Because here we go!"

Working smoothly in unison, Agnes and I each grabbed an
ankle and propelled Wanda forward. She shrieked like a teenager
in a bathtub full of spiders, and like spiders, her hands clung to

the walls as we lowered her slowly downward. We jockeyed her forward until we were lying on our stomachs, and Wanda was dangling parallel to the wall, her skirts fallen about her head and shoulders (alas, I had quite forgotten that today was Thursday).

"Can she reach it now?" I could barely hear myself above an engine gone berserk.

There was no immediate answer, but in a few seconds she jerked like a bass on the line; contact had been made.

33

Somehow we managed to get Frankie safely out of the sinkhole, although by that time all four of us were as skinned and bruised as processed chickens. The woman had the nerve to try and make a run for it, but given her age and general state of health, it was easy to apprehend her. When we got to the car, I parked her in the backseat between Wanda and Agnes, since the two of them were every bit as good as handcuffs.

I was just turning around when the earth beneath the car shook, and black and orange clouds billowed out of the ground to the east. Had I not already known the cause of the conflagration, I might well have assumed that the Battle of Armageddon had begun.

"It blew," Agnes said, stating the obvious.

I executed some fancy steering, whilst pressing the pedal to the metal. "Hang on, ladies. Many of those sinkholes are interconnected by underground streambeds. And some of those caves lead to dead ends where natural gas gets trapped. This whole place could blow up."

"You witch," Wanda said. I could only hope that she was speaking to Frankie, not me. "How could you have killed a good-looking young man like that?"

"His looks were not important," Frankie said.

I switched on the recorder I keep in the console of my car. I am, after all, a mere gatherer of information. Unable—unwilling—to carry a firearm, I carry a big mouth, along with the technology to record what others say in response to it. In this case, I was quite happy to yield the floor to Hernia's very own Rapunzel.

"I demand an answer," Wanda said.

"If you must know," Frankie said, spitting out her words like they were fish bones, "he was blackmailing poor Jimmy."

"Elias was blackmailing James Neufenbakker?"

"Ha, and you probably thought he was some holier-than-though charismatic youth leader."

" 'For all have sinned and fall short of the glory of God,' " I said. "Romans 3:23. That would include you, my dear."

"Strictly speaking," Agnes said, "blackmailing is foremost a legal problem, seeing as how it does not appear on the list of the big ten. Therefore, Wanda, you are the bigger sinner."

"Shut up, Agnes," Frankie said.

"Why, I never," Agnes whimpered.

"There was no need to be so rude," I snapped.

"Save your breath," Wanda said. "This woman ran over a kid with a steamroller. "Do you think she cares about manners?"

Rather than save my breath, I took a deep one. "I know that you and James were close," I said. "Were you lovers?"

All three of my passengers gasped. "Y-you evil-minded sex maniac," Frankie said, barely able speak, so great was her indignation. "We were special friends. No more."

"I saw a photo of you two looking quite cozy; it was in Minerva's photo album."

"And your mind went directly to the gutter? To join Minerva's? We were friends—that's all. A lonely widow and a lonely widower. Soul mates only, but we did not join in the flesh."

"Whew, that's a relief. I've been wanting to poke my mind's eyes out for days."

"Now who's being rude?"

"I'm sorry; I'm only human—despite rumors to the contrary."

"Can we get back to the interrogation?" Wanda said. "I left half my scalp back there in that sinkhole, and it better not all be for nothing."

"Right. So, dear, what was the holier-than-though, richer-than-sin, cuter-than-the-dickens chick magnet blackmailing Jimmy about?"

"It wasn't Jimmy's fault!" Frankie began to thrash about until Agnes half sat on her. "It was an accident! Do you hear me?"

"Of course, dear. The dead in Somerset County can hear you. But they, like me, are going to require details."

"He was leaning over the mixing bowl, see, and his pill case plopped in the batter. It could have happened to anyone."

"Was it open?"

"That too could have happened to anyone. Haven't you ever *not* quite closed something all the way?"

"Yes, of course. But why didn't James just fess up and throw the batter out?"

"Because we were running out of pancake mix, you idiot! Plus he thought that it wouldn't be that concentrated. And anyway, it's all your fault; you're the one who bought the supplies."

I prayed for the strength to stay focused. "What was in that pill case?"

"Does it matter now? Just so you know, Jimmy did his best to pick all the pills out, but he can't see so well anymore, and that's not his fault either."

"I suppose it's mine?"

"Elias saw it happen, but he didn't do a thing! He could have helped Jimmy find the pills."

"And because Minerva was such a glutton," I said, "she ate a whole griddle's worth of hotcakes in one sitting, thus sparing everyone else."

Agnes finally found the nerve to speak. "How much was Elias asking for?"

Frankie snorted. "A million dollars! Ha. Where was someone like Jimmy going to find that kind of money?"

"But Elias was rich," I said.

Frankie snorted again. "Are *you* rich, Magdalena?"

"Why, yes, I am—not that it's your business, dear."

"Well, goody for you. But apparently not everyone who appears to be rich actually is. Sure, Elias owned a fancy mountaintop house, but BUM was about to go out of business."

"The Chinese?"

"The Indians—from India. An enterprising young man in New Delhi has started a company called Sacred Cow Udder Massage. It's supposed to be a superior product, plus it's much cheaper. American farmers are switching in droves from BUM to SCUM. Believe me, Elias was desperately in need of cash."

"And so," Agnes said, "a bad decision that turns out fatal is covered up by murder. Of course, sin can't stay covered up. Doesn't the Bible say that, Magdalena?"

"Be sure your sin will find you out," I said. "Numbers 32:23b."

"Shut up, but both of yinz," Frankie said.

I alerted Sheriff Hughes the second I was within calling range, and we were met by a fleet of squad cars and a flotilla of ambulances before we even got to Hernia. Just how fast the sheriff and his crew drive, I don't even want to know, for fear that I may have to perform a citizen's arrest on one of them sometime soon.

Flannery Hughes is one of the nicest guys you could ever hope to meet, and just because his mama smoked a lot of marijuana while she was pregnant is no reason to suppose that he's not intelligent; he gets his lack of brains from his papa's side of the family, and I mean that charitably. His father sold the family farm and sunk the proceeds into a mail-order business selling pocket-size bags of sand at a dollar each. These were marketed as food for pet rocks, back during that craze. Papa Hughes actually managed to sell twenty-nine of these little bags—all to people from Marin County, California. When it became sadly apparent that his business was a bust, he spent the rest of his life writing unsigned reviews for *Publishers Weekly*.

At any rate, the sheriff insisted on riding in the ambulance with me to Bedford Memorial Hospital, which meant that the Babester had to follow by car. There was no time to find a sitter, so Baby Babester rode with him.

"Sheriff," I said, "I had an epiphany this morning, before I got the call from Agnes Mishler telling me that Wanda Hemphopple was over at her house."

"Miss Yoder is delusional," Sheriff Hughes said to the ambulance attendant over the back of his hand. "Epiphany was in January."

"So it was, dear. At any rate, I have reason to believe that Melvin Stoltzfus, Hernia's most notorious criminal—given that he was once our chief of police—is now posing as a nun, traveling cross-country with a newfound sect called the Sisters of Perpetual Apathy."

The ambulance attendant chuckled politely, but the sheriff laughed outright. "Miss Yoder, now, that really takes the cake!

Even those silly mystery novels my papa used to review wouldn't have plots as far-fetched as that."

"Life is stranger than fiction, dear. But when you think about it, that's a perfect way for him to leave the area without being detected."

"Except by you?"

"I put two and two together. I learned to add in elementary school."

Now the ambulance attendant snickered. This time Sheriff Hughes was not amused.

"And how was it that you deduced that it was Mrs. Schwartz—uh—the woman in custody—who ran over the young, exceptionally good-looking Elias Whitmore?"

"I was working on the assumption that the second killer was also a member of our brotherhood. Then I remembered that Frankie Schwartzentruber's father had been in the driveway construction business. It was a long shot, granted, but my papa was a dairyman, and I *do* know how to milk a cow. Anyway, that was my first clue. Then my daughter—well, she is only my pseudo-daughter at the moment, but that will all change shortly—said something provocative about folks protecting the ones they love, and that's when I remembered I'd seen a photograph of Frankie with James Neufenbakker, and the two of them were looking like a pair of New Caledonian lovebirds. I don't know if you've met James, but the man is held together by Band-Aids and a bad temper, my real point being that I was sure he took a variety of medications." I paused to inhale some much-needed oxygen.

"Miss Yoder," the sheriff said, "don't take this the wrong way, but my papa would have said that you couldn't plot your way out of a paper bag if you had three pencils, a sharpener, and an eraser the size of your fist."

I emitted such long sigh that for a few seconds the poor EMT thought I had gone to meet my Maker. "My dear man, I suppose, then, when you hear that I was able to rescue Mrs. Schwartzentruber from the sinkhole by convincing Wanda Hemphopple to let down her long hair, you will find that part of my tale absolutely implausible. In that case, you will be nonplussed—now *there* is a word that is often used incorrectly—when the others corroborate my story. But just so we're clear now, I had to promise Mrs. Hemphopple that a statue would be erected in her honor, and I do not intend to cover the costs by my lonesome. *Capice?* Murder is a capital offense, so I think the capitol should help out here."

The ambulance attendant chortled behind both hands.

"What's so funny?" the sheriff demanded.

"Forgive me, sir, but this woman's a hoot. And honestly, I don't think she is delusional—but hey, she is a talker."

"She is that," I agreed. But since we had just pulled into the emergency room unloading area, I shut my trap tighter than a clam at low tide.

I left the hospital two hours later, in as good a shape as a teddy bear from the 1930s. That is to say, I'd left a good deal of my fur behind along the lip of the sinkhole, as Agnes and I maneuvered Wanda around in a circle like a human rope. Of course, Agnes was no better off. And as for poor Wanda—well, the intern who treated my abrasions said she was in for some severe headaches, and might temporarily even lose a bit of her bun. If we didn't erect a suitable statue to honor her heroic sacrifice, I would have to give serious consideration to relocating somewhere far away. (I've heard that Boise, Idaho, has a small Mennonite community, and not a single authentic Pennsylvania Dutch bed-and-breakfast.)

At any rate, we had just returned to the inn—and yes, the Babester was with me—when the phone rang. Caller ID gave the number as the FBI office in Cleveland, but one can always hope that it's Drew Carey, can't one? Although I've never seen his show, I've heard he's a barrel of fun.

"PennDutch," I said with practiced mock cheer. "May we help you experience the pseudo-ethnic weekend of your dreams?"

"In your dreams, sis."

"Susannah!"

"Listen, Mags, I don't have time to waste on your silly games. This is my one call."

"Then this is my two call," I said agreeably.

"You see what I mean?"

"But I don't. Please enlighten me."

"Thanks to you, I've been arrested for aiding and abetting an escaped murderer."

I swallowed hard. "They arrested *you*? They were supposed to arrest Melvin, for crying out loud."

"What the heck is going on?" the Babester demanded. The poor man was obviously distressed by my distress.

"They *did* arrest my Mel-kins," Susannah hissed, "but I'm the one who tried to help him get away. You had to have known this would happen."

I staggered to the nearest chair and plopped my patooty down before I collapsed on the floor. "You knew he was dressed up as one of your nuns?"

"Mags," she continued to hiss, "how stupid do you think I am? This whole Sisters of Perpetual Apathy thing was just a ruse to get him out of the state. You know how closely they've been watching traffic across the borders—all those so-called random safety checks."

"But he's a killer! How could you help a killer?"

"Because I love him, Magdalena, that's why. I don't expect you to understand this, and why should you? You're beautiful, you have a handsome husband, and now a baby, so just don't give me any lectures, not when you have *everything*, and I have *nothing*!"

"I don't have—"

"Can you listen long enough to help me? They're about to make me get off the phone."

"Sure," I said. My heart was pounding like a madman on a xylophone, and I felt like throwing up, even though I hadn't eaten anything since breakfast.

"I need you to make me a promise—sight unseen."

"You know I can't if it means breaking the law. And speaking of which, don't you need a good attorney?"

"Forget the attorney!" she screamed.

"Yes, dear," I said quietly. "If it's legal, and not a sin, then I promise."

"You swear on the graves of our parents?"

"I can't take an oath like that; but yes, I'll keep my word."

She sighed so deeply, I could almost feel the breeze come through the receiver. "Congratulations, Mags, you are now the proud owner of a purebred Russian toy terrier."

"*What?*"

"Well, someone needs to take care of Shnookums," she said before hanging up.

Almost immediately the phone rang again. This time it was an FBI agent informing me that I had five days to hie my heinie up to Cleveland to retrieve the repugnant rat in dog's clothing, or he'd go to canine heaven.

I was still in shock when the phone rang a third time. I let Gabe field that call whilst I fed his offspring a much-clamored-for meal. When my husband came into the bedroom to share what had transpired, he seemed more perplexed than anything else.

"I can't believe I said yes, hon."

"Ah, but I was a very persuasive bride-to-be."

"I'm afraid this is no laughing matter. Those so-called nuns—the ones who were taken in by your sister—they're quite serious; they want to continue being Sisters of Perpetual Apathy—in a phlegmatic sort of way, of course."

"How delightfully uninspiring."

"Some of them, unfortunately, don't have much choice, having burned their bridges behind them when they left Hernia."

"At least their new philosophy finds them without regrets."

"So I was thinking, since I'm moving back in here, why don't I offer to let them stay across the road in my house? That can be sort of like a—what do you call it, a covenant?"

"A convent, perhaps? A very inconvenient convent."

"Yes, that's it."

"Tell me, was this Ida's idea?"

"Uh—she may have helped clarify a few things, but it's definitely not her idea."

"I see."

"Seriously, hon, think of the advantages. In her new role as head nun, she'll be so busy taking care of the sisters that she won't have a second to spend interfering in our lives, yet she'll be close enough for us to keep an eye on."

"What do you mean, *head* nun?"

"Oh, that. Well, with Susannah no longer in charge of the group, Ma stepped into the power vacuum and has given herself a new name. From now on, she is to be known as Mother Malaise."

"*Oy vey*," I said.

There were huge challenges to be faced in the months and years ahead, but I was still a very blessed woman. The Babester was finally all mine, and we had our precious son to raise together, and in just a short time Alison would become our legal daughter. As for the challenges: Mother Malaise would be living just across the road, and my only sibling was headed for a criminal trial and a possible stint in the state pen.

And although I intended to keep my promise to Susannah, there was no way, José, that I was going to carry that mangy mutt around in my bra. Shnookums was going to have to learn how to walk. Perhaps Alison could teach him. Lately she'd been hinting that she'd like a cat or dog. She'd said nothing about keeping a rat as a pet, but . . .

I smiled. At least for the moment, the blessings outweighed the challenges.